On the WAY
to the END *of the* WORLD

On the WAY
to the END

of the WORLD

a novel

ADRIANNE HARUN

ACRE

CINCINNATI 2023

Acre Books is made possible by the support of the Robert and Adele Schiff
Foundation and the Department of English at the University of Cincinnati.

ISBN-13 (pbk) 978-1-946724-65-6
ISBN-13 (e-book) 978-1-946724-66-3

Designed by Barbara Neely Bourgoyne
Cover art: images from Unsplash

The press is based at the University of Cincinnati, Department of English,
Arts & Sciences Hall, Room 248, PO Box 210069, Cincinnati, OH, 45221-0069.

Acre Books titles may be purchased at a discount for educational use.
For information please email business@acre-books.com.

For Ali, always, always

I only went out for a walk, and finally concluded to stay out till sundown, for going out, I found, was really going in.

—JOHN MUIR

CONTENTS

Sunday, March 17, 1963

A NOTE TO THE READER

The events depicted in this novel are fictional, but they take place within the framework of a real historical phenomenon known as the JFK 50-miler or the Kennedy Walk or simply the Big Walk.

It began like this: In early 1963, the Cuban Missile Crisis was barely in the rearview mirror, and President John F. Kennedy was casting around for something that would elevate the national spirit and restore a sense of safety and strength. When one of his Cabinet members, Marine General David Shoup, unearthed a mandate from the Teddy Roosevelt administration requiring that Marines be able to walk fifty miles in twenty hours—the norm up until then and thereafter being a mere seven miles in one day—Kennedy's interest was piqued. He decided to throw the challenge to "my Marines," imagining, it seemed, a grand show of superior military grit. But Bobby Kennedy beat the Marines to the punch, immediately deciding he—and the rest of the Cabinet—should do the Big Walk first. A few days later, Bobby and a handful of Cabinet members set off in the middle of the night from Great Falls, Maryland. Bobby, it was joked, must have walked right out of his West Wing office: a winter jacket, no hat, no fancy gear. For god's sake, he was still wearing his thin dress socks and black loafers! The rest of the Cabinet were equally underprepared, and all eventually left the Walk, the last making it as far as twenty-five miles. Except for Bobby. He persevered and finished in Harper's Ferry, West Virginia, seventeen hours later, alone except for the late-arriving company of his Bernese mountain dog.

Soon in every corner of the country, scores of Americans began pouring onto roads and trails and highway edges—military men, nuns, housewives, high school students, solitary wanderers—everyone marching with *vigah*, as the president might say, on their own fifty-mile Big Walks. While the fad lasted only a few crazed winter weeks, the Big Walk did briefly restore a sense of American fortitude and may also have ushered in a new era, replete with marches and demonstrations that continue to challenge and demand more from our national character.

SATURDAY

March 16, 1963

HUMTOWN, 4 A.M.

MILE 0

They begin in the dark as, one might argue, we all must. One car, then another, rumbles across the empty high school parking lot, idling only long enough for an occupant to exit awkwardly and drift under the yellowed beam of a single streetlight. Others arrive on foot, shuffling into view with even less ceremony, already disheveled by damp and wind. At the agreed-upon time, young Warren, instigator and organizer, counts the participants. Nine. Waits for stragglers. Counts again. Two more. So, eleven altogether. More than he'd thought. Fewer than he'd hoped.

Landon Wills, his father's typesetter, hands out copies of a handmade map that no one can read in the dark. Landon appears far too old for this endeavor. Never mind that he claims to have undertaken a similar trek every year of his long adult life. Never mind that it's Landon who traced out a route that bypasses the busiest roads and will bring them to the most appropriate of finishes, a cliffside beauty spot called Spetle Cliff, more commonly known as The End of the World. An ominous sign if you believe in that kind of thing, which Warren emphatically does not.

If Warren had been the sort to believe in signs and if the walkers had had the fortune to leave in the light of day, any one of them might have taken notice of three dead crows lying beneath a scrubby box hedge, steps away from the high school doors. In the meager light reflecting off the streetlamp, only the edge of a single black wing is illuminated, a shadow no one registers. But if they had? *Three* dead crows! Well, even the least superstitious among the walkers might have considered staying home after that. But Warren doesn't notice. No one does. Their minds are elsewhere already.

"Good stops along the way," the old man had informed Warren, when he'd first brought out the map.

"See, right here." He jabbed at the paper. "You got a trail angles up to the highway, comes out not fifty feet from a café and phone booth. A bus stop."

"And here." He pointed again, again.

A café, a state park. Spit Town, of course. No, never far from help, if needed.

As Landon swept his finger across his map, Warren had felt as if the old man was drawing the fifty-mile walk of his dreams. So what if they wouldn't have the support teams other patriotic groups around the country supposedly mustered? The effort would be entirely up to the walkers, a fact that made Warren unreasonably and prematurely proud. With the map in hand, he imagined the walkers as a great triumphant crowd, the flashbulb of his repentant father's camera capturing the end of their Kennedy Walk in that remote cliffside parking lot, miles away from town yet somehow, he imagines, lamplit in the dead of night. As they are now.

He looks around once more. No, not a crowd. But enough, he reckons.

Warren's best friend Denis, a golden-haired track star, breaks away to stretch, as if he plans to run all day. Two junior girls, stars of the high school's Solidarity Club, wearing identical duffle coats, bounce on their toes to keep warm, their eyes on the lean shadow that is Denis. Another girl shifts uneasily within a childlike slicker, a bookbag slung over her shoulder as if she's taken a wrong turn on her way to school. Warren is nervous about her, but even more about the two little boys. The oldest can't be twelve. They mumble their names but nearly shout their troop number. Boy Scouts. Warren relaxes. They must be the Fletcher kids, the mill owner's sons. Heck, they could probably lead the group all the way to Seattle. He doesn't quite recognize the woman with a scarf tied around her hair—feeble protection if the rain begins in earnest—but feels certain he knows her. And next to the Solidarity girls, oh, hell, it's Helen Hubka, the telephone operator. Warren's mother once suggested his father hire her for his newspaper. ("She has such a nose for news," his mother said with a straight face.) One more fellow, too broad-shouldered for a high school kid, raises another worry until he turns to tie a shoe, and Warren notes with relief the distinctive profile of one of the Goodes—the fisherman, he thinks. Add Landon, of course, who had to come along. Warren is grateful for the mapwork, but as he eyes Landon's skinny silhouette and smells the acrid smoke of what will likely be the first of his endless brown cigarettes, Warren sincerely hopes the old man will leave them before daylight.

A little before four in the morning, under a misting rain, the figures in the high school parking lot file into a purposeful group, trooping out from under the solitary lamplight into the black warren of uptown streets, and as they do, another man, woolly cap, long dark overcoat, slips among them. The fisherman nods in the fellow's direction as if he's been expecting him, but that slight gesture of greeting is lost in the dark, and the newest walker joins in without a word. Now they are twelve, and the Kennedy Walk—the Big Walk—has begun, free from all but the slightest suggestion of trouble.

CAROLINE

Trouble? Caroline could tell you about trouble. People say a trauma recedes, as if it's nothing more than a winter wave, bottle green and frothing, hammering a stunned shoreline for a few tear-swept days in late November. "After the initial shock . . . ," they begin. But to her, there was no *after*. The shock lived in her, became part of her, stilled her so completely that her daughter, who should have known better, thought of her as quiet and strong and self-possessed. *You're a rock, Mother*, her daughter wrote after the funeral, misunderstanding everything. No one in town was fooled. Caroline's grief was lasting too long, had taken root too deeply. She'd become worrisome to her friends and neighbors, to the other elementary school teachers. Widows recovered or went mad, and she, it seemed, was on the road to the latter.

In the months after her husband's death, Caroline would wake well before dawn, dress within a sliver of dim bathroom light, and begin an ever-widening circle around the empty downtown streets. Before the town was fully awake, she climbed hills in the dark, feeling the ground tilt and push back at her. She had to lean forward, and yet she persisted, as if by correcting gravity she might arrive somewhere else, in another time, perhaps *as* someone else.

The town was not large, and in the years she'd lived here (all her adult life), she must have traversed every street. She'd walked in love, pausing for stealthy kisses beneath trees. She'd tried out a pair of high heels before a summer dance. She'd pushed a pram day and night and run after a tiny red bike with training wheels. She'd carried damp sacks of groceries home in a rare snowstorm, meandered home with other young mothers after a contentious school meeting, replaying an argument block by block, and she'd worn a track around the uptown streets looking for her renegade teenager the year *she* discovered love. She'd once laughed so hard she'd had to hold on to the slim trunk of a young sycamore on Morgan Street, that same tree that now towered over her as she walked and wept and mourned. *He had died.* He had left and taken enough of her with him to render her useless on this earth. What remained were all these shadow selves, wandering and circling in their old realities, blindly waiting for her to slip by and briefly activate them with her memory. Would there be an end to this? There seemed to be none, just this slippery repetition. Was there, too, she wondered, another future self who would remember this failed and flailing version? She seemed to be wearing the same sweater and skirt she'd had on when she'd met Jay, both of them barely out of their teenage years. Her hair, the same unfashionable bob with too short bangs, the deep red-brown only a little thin and faded. From a distance, she might appear identical to all those vanished versions of herself, but close up, she was courting an early ruin. Her face was wind-burnt. Wrinkles, many more than faint, ringed her eyes. Her chin had reconfigured itself. Jowls, she decided; she was getting jowls. But who cared? She was forty-four and done with the world. She just had to find a way to live within it.

For now, she walked. It was easier to leave the house before dawn, to travel through a weighted netherland that matched the landscape within her. Out in the bay, a foghorn warned away trouble, its incessant blare sounding increasingly useless to her. Raccoons brawled in a verge before slipping like oily water through an open gutter. A screech owl tried to snatch Caroline's knit hat, then harried her for blocks as if blaming her for its own failure. Some mornings, another human silhouette would cross her path, but no one traveling through those hours was inclined to meet and greet. Figures crossed streets, melted into yards. Affairs, perhaps. Maybe even a would-be burglar or two. Caroline wouldn't care. Twice, she nearly ran into a tall, darkhaired boy, dressed in black like a beatnik, carrying a sort of sack and rambling across frost-sheathed lawns. She did wonder until, with a sidelong glance in her direction, he tossed a folded newspaper on a nearby porch, and she was satisfied.

One early morning, well before daybreak, Caroline came across a coyote paused in the center of Bay Street under the town's single stoplight. She'd felt the creature first, a shadow moving in tandem with her up the black, rain-flushed sidewalk opposite. But since shadows were constant companions, she didn't fully accept the coyote's presence until it crossed under the streetlight and hesitated as if to show off the black cat dangling from its mouth. The cat was dead, surely. Its neck snapped in the moment of capture, and yet Caroline did not see the cat as dead, as victim. The limp body, rain-soaked fur glossy in the streetlight, seemed peaceful to her, beyond a graceful acquiescence, and stunned Caroline with longing. To be that dead cat. To be free of this existence, carried with surety beyond feeling or caring. The coyote leapt and disappeared back into the pitch of dawn, and Caroline, stripped soul, felt the blow of loss again. How alone she was! How distant from this world. How ridiculously present.

And she walked.

She worried that in death he would stop loving her, in death he would not only fail to remember he once adored her with a passion that burned and honeyed air, in death he would forget her utterly and feel not the tiniest bit of unnamable loss. Each worry, each hard thought pushed her onto her feet, out of their house.

She walked and walked.

She wrote Jay letters, letters that if they'd arrived at his unknowable address would have been nearly unreadable. Rambling, tearstained pages stung with loneliness and fury. *Why hadn't he taken more care? How could he have left her so deeply alone?*

Her daughter, their only child, Ginny, had answered President Kennedy's call and joined his new Peace Corps. In Tanganyika, Ginny too had joined another sphere. Yes, she instructed children in toothbrushing methods with US toothbrushes and gathered grown women for basic arithmetic and conversational English. But she'd made it clear, at least to Caroline and Jay, that she was *joining* their society, not invading it. Ginny hadn't been able to come home for the funeral, and although her letters were filled with notes of sorrow and love, she also sometimes began them *Dear Mother and Daddy*, as if she might exist in a time where her father still lived. Strangely, Caroline often had the impression that Jay could be in Tanganyika, perhaps digging wells or demonstrating the intricate knots he used on his boat or telling and retelling his ever-embellished stories. These days, too, she imagined the coyote's black cat winding through Jay's newly strong, newly browned legs as he worked in a foreign land beside their daughter. Those brief moments when she could imagine her husband and daughter together relieved her loneliness, the thought of them together in a *place*, a separate but real realm. Then, slowly, and always with astonishment, she'd *remember*, the way you might finally see that what you thought was a memory had in fact occurred during the course of a long, improbable dream.

But then Ginny wrote that she'd seen her father in her dreams. They'd taken a stroll through her village. He'd repaired a broken pump and jerry-rigged a new stove and everyone had celebrated him. She had never been happier than in that dream, she wrote, and *Daddy looked so good!* Despite her own daydreams of Jay in Tanganyika, now Caroline briefly hated them both. How could they leave this world with such joy? How could they leave her behind? She half wanted to curse them, her most dearly beloved. The next morning, she was trudging up Mather Hill. No sidewalk there, but no traffic either. She moved right up the slippery center of the road, her body bending blindly forward in the pitch-dark, and though she'd begun the walk torn to pieces by her daughter's letter, that excluding dream, as she reached the top, she surprised herself by saying aloud, "That was awfully nice of you, Jay, helping Ginny like that." She felt rather than saw him smile. And she smiled, too. It was a kind of beckoning, and right there, she made her decision.

It was, Caroline discovered, harder than one would think. Gun, knife, rope. Who would find her? Poor old Eleanor next door? Letterbox Bob, the mail carrier? No, she couldn't do that to anyone. She wanted to meander into it, a rolling marble finally hitting the grooved track. She imagined that drift, that snapped-in connection. In late February, she tried slipping into the only boat she had left from Jay, a leaky Peapod still miraculously and infuriatingly intact, still tied at a boat haven dock, and began rowing out into a swell of green waves. She'd barely fought her way toward the mouth of the breakwater when another boat slipped alongside her. Charlie Beecher, Jay's onetime partner, and another fellow, paddling like madmen in Charlie's dinghy.

"You're taking on water, Caroline," Charlie shouted.

The big fellow with Charlie, swaddled beyond recognition against the wind, reached out with his own oar as if he could turn her around simply by pointing. And he had, she guessed, because she did turn back, swiveling awkwardly until the wind pushed her to the dock, to despair and disappointment and a curt nod from Charlie, who knew she'd known better, who had to have guessed the course she wanted to take. She bailed out the Peapod, feeling the eyes of Charlie and his silent friend upon her, and, soaked and shaking, she walked home, defeated again.

After that, it was as if the town had conspired to watch her. If she even tripped over the bald edge of carpet at the bank, a hand would be at her elbow, and someone would offer to drive her home. At the grocery, she had to endure a lecture on avoiding the ferry traffic while in a small boat. Letterbox Bob lingered outside her door to advise sturdier shoes. More than once, she was sure, too, that the new paperboy had been pressed into service, his rangy shadow crossing hers in the night as if his route had been altered to dovetail with hers. A car with a ticking engine sometimes seemed to tail her block after block until she returned to her own street. Even ancient Eleanor-Next-Door wobbled out into her side yard to impart to Caroline not words of solace but of instruction. Her rowing technique, she was informed, was fully backward.

Alone, she reveled in the moments when she'd bang a shin on the bed-post or burn a finger on a hot pot, the pain allowing her to weep uncontrollably once again. Still somehow, they all knew. The phone would ring. A knock would sound on the kitchen door. She would wind down swiftly, as if her grief had been switched off, as if it hadn't gone underground once more, as if it weren't still calling, calling to her to leave, to fully check out. One neighbor whispered an offer of a single insipid sleeping pill. Another suggested a dog. Still another in almost comical sincerity directed Caroline, lifelong Methodist, toward a chat with a new young priest at St. Anne's.

She would have to pretend, she realized. Put on a show.

How do you play the part of a recovered widow? Was there such a person? She'd borne her parents' deaths, cried only when she was alone with Jay. Hadn't she pretended she was fine, death simply the way of things? *Goodbye, Mother. Goodbye, Daddy. So long, brother John.*

Yes, the unfortunate state of being contained and held by this town, Jay's town, an untenable state, as if she'd managed to nick her wrist, deeply but narrowly, a near-invisible wound that must bleed and bleed and bleed at an almost unendurably slow rate, not a gush, not even a trickle, but a constant pain, sharpened by each quickened glance, a single stinging touch of breath.

Caroline did not go back to work after the holidays. The school hired a substitute—retired, stern—and the principal made noises about advertising for a replacement, but no one wanted to let Caroline go. Her class had cried when they learned she wasn't coming back—a roomful of weeping and wailing five-year-olds—and yet now, when she met one of her kindergartners at the market or the park, they did not run to her as they once did, to be hugged, to be consoled. More often, they stopped inches away from her, frozen by shyness, as if her terrible grief was a wall even they could not breach. And she could not, she *would* not, move to comfort them.

Without a plan, Caroline immersed herself in an early spring cleaning. She sorted and stacked and finally wrote an ad and braved the newspaper office. As always since Jay died, she felt exposed in public. So she tied a scarf over her untidy hair and wore one of Ginny's old winter coats, her new reading glasses hanging awkwardly on a chain around her neck. A meager disguise but one that let her shuffle downtown in daylight without inviting scrutiny from pitying eyes. The new secretary at the paper, a frazzled young woman, didn't seem to recognize her, which was a relief. She began to read the ad aloud, slowly, laboriously, to make sure all was right. Even so, Caroline had to correct her more than once.

"How 'bout you read it to me, hon," the secretary said, thrusting the note back. "It'll go quicker."

At first Caroline's voice wouldn't work, and she could hardly read her own writing. She whispered, then as the secretary frowned, Caroline remembered the reading glasses. Honestly, she did look half mad, stammering as she delivered the ad. She hadn't brought her wallet, only crammed a few dollar bills in her pocket, and they emerged wrinkled and sticky from whatever old candy a high school version of Ginny had secreted in her coat pockets.

"Hold on," the secretary said. "I need to get you a receipt. Oh, dear, I ripped . . . oh, and now that darn carbon is missing. Just have to run to the basement storeroom. Won't take more than a few minutes."

Could anyone move more slowly? Caroline lamented. She was desperate to leave. She could hear other voices, voices she recognized.

In the newspaper's side offices, Warren was trying without success to get his father to agree to more than the tiniest of announcements, those few lines shoved between the weekly Mill Record, which almost no one read, and an account of a charity luncheon.

"Not even two lines!" Warren said. He read them aloud as if to illustrate their paucity: "A fifty-mile Kennedy Walk will begin on March eighteenth at three forty-five a.m. at Humtown High School's west parking lot and end at Spetle Cliff."

"If the school won't sponsor the walk," his father was saying, "I can't pretend it's official."

"You could have put my name and our new phone number in, in case anyone had questions."

His father snorted. "This week? No one would get through with your mother trying out everyone's new number."

The telephone system had shifted to dialup three days ago, and the novelty of having a phone number—a private number—was still strong. Caroline had hardly paid attention.

His father went on: "Didn't you pass around that *Life* magazine to half the town? Anyone who wants to go on a 'Kennedy Walk,' assuming they are not idiots or felons on the run, will certainly be prepared."

"Who will even show up?" Warren protested.

"I've done all I can, son," his father said, finality in his voice. "I'll be there at the end with the station wagon. Your uncle's offered to pick up anyone who needs to quit along the way. Enough already."

The president had thrown out a challenge. *Life* magazine made a fuss. Caroline had missed it all. Yet had she? Even after the flustered secretary returned and painstakingly delivered a receipt, Caroline lingered, a plan rushing into place.

A walk. Far away from the prying eyes of town. A walk that would end in the deepest part of night on a cliff where she and Jay once perched in the moonlight, a lifetime ago. The synchronicity could not be more perfect. Yes, finally, a real plan, and only two days left to wait. In the meantime, she boxed up the wedding china and once-treasured pieces of silver and crystal. They might as well have been sticks and rocks, she cared so little now. She set aside her mother's pearls, Jay's father's watch. She wrote one short letter after another on her best Crane cardstock. It was a bit like Christmas. Room after room. Her sewing machine would go to a neighbor, along with boxes of fabric, some saved since Ginny was a baby. The car to a young father down the road. Of course, Charlie Beecher should have Jay's tools and everything salvaged and stored in Jay's port shed, from his old sextant to the carefully coiled ropes. She emptied closets, stacked boxes, delivered her storehouse of school supplies to her old classroom late the following afternoon after everyone, including the substitute, had gone home. She worked well into each night until both she and the house were duly lightened. Could she admit the joy she found in leaving her house, in scouring what was left of her life, the downright beauty of emptiness she engendered? Mercifully, her garden was late, barely stirred into spring. So much easier to say goodbye. Caroline wrote Ginny a letter on whispers of airmail paper, addressed it, left it on the kitchen table with change for the foreign postage, and readied herself for her last walk.

HUMTOWN

In a place as small as this one, miles away from any other, we do live in
one another's pockets. The town, like most around here, has an official
name, but most people call it Humtown. A few Chamber of Commerce
types have tried to sell our community by skewing its name to Hometown,
but nearly everyone, not only the notorious wags, knows Humtown suits
us perfectly. You can stand on a street corner and practically hear the subterranean chatter of gossip. We know something of everyone, including all
the dogs and most of the cats. Our information is not always correct, but
once we own it, it's ours and very hard to relinquish. Yes, we keep track of
who drives what vehicle and when and where that vehicle might be parked,
particularly in the early morning. We observe and note the conditions of one
another's houses: the progress and abundance (or lack thereof) of vegetable
gardens, the proliferation of roses, the trees we have labeled not according
to type but by the family who shares space with them: the Duffy Yews, the
Kendall Willow, the late lamented Malonardi Monkeypuzzle, felled only
months before in the Columbus Day storm. We keep track of each other's
relatives and are well-acquainted with numerous strands of family lore:
black sheep who have fled town, black sheep who stayed and reformed,
black sheep who have gone underground. Long-lasting grudges between
cousins and neighbors and, yes, cats. We know who is stepping out in a
marriage, what bastard raises his hand to wife, whom not to leave alone in
a room with an open purse or child, where to carefully count your change.
Those we don't quite know, we still surveil and categorize. Newcomers are
given nicknames that sometimes stick for years. Nicknames are actually
our key identifiers, linked as they often are to occupation. Rick the Fish
runs the cannery market, of course. Dandy Dan is our barber. Sparky Hipps,

the electrician. Thunder Bob used to drive the heavy quarry truck. Now he manhandles garbage cans in the dawn route as if determined to keep earning his name. Each week, the newspaper chronicles the doings of the town elite, such as they are: the higher-ups at the mill, the business owners, the school principal, the doctors, and the elected members of the numerous civic societies that keep up the pretense that we are a vibrant community burbling with events.

The week before the Big Walk is an exceptionally newsworthy one in the dulled environs of the local paper. The school board holds an annual dinner and presents awards to one another. Reports warn of a man and woman, posing as a pair of missionaries, going door-to-door out in the county, soliciting donations for "heathen conversions." Another visiting sailboat lost its mooring and went aground behind the old cannery. *Dial M for Murder* and *The Manchurian Candidate* have finally arrived at the theater.

Two paragraphs are given to the discovery of a steel box, which appeared on Gold Egg Beach. So much has washed up since the Big Storm, the Columbus Day Storm, the "Storm of the Century." And so much is still missing, lost in the storm surge that engulfed the boat haven and part of downtown. Suddenly being a scavenger isn't for the faint of heart. Closer to Seattle, for instance, a child's body washed ashore. But some are still compelled to roam the beach, remembering the last time real valuables had been swept up. A box, wood and iron, reputed to be part of the much-sought-after treasure from an old shipwreck. Inside, gold eggs, a baker's dozen. That was back in 1941, the war years, when honesty was patriotic. The gold eggs, according to old stories, were swiftly delivered to the heirs of the embossed name on that box, who, astonished and grateful, donated one—lucky number 13— back to the town museum, where the curator promptly locked it away in a drawer. It was years before most of the town realized the artifact wasn't an egg at all, but a dumpy, flattened sphere, possibly a primitive figurine, its waist encircled by a deeper gold band, as if the object were meant to be opened. Did anyone make the attempt? Was the object hollow, and did they find more treasure inside? Was it indeed gold? The same museum curator, still guarding the treasure in 1963, albeit with less constancy, was reluctant to allow examination. Wasn't the glorious story enough? The true legacy of the shipwreck and gift turned out to be the renaming of the old brickworks beach, still the most popular for scavenging, especially after winter storms. The original native name, long subsumed into white-people translation, was discarded without a second thought.

Hopes for this newly discovered box on Gold Egg Beach, however, are dashed only a paragraph into the newspaper article, because all this new container holds are a few dusty bottles of undrinkable port.

If you'd happened upon Humtown that particular week, you might have mistaken our tiny burg for a bustling hub—underpopulated but soaked in curious happenings. In truth, we are the end of the road, immeasurably bored, enlivened only by gossip. Our key source has, for so very long, emerged from the telephone. Almost the entire town has been on a party line—more accurately, a series of party lines—so that often you are not quite sure whose conversation you're hearing when you lift the receiver. One could spend an entire day cradling phone to ear, of course, locked in place by the kitchen wall or hall table. More commonly, a housewife would pick up the handset to call in an order to the market or reach her sister across town, and before she could ask for the Operator, she'd hear a conversation already underway. Rarely have these overheard fragments been interesting, but occasionally an event occurs that is so perplexing or shocking or thrilling that it seems the whole town wants to weigh in, to piece each stolen nugget of information to another to create a near-seamless narrative, the silent story told in whispers or in the bedroom or better yet on the goddamn phone.

So the big news, the truly stunning news of this tremendous week, is the upending of this pastime due to the long-planned-for switch to dialup. Now, you wouldn't have to be rich or important to get a direct number. No longer would you have to involve the Operator. Nearly a full page in the weekly newspaper is given over to timetables and logistics. If *The Recorder* could have printed the entire new phone book, it would have. That is the nature of public news, the dry obscuring the sensational while other better fodder circulates away from the printed page and its guardians.

As the countdown to dialup begins, gossip burns the wires, as if all must be laid bare at last. Conjecture becomes possible, slides right into certainty. Every lift of the receiver offers a shocking sliver that must be shared again and pieced together with all the others until the full picture emerges. Affairs aren't uncommon, but they are only intimated over the phone. Hard to keep such assignations a secret, though, once a breath of rumor has begun. The next town is a forty-minute drive away, and even there, you might be recognized. Even the most circumspect of illicit lovers has to know how quickly their trysts will become common knowledge, common *currency*. But all that is changing. If you have a secret, well, well, what a marvelous convenience, of course, that dialup is going to be. A real boon!

Helen Hubka, who runs the telephone service almost singlehandedly, would beg to differ. The real news, what folks really needed to know, you couldn't find that in *The Recorder*. Take the latest, not a whiff of which appeared in print, but which, thanks to Helen Hubka, is circulating, gaining substance with each round:

For instance, what isn't mentioned in that article about Gold Egg Beach is an unnerving coincidence, the stunning revelation that the museum's own gold treasure, the non-egg, the mysterious sphere, is missing, replaced by a poor facsimile, spray-painted a lurid mustard color. How? When? No one has answers. The switch might have happened days or months or even a year ago. The last time anyone pulled out the treasure was almost two years ago for a twenty-year celebration. The distraught curator vividly remembers the ceremony that accompanied the object's return to a vault. The sheriff's office seems stumped, which sadly doesn't surprise anyone. Talk is going round of a private detective, an insurance investigation. In whose pocket has that treasure landed? Keep an eye out, the whispers go, for a sudden journey, say, a curious need to visit a sick, out-of-town relative.

Also . . . a man shot on his own boat. Knocked into the water. But he survived. He wasn't local, this fellow, although the man who shot him was. One of the Cravens. Had a woman been aboard? Had they all been drinking? A debt had gone unresolved, threats issued and delivered. That wasn't all. The boat had run aground after the shooting and all the hullaballoo that followed. Wouldn't it have been Craven Hauling that used a kedge anchor to tow it to the boat haven? They claimed it, of course. Salvage rights, they declared. Just as they had with that doomed Canadian sailboat last fall, the one that took away Jay Weller. The real owner of this new snakebit boat might have raised a ruckus, but hadn't. The sheriff himself escorted the stranger straight from the hospital—superficial wounds—to the bus station, a debt possibly settled. And the older Craven boy walked into the courthouse and right out again, uncharged in the end. He was back at the café having breakfast before you could say "boo," and the Cravens, taking no chances this time, had their new vessel hauled out and into dry dock where they could keep an eye on it.

Something hinky was going on at the courthouse, anyway, wasn't it? An outside auditing agency had been called in to comb through the last few years' worth of books. Now, what was the story there? Someone should ask the sheriff's own wife, Peggy. Wasn't she the gatekeeper of the courthouse books? Or maybe look into one of the newer employees, especially one suddenly dressing to the nines and acting haughty, as if she'd just come into a much-awaited inheritance.

And this one: months before, only the day before the calamitous Columbus Day storm, a sheep farmer named Remy Gussie, leaving his barn after a middle-of-the-night emergency with a sick ewe, claimed to see the lights of the family car retreating down the dirt driveway. His young girl-wife often drove their daughters—a toddler and nine-month-old baby—to her parents on the other side of town, those trips usually following a night of what the farmer called "spats," but not in the middle of the night. And nothing like that had happened for days, he said. By the time he'd finished seeing to the sick animal, it was dawn, and he carried on, watering and feeding the sheep before returning to the empty house for breakfast. The car and his family were still gone at suppertime as the storm came up, and all hell broke loose. He'd lost four ewes that night, and hardly cared that his family still wasn't back the next morning. In fact, he was, he claimed, damn tired of her moods, so he waited another day before showing up at her parents', who said they had not seen her for a full week (as he well knew, they wanted to add). The parents called the sheriff, who so far had found no sign of the wife, the children, or the car. An odd duck, that Remy Gussie. A swaggerer, convinced of his own charm, unpredictably brutal with everything from farm animals to borrowed tools. He shot wandering neighborhood dogs on sight and darn-near killed that kid last year, the one picking blackberries on a nearby property line. No one would blame the young girl-wife if she had fled, but then who could believe a word that man breathed? No real investigation had taken place, but rumor had it that now, four months later, one of the wife's brothers had engaged a real detective, a move most of the town, if not the recalcitrant sheriff, would certainly applaud.

Of course, that rumor might have been conflated with another, the detective might be one of the FBI agents who had supposedly returned to town, undercover, and not because of the jailhouse still or a boatyard smuggling ring. They had a local informant, apparently, and were following his lead that one Richard James Young, age thirty-four, one of the FBI's ten-most-wanted criminals—a real bank robber—had found seasonal employment repairing furnace ducts throughout the county and, speculation had it, might still be around, waiting out the winter before fleeing by boat, just another pleasure-seeker or fisherman.

If the Operator, Helen Hubka, were in charge, you could imagine exactly what she'd do. She'd set up a regular roadblock at the edge of town and interrogate everyone who attempted to venture past town limits, because certainly more than a few would be on the run. She'd shake out that stolen egg and the fugitive and the squirrelly secrets of those Cravens and scour out the wheres and whys of the farmer's girl-wife and that bank robber, too. They might even be all together, now that you think about it. But who listens to Helen Hubka? They *hear* her. Her whispered insinuations (*Have you heard?*) lie in the shadows of every conversation, but do they listen? Who could blame her for sometimes simply taking things into her own hands, as she has time and time again?

Yes, in a town as small as this one, miles away from another, we slip into one another's minds, as surely as the Operator herself waits in our homes, coiled within the black cradles of our hall table telephones, listening, following along until we nearly breathe together and speak for one another, ventriloquists all, until suppositions twine and, enthralled, we pass off a story to one then another and another, until a fulsome shape emerges, until at last we can claim the terrible truth of the mischief at hand.

THE FIRST STOP

MILE 6

Though it had rained heavily throughout the night, by the time the walkers set off, what had been a torrent has eased into a steady mist that, only a few blocks in, becomes barely noticeable, a familiar tickle on the face to which all of them (with perhaps one exception) are accustomed. The walkers troop through this uncanny version of their ordinary streets, relieved by the occasional illumination of a streetlight, cheered by the reverberation of their own footsteps. A foghorn nudges, and the faint scent of woodsmoke soothes. Soon their eyes adjust, the mist passes, and the walkers look upward to track the passage of night clouds skittering above, revealing slivers of a star-laden sky beyond.

"How beautiful!" one of the Solidarity girls says, stopping to tilt her head back and gaze.

It's a fact Caroline knows well, but more than a few of the walkers are surprised by how easy it is to claim the night. They drift from the edges and soon are meandering down the middle of the road as if they're on parade. They are the opposite of a mob, a moving silent prayer. The houses remain dark. Even the dogs sleep on, unperturbed.

When the walkers leave the uptown houses behind, the group that sprawled across the narrow uptown streets funnels into a single line along the narrow shoulder of the main thoroughfare out of town. They must brave the main road for the next mile or so, but Warren isn't worried. Other than a single car, which cruises by twice and which he suspects may be his father's, and the rattling milkman's truck, they encounter no other vehicles as they ascend the last hill out of town. The man in the blue woolly cap begins to sing "Rambling Rose," confusing Warren, who only now notes his presence, but making the others smile. Soon the Solidarity girls shift positions to walk nearer him. The fellow's voice is clear and sweet, and when he shifts into Ricky Nelson's "Travelin' Man," at least one of the girls falls instantly in love.

Sadly, romantic notions are short-lived. It is still dark, possibly even gloomier, when they reach Toby's Tavern on the far edge of town, the six-mile mark, where Warren's uncle is waiting. The rain has begun in earnest once more, tapping endlessly on bowed hoods and hats. Necks are aching. Trousers and feet are drenched. They've been walking for not quite two hours, but that's enough for the Solidarity girls. The pure magic of traveling through the night has worn thin for them, overcome by real discomfort and boredom. One is wearing tennis shoes, now completely soaked through, her feet so chilled and stiff that even though she knows she is being irrational, she can't stop thinking about frostbite, about the horror of being toeless in her white summer sandals. The other is astonished to be struggling in her school saddle shoes—she wears them *every* day!—and despite the layering of two pairs of thin socks, her toes and heels burn with oncoming blisters. Each step pierces. And her legs! Those three bare inches between the hem of her skirt and the top of her socks are chafed and numb with cold. More importantly, neither Warren nor Denis is paying any attention to the girls, and the fisherman, Jaspar Goode, as brooding as all the Goodes, actively avoids them, drifting away each time they draw near. They each had hopes for the other fellow with the lovely voice, but he hangs back with that old man, not far from horrible Miss Helen Hubka, and they're not about to walk with *them*. When they make out the headlights of Warren's uncle's car, the Solidarity girls leap toward them as best they can, leading the pack to the first rest stop, the last scheduled one before the fifteen-mile mark. Time to call it quits. For them at least.

The walkers huddle under the tavern's canopy. A few sip hot chocolate from the styrofoam cups Warren's uncle hands around. The Scouts bolt down the warm cinnamon doughnuts Warren's aunt has made. Others nibble. It's too early to be truly hungry, but they all feel justified in calling this breakfast. It's certainly not too early for other needs. After Warren's uncle leaves with the Solidarity girls, the singing fellow who's been walking in the back with Landon tries the back door of Toby's Tavern, and to everyone's surprise, it yields.

"I have a knack with doors," he jokes, "especially when I need to hit the can."

The unfamiliarity of his speaking voice confounds them all as he disappears inside.

But Landon follows, and by then, everyone has to go, a line forming. Warren takes the opportunity to count once more, a show of organization, and either the coming and going from the tavern toilets confuses him or his earlier count was off. (He does briefly overlook Helen Hubka, a Herculean achievement, while she's been seeking relief, assuming incorrectly that, her chaperoning task over, she must have left with the Solidarity girls and his uncle.) Eleven minus three equals eight. But now they are ten, a mathematical surprise that rattles him a little. What else can he have missed?

"Hello, Denis," the woman in the scarf says as they edge past each other at the tavern door.

"Hi, Mrs. Weller." Denis half ducks as if attempting a bow.

Denis does not seem surprised to see Caroline Weller on the walk. He actually looks relieved. Her presence has always been a kind of balm. His beloved kindergarten teacher. Both he and Warren had vied for her love, and she'd easily maneuvered that competition into a friendship, pairing up the boys whenever she could. Yes, Denis and Warren have known each other since they bumbled into Caroline's classroom, with spanking-new crew cuts and near-matching plaid shirts. Jolly boys, half toddlers. On the playground, they'd tussled together like a pair of Mutt-and-Jeff puppies, rolling in the dirt, the playground supervisor constantly setting one or the other upright again and dusting him off. Caroline remembers serious Warren, always playing by the rules, yet breaking every one to whisper through naptime to teach Denis his letters, and little redheaded, freckled Denis, a quicksilver boy, tamping down his own energy to patiently illustrate for a more awkward Warren the best way to traverse the monkey bars.

Their fathers had gone to school together, too, Caroline remembers, and while those two have never been the best friends that Warren and Denis turned out to be, they'd accompanied each other throughout their own boyhoods and now each has taken a place as a town leader. Caroline is amused to see how much the boys now physically resemble their own fathers. Although Denis is still the slighter figure, he is growing into his father's wiry strength and—she can see—already practicing the sheriff's habit of silently (and lengthily) assessing, while one hand idly rubs at his jaw.

The sheriff came to see her after the storm. To express condolences, she thought at first. Later, she remembered how his eyes swept around the room, how he waited patiently after she replied to his questions: that she was as well as she could be, that yes, Jay's workshop survived the storm intact, that no, Jay had no one working with him these past months, relying on Charlie Beecher only when he needed help. Just making conversation, she thought, but he sat in silence after each of her replies, as if suggesting she was holding something back. But when *she* asked him about what he knew about Jay's last moments, he only shook his head. "It's a mystery to you, is it?" he finally asked, as if he'd been expecting her to tell him why Jay was down at the docks that exact moment. She remembered then why Jay refused to play poker with the sheriff: "The fellow takes forever to place his bet. Makes me jumpy as hell."

On Denis, however, the sheriff's contemplative gestures seem sharper and sweeter—a more inward calculation, as if he's continually taking his own measure, not the other fellow's. While Warren pushes forward, as single-minded as a sheepdog trying to corral his flock, Denis seems to have his nose in the air, jaggedly alert, ready to offset trouble before he even finds it. A good boy.

They both are. Warren is a near-spitting-image of the newspaper editor, a broad-shouldered man with heavy eyebrows. Yet, he, too, clearly differs from his father. Look at him, Caroline thinks, with almost proprietary pride. A born leader. Not like his father. No, not at all.

The boys' fathers might be big shots in town, but both the sheriff and the newspaperman seem determined not to draw attention to themselves. They are public servants. They are *of the town*. Like Jay, but then nothing like Jay, who would jump to lend a helping hand, regardless of the mess he'd find. Obviously. In contrast, neither the sheriff nor the newspaperman is given to stirring the pot, stubbornly pursuing what they perceive as their respective roles of peacekeeper and recorder. In fact, the only thing that can rankle either one of them is meddling from outsiders. For the sheriff, that means he will not brook any state or federal interference. While the newspaperman remains myopic, a frequent whitewasher of difficult news, dedicated to a straightforward reporting of local society dinners, high school sports, and upbeat business reports.

Caroline remembers, too, how Warren's mother could be counted on for any classroom help, but Denis's mother, Peggy, a secretary at the courthouse in the auditor's office, couldn't spare a moment. She still handles all the property tax payments and collects fees for vehicle and boat registrations. Drawers of cash that must be carefully counted, locked in a safe, and then bundled into a zippered leather pouch and delivered in hand to the bank each Friday. An important job, the kindergartener Denis informed her. Back then, he'd been so proud of his father with his badge and his mother with her bank-bag duty, and Denis hadn't minded at all that he often went home with Warren. Of course, Denis would be on the Big Walk with his best friend, but Caroline can't help wondering what the sheriff thinks about this walk and whether he'll be there at its ending and how he will deal with its outcome, all the trouble she'll have caused him.

After the two girls depart, the group seems to take a deep communal breath. It's not yet light, but their eyes have adjusted, and only a few are using their flashlights now. The rain is letting up, *again*, but hats and hoods remain in place. They are heading west, the smudged sky heavy, a rising wind slapping at their faces, yet behind them a faint glow, the new day shouldering through, and as the light it brings gradually creeps around and over them, they can make out the contours of figures, put voice to shape if not face as bits of conversation burble and drift.

In those early miles through the night, Helen Hubka had been kept busy eavesdropping on the Solidarity girls' gossip and trying to suss out possible reasons why three grown men—that singing fellow (Danny?); one of the Goodes, Jaspar, the least sociable (he'd run away somewhere, hadn't he?); and that old tomcat Landon Wills—would choose to undertake this tromp. Certainly she knows about Caroline Weller's constant rambles. Who doesn't? A surprise to see her here, but not a shock. The poor woman is unhinged. And of course, no one has asked Helen *her* reasons, and she wouldn't tell the truth if they did. Her admiration for her young President is deep, private, and abiding, one of the few secrets she thinks she can keep. In a metal box beneath the switchboard are her "Kennedy cards," photograph postcards she's been collecting since before the election, featuring handsome Jack and (sometimes) his elegant child-wife. Helen Hubka snaps up the cards as they appear and, with each new addition, marvels at the young President's relentless courage. He's very ill; she knows that. Addison's disease, back pain, lingering injuries from the war. Yet look how hard he works! When she first heard of the Big Walk and saw how the President's brother Bobby leapt into the task, Helen Hubka felt a strange stirring inside her as she sat beside her narrow switchboard. That *emotion*—it wasn't anxiety or longing or even distant admiration. No, Helen Hubka was overcome by something closer to what she imagined her President might have felt as a naval lieutenant on the PT 109 as he threw himself into keeping that boat and crew safe in the bomb-strewn South Pacific. She felt *called. He'd* called her to action, and by God, she was ready, already humming Jimmy Dean's fabulous tune about the PT 109 to herself. Yes, she would walk and walk and walk and wait for whatever noble task appeared. But would it hurt if she gained a little useful information along the way?

Who's left? All these boys—which makes perfect sense. The girl, though—What is she? Twelve? Thirteen?—this child is a mystery. Shouldn't she have left with the other Solidarity girls?

As Helen Hubka sidles up to link her arm with Caroline's, anyone might make out the slight recoil, the dismayed drooping of Caroline's shoulders as she reconciles herself to the gossip's company. But Helen Hubka is disappointed to learn that Caroline, who's walked side by side with the girl, has only learned the child's first name—*Avis*—and the fact that the girl's family is new to town. Her father? Her mother? Does she have more family nearby—siblings, cousins, a grandmother?

Caroline shakes her head. "I don't know." She almost snaps, *Ask her yourself*, but restrains herself. No one would wish Helen Hubka on the unsuspecting, especially if her quarry is an innocent child.

Everyone but the girl, this Avis, and the singing man knows Helen Hubka. Warren and Denis have been schooled not to mention anything near her, not even what they ate for supper the night before. "She knows what you had for lunch before I do," Warren's mother has complained. Caroline learned long ago not to say much to anyone but Jay. News travels so quickly in town that the edges burn off and other bits floating by can stick, obscuring and rearranging, so that each time the news lands, a different shape emerges. She was hugely dismayed to see Helen Hubka on the walk. A mouth full of kindling awaiting the tinder box, the flint, the snap of the flame. The trouble that woman has caused. Marriages set alight, families ashed. It was Helen Hubka who passed on the erroneous information that sent the best teacher Caroline had ever known running from town. "Light in his loafers." "Not the marrying kind." "A *friend* in the city." She kept it coming over the party line until she had a cluster of parents squirreling around to find real fault. The poor fellow. Nothing Caroline or any other teacher could say would quell fears or dissuade that good man from leaving. Who could blame him?

Helen Hubka's surely spread a rumor or two about Caroline and Jay. In fact, Caroline probably has her to thank for her continued surveillance by half the town. Maybe that's even why the woman's on the walk. Caroline resolves to keep her own mouth shut.

Helen Hubka tries to eye up Avis through the speckled dark. Astoundingly, she doesn't seem to know the girl or her people, and Avis isn't helping. Yes, she lives in town. On Bryant Street. The yellow Victorian. Caroline feels a little pinch at this revelation. Avis's house is a special one. Everyone in town, Caroline thinks, fosters a secret wish to one day own that house with its yew and rose garden, widow's walk, its multipaned conservatory and notoriously cavernous basement. The house had been empty since late last summer, the sales price well above any local's means.

"The Mudge House?" Helen Hubka says. "You're the ones that got the Mudge House?"

Infuriatingly, the girl appears puzzled.

"*Our* house," she finally says.

"It's haunted, isn't it? An unlucky family, weren't they, the Mudges? Despite all that shipping fortune."

The impossible child only stares rudely at Helen Hubka, not one clue offered.

Helen Hubka seems to struggle with herself over how much to interrogate outright. She knows the new owner of the Mudge House works at the mill, but unforgivably, she knows nothing of the man's wife, whose voice she cannot recall hearing once. Her mouth fills with questions, even as she scours her own considerable storehouse of stolen conversations for clues: *Who is your mother? Does she belong to any clubs? Have you any brothers or sisters? Where did you move from?*

Who are your people?

What are your secrets?

How did you steal the Mudge House away from us?

The girl isn't biting. Not when named ghosts and other seductive wraiths are offered; not when a nonexistent shed filled with the Mudge-enchanted fishing nets is mentioned; not even when the Operator begins the tale of a blind cat who haunts the Mudge House with a peculiar yowling. The girl does look up at this, but stays silent and soon alters her pace so that she walks either in front of Caroline, falls back beside Landon, or hustles up next to the fisherman. Helen Hubka steers clear of that particular Goode and thinks the girl should as well, but she can't walk fast enough at the moment to correct the situation. And Landon won't stand for her nonsense. She can almost hear him.

Scat! he ordered her once, when she came sniffing around the newspaper office.

The wind rises and washes out every other attempt at real conversation as they turn onto Quarry Road, which doesn't feel like a road at all, but a forgotten byway whose corrugated pavement could use attention. The gray figures of the walkers spread over the empty street once more, one or two flashlights pop on again.

Frustrated, Helen Hubka half hollers to Caroline: "*Ginny still canoodling with the savages?*"

Before Caroline can say a word, the distracted Operator trips and is saved only by Caroline's firm grasp. A selfless act. The woman latches on to Caroline, linking arms firmly once again. For now, at least, Avis is safe from interrogation. Not a terribly big deal, Caroline thinks. After all, what secrets can a child have that would interest Helen Hubka?

AVIS'S SECRETS

SECRET #I

Avis's brother is broken, and that brokenness is the reason they've ended up in this tiny, grim Northwest town. Her father maintains that Teddy's problems were ignited by overcoddling (her mother's) and censure (those damn nuns) and avoidance (his own relations). He's stopped short of blaming Avis, too. As far as he knows, despite other claims, she has been nothing but mere witness from birth. Teddy's not talking. Teddy's all action. He hasn't killed anyone—*don't be hysterical, Avis, of course not!*—but he's come closer than anyone (other than she) knows.

Avis remembers the Saturday morning they'd stood in the long line at the public high school—an alien place, a public school—to get their sugar cubes soaked in polio vaccine. How Teddy had tried to get her to distract the nurse, his constant nagging in her ear. His plan had been to snatch as many sugar cubes as he could and substitute them for plain ones in the convent dining room. How he planned to get into the convent without a nun noticing was not clear to Avis. But she didn't question that if he did manage to get the sugar cubes, he would do it. He would poison the nuns. Teddy hated them all, even kind Sister Redempta, whom no one could fault, who'd once loaned a sniffling Avis her nun handkerchief and told her to come find her any time she needed help. A big phony, Teddy called her, the worst. They'd been separated at the end of the vaccine line, and of course, Avis hadn't been able to assist Teddy, but in the car on the way home, he opened a now-familiar linen handkerchief. In its center, three oddly translucent sugar cubes. He'd been eleven then, a sweet-looking, bright-eyed boy. Teddy is seventeen now, his birthday the first of January, and this is his New Year, her mother says.

Everyone but her father has been slow to make acquaintances in Humtown, their anonymity a condition her mother seems to relish, but if anyone does ask, her mother briskly informs them that Avis's father is the engineer at the paper mill. She does not mention they've moved here because the town and job are three thousand miles from her own family and Teddy and Avis's old school and a chatty neighborhood where doors shut and locked when Teddy sauntered outside, where Avis's former friends rode their bikes, at speed, away from her daily. In private, Avis's father says they've moved here because the Northwest is an honest, no-frills reality, unlike the East Coast, which is rife with pretense, neurosis, and unreasonable expectation. A boy can practice with his archery set or master a BB gun or play teasing games with a stray cat without a bunch of Nervous Nellies raising alarms. A safe place, too. *You think the Soviets are ever going to aim missiles out here in the wilderness!* her father's proclaimed. *Not enough people for their trouble.* No, her father couldn't imagine a better place to weather a crisis, any crisis. Trying to jolly them, her father went a step too far: *Who needs a bunker,* he added with a laugh, oblivious of her mother's discomfort, *if the town itself is one?*

Yes, let's say they moved here, too, because a hard-earned dollar goes a lot further, so much so that her father's salary and the proceeds from the Philadelphia house grew more and more majestic as they'd traveled east to west. They've moved here, one might even imagine, so that her mother could achieve a dream, the Victorian house, period details fully intact, astonishingly not in need of substantial work but rather only *deepening*, her mother said, which, given the endless catalogs and wallpaper and fabric swatches that arrived in the mail, certainly meant *decorating*. Some days, she hardly shifts from the dining room, which resembles nothing so much as the back corner of a cluttered hardware store, with rolls of old wallpaper and bins for oddities like the tiny screws that secure the house's glass doorknobs in place. This is her mother's job now, the restoration of an imagined time, and she has never been happier. Or more oblivious.

Because clearly the house demands more. At night, wind whistles through cracks in the sills and radiators clank with wild abandon. A faint mewling crawls within the walls. Foghorns join this syncopation, which might also include a clattering that her father teases must be the windblown rigging of ghost sloops anchored in the bay below. To Avis, the house itself feels like one of those ships, but not one safely moored in the bay. No, this ship is broken and adrift, hanging on through the elements with brittle timbers and tilting masts. Still, her father raves about *the history! the promise!*, totally blind to the fact that those two qualities must necessarily cancel each other out. Her mother persistently confuses decay with charm. Avis has come to realize that her parents' preferred state is a kind of limbo, a floating place seemingly immune to visible conflict, and that in moving here, they believe they've landed squarely within its borders.

A perfect fit, because as Avis knows, the most important reason they've moved here is that everyone is a stranger to them, and no one knows anything about Teddy . . . or Avis . . . or, well, any of them.

Is it a coincidence that they've arrived, too, in a season of limbo: the middle of the school year, the dimmed heart of winter? Back home, as Philadelphia greeted weeks of snow, followed by days of sharp blue skies, Avis would revel in the adventure of a walk, the thrill of becoming snow-blind as she tromped off unshoveled sidewalks, over slushy gutters, her salt-stained boots squeaking with every step. Here, despite the idyllic-sounding location—*on the water!* her father had exclaimed, *beside the mountains!*—winter means nothing; it's a ghost of a season. Avis is continually lost in this sunken, end-of-the-road gray village, assaulted by bitter wind and constant rain and bottle-green waves. No one mentioned to her, either, that because they'd be that much farther north, the light would not appear until well into the school day and be shut away before she got home. Yes, here, they are formally setting up camp in a kind of Purgatory, right next door to Hell, which is a step up, she has to admit, or, more accurately, a relieving step back from the precipice onto which Teddy propelled them all.

As if to keep up with the Victorian dream he'd satisfied for her mother, Avis's father has claimed his own dream, his own outsize plans. In addition to his new job at the mill, he is now researching a sunken ship, a fascination sparked by a new friend at work. For the first time, wonder of wonders, Teddy's interest has been piqued, and whatever anger her father imagines Teddy harbored from birth has been vaulted at last. Her father, of course, has always believed he and Teddy were destined to be buddies, so despite what must be his better judgment, he welcomed Teddy into the project.

One full section of basement walls is covered with hand-drawn charts that Avis herself discovered behind a false wall in a bedroom cupboard. (*A real find!* her father congratulated her.) A long table holds a plaster-of-Paris topographical map that Teddy may have made or may have stolen in pieces from the musty, seldom-visited town museum. No, not a topographical map, her father corrects, a *bathymetrical* map. This rendering shows the depths of the ocean, a completely hidden seascape, laying out what her father calls "the shipwreck trail, the Graveyard of the Pacific." A commonplace event, it seemed, in the latter part of the last century, to pack a trunk and board a steamer in full faith of arrival, despite unpredictable winds and high seas and rogue storms and constant news of midnight shipwrecks. Ships fell to collisions with lightning or rocky shores or even other ships. Boiler fires, shattered masts. The waters here so deep and wild that, once lost in the waves, few bodies were ever recovered, even in current times. The worst of the stretch from San Francisco to Victoria, British Columbia, lay in their new nautical backyard, along the Pacific coast between the Columbia River and the Strait of Juan de Fuca. The town museum, her father declares, keeps a log listing near-monthly catastrophes for decades. Either the original or a copy of that log now lives in Avis's basement. Steamers, trawlers, schooners. Pick one. Her father and Teddy have. They are only interested in one dramatic ship, laden, of course, with a singular treasure when it went down. Her father has interrogated his equally obsessive friend at the mill. He has performed calculations. He consults charts and logs and weather patterns. Teddy has trawled through borrowed books to make lists of that particular sunken cargo. Avis doesn't quite understand their passion. Even if her father manages to accurately pinpoint the current location of the shipwreck (if it were still intact), how would they reach it and who would want ancient bottles of whiskey and port?

"There's much more to it than that," her father says while Teddy practices a quiet grin, his new impersonation, this one of a wholesome Northwest teen immersed in a dreamy, boyish hobby.

Avis isn't fooled. An image of a ghostly Teddy plundering beneath the sea floats by her, a giant in the ship's close, flooded cabins. In the weeks since they moved, Avis's brother has grown full inches and leaned out even more, and now he looms over even her father, who has to reach up for his awkward pats on Teddy's shoulder.

"Weeks after the shipwreck, a tiny metal box washed up on the beach by the Point," her father informed Avis not long ago.

"Gold Egg Beach," Avis said, showing off her new local knowledge.

Her father was still talking: "The people here, of course, tried to restore what they rescued to the heirs of the family whose name was engraved on the box. But I guess they didn't have much luck, because the town ended up keeping their prize. We've seen it, haven't we, Teddy?"

The new grin again, shaded just a little.

"It's not on display, but Teddy found a photograph in the museum archives. It's probably been locked in a drawer downtown for decades."

"Would have to be," the newly agreeable Teddy concurred.

"And it's not an egg at all. In fact," her father declared, "as far as I can figure, it most closely resembles a Klerksdorp sphere. Absolutely ancient, those spheres, billions of years old, but Klerksdorp spheres are pyrophyllite, not gold like this one, and extremely rare, found only in isolated parts of South Africa. Still, the resemblance is uncanny.

"The thing is," he went on, "that gold knickknack, that Klerksdorp shape, was part of a larger set of gold valuables. All the cargo was lost except that one little box. Maybe it was all they could grab during the chaos of that night. The rest, you see, must have been secured in the ship's hold and is very likely still there."

"What happened to the people?" Avis asked.

"What's that?" Her father leaned in, as if now she were the one presenting a puzzle.

"The ones who owned the gold. On the ship? Was anyone rescued?"

"No one claimed the treasure," Teddy said. His voice held a warning only Avis seemed to hear.

"Fair game for one and all," her father added.

Her father's new friend at the mill confided that he knew of an expert team of divers who specialized in shipwrecks. *They'd love a good look at those charts you found,* his friend had said. Avis's father spoke as if this intrepid team were only waiting for him and Teddy to reveal the spot where the shipwreck had drifted before, like every other vessel that met misfortune out there, it sank so deep it might as well have vanished. Holding forth, her father radiated an uncharacteristic swagger, as if he believed his ingenious engineering calculations would lead them to the exact spot the divers needed. Avis couldn't help thinking, too, that her father half believed he and Teddy were slipping through time to become rogues together in this outpost of a state, a onetime haunt of outlaws, where a character like Teddy, recast as an adventurer, would certainly have prospered, flitting from one grand, illicit scheme to another. Yet even her father would have to admit that limits had been set, that laws would prevail, that even a broken boy, beguiled by history, must face justice eventually.

SECRET #2

Say, for instance, a single gold relic of a long-ago, misbegotten journey became the prized possession of the town museum, and if, one day, the curator noticed it had been replaced by an ordinary toy, spraypainted gold, well, the thief would certainly be pursued. But say, too, that particular sort of thief was the kind who would react very badly, enacting a bitter revenge even before, or perhaps to prevent, being caught and punished. Some things didn't change. Her parents might have fooled themselves, but Avis knew that all too soon Teddy would come for her again, dragging her further and further into his troubles, and if she dared to gasp a complaint, he would only smile and say, *You're in as deep as I am.*

Once again, Avis was swimming in a dreamscape wherein she must constantly search, accumulating clues to solve a mystery that hadn't yet arrived, a mystery that, once exposed, would unravel this tentative ease, that would break her family once and for all. So she'd been reading Humtown's weekly newspaper cover to cover to keep abreast of potential enticements, to keep real destruction at bay, and when she had to, she would cut out an article and hide it in her geography textbook, so that Teddy wouldn't run across certain information or her parents note the familiarity of certain petty thefts, discoveries that were sure to end with blame raining on Avis from all directions. When she spotted the bland article about the latest discovery on Gold Egg Beach, the near-empty box that should have held treasure, of course she acted. That evening, her father groaned as he turned a mutilated news page, a missing rectangle in one corner.

"What? Are we being censored in this house?" he said.

"Recipes," she told him with a manufactured sigh that implied she could not account for her mother's bad habits. "Fish cakes. Chowder."

The next afternoon, as the rumor about the missing egg began sifting through town, Avis found herself alone in the house—*with* the house, she might have said—her father at the mill, her mother seduced downtown by a paint store advertisement, and Teddy momentarily held tight by a dentist appointment. Alone for at least an hour. A sign, for sure. She didn't bother searching Teddy's room. Other boys might compile their stolen treasures and hide them within a stuffed cigar box held closed with a rubber band. Not Teddy. He believed the surest way to hide something was to place it in full sight, preferably wrapped within someone else's belongings. *Who's to blame? Not me!* Avis rummaged through her own bookcase, her mother's desk, the top of her father's highboy, familiar objects out of place in these high-ceilinged narrow rooms. She crawled through the backs of closets, lifting flaps of old wallpaper, tapping on cupboards and loose stair boards. One narrow room off the kitchen had long been used as a kind of in-house shed, the sort of place in their old house Teddy would certainly use. Here, he physically recoiled from that space for reasons Avis hadn't yet fathomed. She searched it anyway. In the kitchen, she peered into saucepans, stirred the sugar bowl, even examined the refrigerator egg tray. The deep corners of the cavernous basement, damp-smelling and shadowed, did not deter her, but again, she found nothing, and she would have left off her search there if she hadn't caught sight of a faint but noticeable crack along the highest range of the underwater plaster-of-Paris mountain, a change that not a soul other than Avis might spot, Teddy's joke slowly dawning on her: the gold hidden again within the sea. Under the plywood table, her father's flashlight in one hand, his utility knife in the other, Avis was able to pry out the neat door her brother had sliced into the plywood base, put down the flashlight, and with a measure of pride and terror, reach up through crumbled plaster until her hand closed around the prize she knew she'd find.

Now what?

Avis didn't dare examine the treasure in the basement. She replaced the square of plywood, wedging it tightly so it would not fall out, swept the bits of plaster dust into a dustpan she emptied in a spidery corner, and cleaned her own hands on a rag on her father's workbench. She didn't dare examine the gold egg then or even brush off the plaster dust still clinging to its gleaming sides. Instead, as calmly as she could, she carried her find to her bedroom. She allowed herself one terrifying minute of observation, turning the object around in her hands, before she dropped it into the end of one of her long gray knee socks. Then she rolled the sock together with its mate and stuck the sock ball at the front of her dresser drawer. A completely ordinary, if alarmingly heavy, pair of socks. Avis moved through these tasks with unerring purpose as if, she felt later, she'd been instructed, and remarkably, for that entire afternoon, she did not feel the usual despair that came with daring to touch one of Teddy's "discoveries." On the contrary, a glorious peace entered her, as if she'd done a very good deed, performed a kind of rescue that also rendered *her* grateful. But what had she done? *Nothing*, a thrillingly calm voice inside her nudged. *Yet.*

Of course, any suggestion of serenity evaporated as the hours passed, and Teddy and her parents returned. What *had* she done? What should she do? She couldn't put her find back; she couldn't keep it. Certainly, she could not restore it to the town. She knew the turmoil that would ensue once Teddy decided to reclaim his prize from its hiding place—and found it missing. He might leave it untouched for a few days or even a week or two. And he might, Avis tried to believe, blame their father. Or maybe he'd suspect locals—the gasman or any of the extended family of broad-shouldered handymen her mother threatened to telephone weekly or even his father's inquisitive friend from the mill. He might even consider the ghosts in the house, the unseen ones who opened and closed doors and chattered indistinctly in the empty halls throughout the night. So many possibilities. But all too soon, Avis knew, he'd light on her.

SECRET #3

That same Wednesday, Avis spotted the tiny announcement of the Kennedy Walk, also in the pitiful local paper, and, as she lay in bed worrying, the sweet synchronicity hit her. She'd read most of the President's speech in a national newspaper in the school library and pored over every photograph of the Big Walk in *Life* magazine: Bobby Kennedy in his black loafers walking along a frozen towpath in Maryland with his Bernese Mountain dog,

California teenagers in tattered shorts and sunglasses, housewives bundled up in Minnesota, Boy Scouts and soldiers—the whole country taking up the President's challenge. "Walking Madness," the *Life* article called it. That Wednesday night, she scoured the battered, unpacked boxes in her closet to find her summer sneakers, hoping they'd look like the pair of Keds one weary girl from California wore, the one who had almost set a record. In the end, Avis pulled out the sturdy black shoes she'd worn every day to St. James before the so-called accident that removed her from parochial school and the near anonymity that a daily uniform provided.

Fifty miles. Yes, she thought, that should be far enough.

All were sleeping when Avis pushed away. Even the night chatter of the house itself, those constant hallway murmurs Avis had almost become used to, had ceased, as if the house were holding its breath for her. After dinner, while Teddy and her father were colluding in the basement and her mother was soaking in the deepest clawfoot bathtub, Avis had managed to put together two peanut butter and jelly sandwiches, wrap them in wax paper, and fill an old canteen of her father's with water. From the bathroom's creaky medicine chest: a Band-Aid tin and a tiny bottle of Mercurochrome. All efficiently set within her red plaid bookbag. She had thought about using her only piece of luggage, a square blue box with a wide handle, a Christmas present from her grandmother. A train case, her grandmother called it. Her mother referred to the little suitcase as a cosmetic bag. Neither use was right for Avis. She wiggled two rolls of Life Savers—5 Flavors and Wint-O-Green—into her coat pocket, then, almost as if to hide them, added her tiny spiral assignment book and two pencils. She might, she reasoned, need to jot down directions. And then, light-headed with fear, Avis eased the pretend pair of spare socks into a bottom corner of the near-empty bookbag. To be safe, she tucked the bookbag under her pillow. After saying goodnight to her parents, she changed out of her pajamas, layering one cotton blouse over another and dragging on an old pair of Teddy's outgrown dungarees.

Did she sleep?

Of course not.

No, Avis embarked on the walk right then, mentally charting an imaginary course, drifting and startling from the lightest of dozes even as she pretended to court rest. She worried a scab on her arm, relieved by the sharp, distracting pain, the trickle of blood so small she could lick it away. Doors and floorboards creaked continually. A radiator rumbled and clanked as if about to drum into song, the fractured almost-music of this house a near explosion she never heard during daylight hours. Avis waited for another shift, waited and waited, until Teddy finally shut the basement door behind him. He hadn't been in the basement all that time. She was sure of that, and yet he always returned through that underworld route. Teddy owned the night here in Humtown and would never guess anyone else in the family would dare to claim it, especially not Avis, who was wary of this place and seemed incapable of remembering the few street names. He'd let her alone these past couple of months while he himself unraveled and beguiled Humtown. He did not know she'd gone inward, that she'd been busy learning all she could about the house, about how her family used it, and how the house received them. She could pinch out the sound of her brother's footsteps, light and quick on the stairs, wait for his door in the attic to ease shut with a clear snap. Wait until the house adjusted, gathering in Teddy, a wire of tension rising with him, then slowly, slowly ebbing until he finally slept. Even so, Avis knew enough to close her eyes and wait some more, deliberately ignoring a faint but clearly audible purring coming from inside the wall behind her bed.

A little after three in the morning, she pulled on a sweatshirt, strapped her bookbag like a rucksack on her back, dragged her blue-checked rain slicker over all, pulled up her hood and tightened it. Passing the hall mirror in the dark, she glimpsed her ghostly outline and smiled at the thought that she might finally be capable of startling even Teddy. Still, the journey to the high school parking lot might have been the hardest part of the whole trek. Even as she put one block behind her and another and another and began the climb toward the high school hill, she felt her mother's dream house looming behind the walled night, and she couldn't help wondering if it would tell on her. She couldn't help imagining Teddy roused from his subterranean dreams, his hands clawing for his treasure; Teddy, stirred by the mischievous house; Teddy, waking and knowing immediately what was missing and setting out to get it back.

DRIFTING

Three lonely houses along Quarry Road, and at this hour, even lonelier with curtains drawn, rooms unlit, and one lone dog fruitlessly signaling their passage. In this March morning, overlaid with gloom, true sunrise is still an hour away, and as the badly paved road gives way to what should be gravel, conditions underfoot change from bad to worse. The few patches of navigable ground are islands within troughs of mud, of deep puddles too wide to leap. Warren shouts back warnings over his shoulder, purposefully slows as he leads the walkers to the high, dry edges of this broken road.

Jaspar Goode offers assistance to the women, but neither Helen Hubka nor Caroline registers his outstretched arm, only the halting shadow in front of them, and he puts his big hand down as the women edge by him. Avis slips among them. Caroline worries about this remaining girl, who seems not much more than a child. It's a forgotten sensation, that worrying, and Caroline is surprised and a little irritated by how much she welcomes it.

Are you okay? she wants to ask, but the teenager is intent on moving forward and clearly insensible to everything but the troublesome ground beneath her own two feet.

Not true.

Avis can hear the men and boy behind her. One is humming, one is lightly sniffling, one has an occasional barking cough. Only the fisherman is silent, and she will be surprised to see him when they all meet up again. She won't have counted him in, and that will add to her growing sense of dislocation. She nearly slips, nearly has her own fall. As she recovers, Avis looks through the gloaming light to see a disgusting sight, a glistening blob oozing on the side of one shoe. A giant worm? Worse, more appear strewn over the ground. The other walkers deftly bypass them, hardly paying attention, but Avis, who wants to leap over and tiptoe around simultaneously, develops a tangled walk as she tries to avoid the creatures.

"Watch out for slugs," Warren calls out belatedly.

What a mess this road is. Warren thinks of his originally planned route over main roads, paved roads. Geez, why had he listened to Landon?

"See here, boy," Landon had half growled as he spread out maps and took a pencil out from behind his ear. "If you take Quarry Road to Forgotten Bay"—he drew a line—"you can pick up the tracks."

Not the tracks, exactly, but the flat access road that follows the old railway. It would be easy then to chart their progress using the railroad markers. Of course, it made sense when presented on a piece of paper. A better route, no question. But had Landon mentioned mud? A rock strewn gully? Early March rains always create vast puddles—why point out the obvious?—and who can't figure out ways to skirt those? Other damage, most likely inflicted way back in October during the biggest storm of all time, the Columbus Day disaster, well that residue, Landon would have to agree he didn't anticipate that, and it's proving far harder to overcome.

It's not long before an insurmountable problem emerges. The road ahead is blocked by a near wall of fallen debris, as if a tractor pushed it there. If what they're seeing with their flashlights is right, beyond that is a washed-out section, too large to leap across, the very edges sheared away, impassable, it seems. The first walkers (the Scouts, of course) hover, waiting for guidance. Warren works his way back to Landon, who knows every inch of this area and carries a thousand maps in his head. Landon lights another slim cigar, spits into the chalky light. If he's shaken by the idea of a vanished road, he doesn't show it.

Landon hasn't been out this way since the epic storm—who had!—had no clue about the damage, which is immense, but that's life, isn't it? One damn thing after another. They can walk all the way back to the highway, he finally tells Warren, which will add miles to the walk and upend the course altogether. Or take another slight chance and backtrack a bit to follow a farm fence that parallels this track and eventually should let them loop back to Quarry Road. The whole dang thing can't be washed away!

Landon jabs at Warren's damp map to show the revised route, but honestly Warren isn't completely following. "Circle back here," the old man says, and Warren only sees the round flashlight beam owning the map's center. Rougher going than planned, and Warren hasn't bargained for injuries. One broken leg or sprained ankle and they might have to call the whole walk off. But what choice do they have? Landon shepherds them back down the way they'd come and soon leads them off the road, tromping high weeds that scratch their hands and snatch at their trousers until, mercifully, they reach a wire fence, a bristled field on the other side. The old man expertly bends the wire fence, a feat of magic, and waits for each of them to squeeze through before easing through himself and setting the fence back in place.

"Make 'em all stay close to the fence line and each other," he tells Warren, advice the boy almost immediately forgets in his hurry to get this walk back on track.

Caroline drifts. She puts a little distance between herself and the others. A little more. Soon, she is farther out in the field, and maybe she's alone. She feels alone. It doesn't matter. You could stay as close together as you liked, and trouble would still reach you. Caroline and Jay. Jay and Caroline. One unthinkable without the other. The widows in town came to visit Caroline, one by one or in little groups, as if to bring her into the fold. They put away dishes in the kitchen, folded towels in the bathroom, smoothed the cushions on the sofa. They made strong tea, cut cake, arranged flowers. One lady from church even surreptitiously read fortune-telling cards for Caroline, who, God help her, briefly believed in a future. Always she worked around the women, sweeping a floor, pinning damp clothes to a swinging clothesline, while they sang their familiar chorus. Caroline has learned most of the words by now, but can't seem to find the right order, if there is one.

The empty side of the bed
A single plate on the dining table
A sock drawer, boots in the hall
The rattling sound of a pickup truck

They meant well. Laying out the traps, so that she wouldn't be caught unawares. But is there anything that won't assault her?

Whiskey over ice

A whistling man

His winter jacket with its pockets full of wish rocks plucked during beach walks

Woodsmoke

Couples holding hands

Wind, she thinks. *Rain.*

The whole damn world.

She's exhausted. Maybe she could lie in this field, she thinks, and will her heart to stop.

She's learned from the widows' whispers that in the early days of intense mourning shock can damage a heart so badly it can just stop—if you let it. Some of the widows seemed to be warning her. Others appeared wistful. Caroline is still furious. She remembers two days after Jay's storm when her house was full of neighbors and she'd slipped off to lie alone in their bedroom for a few minutes. Overcome, overcome, she felt the room spin wildly, rushing away from her in bits so that she seemed to be standing on an open threshold, in a grayed field not unlike this one. Something had been offered to her then. A release. A split-second opportunity. She realized that too late, of course, and even as she regained her balance and began contemplating the strangeness of that fractured moment, a knock interrupted. More tea? A blanket? A little soup?

How about now? she wants to plead to whoever had cracked that door open for her. *Now would be good.*

A tiny flash of light in the gloaming sends her heart soaring, but it's only a flashlight reaching toward her much the same way the rangy man in Charlie Beecher's rowboat had, pointing her back to safety. Another man appears beside her, an abrupt materialization that shocks her and makes her heart thunder promisingly. She stops short, but when he reaches out to steady her, she sees it's the big fisherman, Jaspar Goode. Here we go again, a flustered Caroline thinks, because, although neither of them says anything, Caroline understands she's gone astray and he's been sent to fetch her, to set her back in line. Only then does she register a distant scraping sound and see the winking lights of what she supposes to be a tractor off in the distance. The morning is here. She's too late, as always. She shifts course to walk beside the fisherman until she can make out the outlined figures of the other walkers, and, corralled, stride into place behind Avis, resigned once more to the miles she must yet walk. Her own finish line.

IN FULL LIGHT

For a while, the going isn't tough at all. The ground is like the sheared back of the sheep that must graze here. Rough in stretches, woolly and tangled. Patches of flattened grass, mud, manured straw. The walkers learn to find the high, mud-free spots, to dance from one to another, everyone following Warren's lead, in his exact footsteps. The wind, which had all but left them alone in the woods, picks up as they lumber along the fence, but that's all right, too. The wind eases the stink of sheep. It's near daylight, and almost to a person, they are feeling revived. Well, except for Avis, who's locked in a never-ending daydream.

The promise of full daylight teases as they thrash along, and as if to emphasize the strangeness, here is that distant but constant chopping, drawing closer and closer to the group. Yes, Avis is dream-walking, and with her newfound country knowledge, she decides that noise means someone is shoveling a deep hole in hard clay. Maybe her father, who has been struggling to dig out a row of what he calls invasive blackberries—as if that were a thing!—and when he tries to persuade Teddy to help, his demonstrated efforts produce the same escalating, painful sound she hears now. In the garden, her father attacks with wild abandon, hopelessly slamming an old spade under the brambles. Outside her bedroom door, Teddy skulks before taking up his own version of a pickaxe. *Chop, chop*, he hacks and hacks away at their new safety. He thinks she is clueless, but his breath, the shuffle of his feet, suddenly too large, can't navigate the creaky halls of this old house, their "new" house, without signaling his every move. *Chop, chop*, and Teddy is out, roving. *Chop, chop*, and Teddy is waking up. *Chop, chop*, and Avis's step quickens. Teddy is looking for her.

* * *

Old Landon has taken up the near end of the line once more. Later, he might wish he'd been the one in front, the first one to glimpse what the Scouts thought was a lantern and what Warren and Caroline correctly took to be the lights on a tractor in the field beyond. The first one to hear however faintly the grinding of a stump, a thump and scrape. Landon would have acknowledged straightaway, even without fully knowing, that they'd trespassed into trouble. And then, too, he'd realize how close they were to Remy Gussie's back land and how strange it would be for a man like Remy, a sheep farmer, to be driving his D6 Cat beside this near-forgotten edge of property at this hour. He surely would have noticed, too, the way that light was swiftly extinguished as the group crept closer to the fence line, flashlights darting. Landon would have turned them around, no matter the time lost, and rerouted the entire walk. Remy Gussie had a reputation for violence and an unholy need for privacy. But Landon misses the signs.

By seven, as a gray-sheathed daylight finally slips among them, the walkers come uneasily to the end of the fence. The chopping noise—tractor? axe?—has ceased, or perhaps the wind and a few caterwauling crows have only taken its place, hurrying them forward so that all are suffused with a sense of unspoken urgency.

Get out of the field.

The Scouts don't wait for Landon's cleverness with the wire fence this time. They improvise without a word between them, creating a kind of ladder from rocks. Two steps and an easy hurdle over a fencepost. The others follow, managing with varying amounts of awkwardness and effort. Once on the other side, Landon points out a deer path leading back into the wood, away from the cresting day, as if folding back into those minutes before dawn, all that stippled light, but no matter. They've become used to navigating shadows. The ground is spongy but not terribly muddy, and without the bitter edge of wind that assaulted them beside the field, they hike obediently, intent upon following in the footsteps of their leaders, avoiding roots and fallen logs with their swaths of slippery moss. Tricky spots are noted, warnings called back. A low branch swipes at the tall fisherman's face, the singing fellow's ridiculous pack, the others too short or contained to notice. They can truly hear once more—the echoing shuffle of their footsteps, the slight trickle of leaves, dislodged by wind, descending, and now, too, *the birds, the birds, the birds*—such an unholy clatter, as if the whole world must know a new day has begun. To everyone's relief, they soon reach a scrabby section of half-grown alders, and with a few more steps, they arrive back on the ruts and gravel of the quarry access road. This higher section of the road is also puddled and rough, but blessedly whole. The walkers feel liberated, heartened to see that they have arrived at the defunct quarry's gate. "All downhill from here," Warren sings out, and briefly it does seem that way. Soon, they'll reach Forgotten Bay and the train tracks and a straightforward trek to the End of the Walk. But it's not until they pause beside the defunct quarry's locked gate that the walkers can finally see one another fully in what passes for daylight and put voice to figure and face. Warren is slightly jarred to realize that with the loss of the Solidarity Club girls, there are now as many adults as students. And in daylight, a few more surprises:

The rough fellow in the wooly cap, the man with the beautiful singing voice, *Danny*, is a priest, wearing an actual white collar under his long black raincoat. *Father Dan*, he introduces himself now as Helen Hubka's eyes widen and Jaspar Goode shakes his head.

The two Boy Scouts are not the sons of the mill owner, but possibly Swenson cousins from Spit Town, with their light gray eyes, white-blond hair, and jerry-rigged, hand-me-down Boy Scout packs.

Caroline, the wraith-thin woman in the bluebird scarf, is Mrs. Weller, Warren's onetime kindergarten teacher (*how did he not see that?*).

Avis is not another member of the Solidarity Club but a wisp of a girl in baggy dungarees and a near-useless blue-and-white-checked slicker. She is—Warren is almost positive—the younger sister of that odd new kid in his class (Edward? Eddie?), the one who has all the girls fluttering. The new boy is exotic, more handsome than a famous Italian movie star, Warren's gathered from overheard gossip. The new boy might be a Russian or even an Indian. His sister has the same glossy black hair and turquoise eyes, although Avis, her hooded head

47

perpetually lowered, seems less inclined to put these striking features on display. Her nickname (Warren knows, although Avis does not) is Ghost Girl. She's been glimpsed in the oddest places, it seems, places she shouldn't possibly be able to access: the courthouse clock tower, for instance. A seaweed-covered boulder well off Gold Egg Beach. All mere rumor, of course.

The Operator, Helen Hubka, who he'd supposed was the Solidarity girls' chaperone, has certainly not departed and is clearly on her own.

Denis has a black eye, a real shiner.

And Jaspar Goode, the big fisherman, is wearing head-to-toe camou-flage.

Only Landon is as usual, wizened and tough in his stained brown canvas jacket, his endless slim cigar in hand, familiar half sneer on his face.

In this pause, the Scouts use their compasses. One consults what looks like a pocket watch.

"Eight miles," the first says.

"Eight point four," pronounces the other, holding up what Warren now sees is not a pocket watch but a real pedometer.

"Nice," Warren says, and the kid gives a sharp nod, fighting a proud smile.

"We should hit the ten-mile mark at Forgotten Bay, the loading dock," Warren tells them.

The Scouts are disappointed, clearly worried that already, not ten miles in, they've lost all claim on beating any records or even making a good time, but Warren reassures them that every Big Walk so far has counted only the actual walking time, deducting break and rest times. This, this recalibration moment, their detour, should be considered as a rest time, like the half hour at Toby's Tavern. Warren isn't sure that's true, but it's too early in the walk for more disappointment.

"Who is keeping track?" one of the Scouts asks.

"Track?" Warren frowns.

"Of our times," the other boy says.

"So we know how long we took," the first boy adds. "You know, the walking time."

Avis finds herself volunteering, even as skeptical glances are thrown her way. *And who will do it once she drops out?* She can almost hear that question, which fortunately is ignored. One thing at a time. She pulls her pencil and tiny spiral notebook from her pocket, and the Boy Scouts seem relieved to believe that she's been prepared all along.

"Don't forget the first stop," the smaller one, Karl, tells her quietly. He is barely eleven years old and, despite the sleep still in the corners of his eyes, wired with eagerness.

Avis draws three columns and labels them. *Time stopped. Amount of rest. Time resumed.* Consults the slim Timex on her wrist—a consolation present from her father for the move—and prepares her first entry while Helen Hubka strains to see what else the girl might have written in that little notebook of hers and the two Scouts look on with identical expressions of approval.

DISCOVERY

Oren and Karl are indeed Swensons from Spit Town, brothers not cousins, their birthdays a day and a year apart in March. Brothers like Jack and Bobby Kennedy, Karl would like to say. Their sister woke with them in the middle of the night and drove them from Spit Town to the Humtown high school, staying on the far side of the parking lot with her lights off until the walk was underway. After driving back out of town, she doubled back only once to see them walking with the others in a straight line up the highway. Idiots, but she was proud. Since their dad died, she and her mother have worried about all that these fatherless little boys would miss. But then the two had entered into scouting with such vigor (or *"vigah,"* as the President would say) that they had been teased endlessly as they accumulated badges for stuff any fool would learn along the way to adulthood: Can you tie a knot? Find a star? Paddle a canoe? *C'mon!*

"Hey, Oren. Hey, Karl," her cousins would shout, "you wanna eat with us, or you gotta get a badge for that?" Their sister believed her brothers actually might have gotten a badge for eating Sunday dinner with their granny, some kind of cultural badge. Karl told her in the car that they need sixteen merit badges to become Eagle Scouts. This one will be for Citizenship. She worried that once the town kids saw how young they were, they would be teased anew. She worried that despite their strong wills, their indefatigable determination, they would be left far behind to struggle as the night turned to day to night. She could only guess their route, but knew it would have to pass the highway café where she waited tables, and she would be there, looking out for them.

She had saved and saved for their Christmas presents. Her widowed mother, she knew, would concentrate on the practical—new socks, knitted hats. Their mother wasn't entirely blind to the boys' desires; she simply felt fulfilling dreams was the job of the dreamer. Their sister, though, felt every vibration of their longing and always, always searched out the perfect gift for each boy. This past Christmas: a first aid kit for Oren, stuffed full of gauze bandages and ointments, scissors and tweezers, bells and whistles. A pedometer had been Karl's dream, but she couldn't find one in any local store. Then she'd overheard Oren telling Karl about how another Scout had seen an address in *Boys' Life* for a place that sold official pedometers. She had flipped through every issue she could find in the boys' bedroom until she spotted it: Goldberg's, 202 Market Street, Philadelphia, PA, a walloping $5.75 + 30¢ for parcel post. She jotted down the catalog number: *E365*. Of course, no package arrived in time for Christmas. All she had for Karl then were some obscure trail maps she'd conned off a forest ranger who'd come into the café and a star chart a smitten suitor had once given her. But last week, a tiny brown-paper parcel appeared in the mailbox. And his face! He'd strapped the pedometer on late last night as he'd readied his rucksack and checked it again and again this morning on the ride into town. He would reset it, he told her, the moment the walk began, so they'd know for certain how far they'd walked. As Avis flips her notebook closed, Karl consults his new tool with satisfaction and without another word shuffles back into step with Oren, the two of them leading the pack, just as in their dreams.

Hardly any time passes before the Scouts imagine they can see a shimmer of water through the trees, the bay ahead. So close! Oren shakes his compass. He'd reckoned the bay would appear farther to his left—that is, to the west. But the Scouts almost tumble over each other with pleasure. What good time they must be making after all! They might yet break records. Their daydreams of glory are dashed when the glimmer turns out to be, not Forgotten Bay, but weak March sunlight calling out chrome and glass within the trees. As they approach, Warren's first thought is that his father has been won over and come to offer support. A little early, but okay. He's about to shout out when he realizes he's dead wrong. The car isn't even on the gravel road. It lies well beyond the scrim of trees, deep in the mud. No, Warren doesn't recognize the vehicle. Such an odd spot to leave a car—up this abandoned track, cedar branches nearly covering the windshield—that they all feel uncomfortable as they register the dark dusty green Plymouth, especially when Helen Hubka says, "I know that car. It's the Gussies.'"

"Boyo." She pinches her nose. "You can smell the sheep manure from here."

Only a few of them know immediately what she's referencing. But the Scouts sense trouble, and although they remain eager to keep moving, their Scoutmaster has taught them to always be prepared to help in any circumstance. They don't hesitate to follow Landon as he barrels toward the old dented Plymouth, Denis and Jaspar Goode with them.

Helen Hubka holds one arm out as if to shield Caroline and Avis. A moment before, the woman had been lightly panting, wheezing from the effort of clambering over fences, along a field, through the woods. All that has vanished. Helen Hubka is revived.

"What's happening?" Caroline asks. "Is someone hurt?"

"Aileen Gussie," Helen Hubka says, her voice thick with alarm-laden joy. "And those poor little girls."

"You must remember?" she says, delighted at Caroline's look of puzzlement. "Well, let me tell you."

Avis, who has scoured every issue of the local newspaper, has no idea what Helen Hubka is babbling about. Caroline might have caught the drift in other times, but of course she remembers so little of those weeks after the Columbus Day storm, after Jay, and has purposefully absented herself from town talk. Warren feels an itch, remembering the embarrassment of an older man weeping at the newspaper office, his father nodding in feigned commiseration, but clearly stalling with faint promises, and once the man left, Warren's father shaking his head at Landon and Chrissy, the secretary.

"Domestic matter," Warren's father said, shutting out any further conversation.

Beside the found car, Denis is vibrating at full, furious attention. No question that he knows exactly what they've stumbled across. He's been witness to more than one twist in this story so far, and hasn't forgotten any of it. Back in October, Remy Gussie's brusque, belated call to the sheriff's office had been followed by an emotional visit from Mr. Johansson, Aileen Gussie's father, that man in such distress, but even his flat-out plea hadn't inspired Denis's father to action. His father had decided to "wait and see," and he would declare to any who questioned his decision that *a man and wife were entitled to a measure of privacy,* that *things like this tended to work out; you get married, well then, you make your bed and you lie in it.* But then, just this week, his father had heard that the Johanssons had hired their own detective who wouldn't back down, who had contacts with the FBI, a local office that didn't think the disappearance of a young mother and two babies should go uninvestigated. Denis's father was furious at the intrusion and determined to get ahead of it, to show his department had done due diligence. So he arranged to send a team out to search the Gussie property thoroughly, unlike all those months before when they'd merely glanced inside, as if to say, *Yup, they're not here.* This new search would be a clear reproof to whatever interloping detective showed up, and he could send the bugger on his way. But Remy Gussie got wind of the sheriff's plans, and soon, there he was on Denis's porch, that creep, hawking onto the porch floorboards. Denis's mother wouldn't let Gussie inside, of course. *Policy,* she said. *He'll come out to you.* Denis saw from the side window how the man side-eyed his mother, cocked his head, lolled his tongue in his cheek. His mother must have fought the urge to lock the door. She did shut it firmly in his face and then rapped evenly on the bathroom door.

"Get out here, Chester," Denis's mother murmured. "Remy Gussie is outside."

His father emerged, newspaper in hand, cross from the start. He didn't invite the farmer inside either and, in fact, even walked him off the lit porch to talk in the yard, the two of them standing in the spitting rain. His father lingered even as Gussie stalked off, and when he finally came inside, he bypassed the kitchen where supper waited to head to the hall phone.

"I said call it off," Denis heard his father say. "Yeah, well, he's not in charge, is he?"

Denis's mother shook her head as they listened, but held off until after grace was said and supper half over.

"She ran off," his father said when his mother pressed him.

"With those babies?" his mother said. "Chester, you can't think she would . . . or could. She's not much more than a kid herself."

True, Aileen Johansson Gussie was barely nineteen. Denis remembered her from school, a tall, shy girl with long, curly auburn hair. One of the horse girls, she'd left school two years ago to marry Remy Gussie, a farmer in his thirties who raced his horse to sweats every Sunday at the fairgrounds. A real creep who canoodled with the high school girls and played mean tricks on the few boys who hung around, hoping themselves to catch the eye of a horse girl.

"Fool's errand, wasn't it? What could we hope to find at the house? She took the car, didn't she? That gal's miles away."

"Her family . . . she wouldn't have gone without telling her mother. All these months. Her mother's been going crazy with grief."

"Enough," he snapped, raising his own fist. "Be quiet about this, Peggy. Stay off the phone tomorrow. And for god sakes, don't mention it at the courthouse."

"For your own damn good," he added pointedly. "You, of all people, will regret it if I have to open this can of worms and the gossips get back to work. You want that kind of attention?"

His mother blanched. Was his father threatening *her*? It didn't seem likely, but Denis had noticed a strange tension around his mother's job. Conversations that petered out when work was mentioned. A summons to an urgent Saturday-morning meeting. His mother had been working at the courthouse since she graduated from high school, moving up from permits and licensing to secretary in the auditor's office. Among other things, she oversaw the collection of property taxes. People were always jokingly complaining about her. The Tax Lady, they called her, doesn't break a sweat when she takes hundreds out of your wallet. The Permit Queen. Why, you'd have to have all your ducks in a row before you brought your plans up to her office. His mother usually *was* calm and steady. Now, she hovered, her hand shaking as she handed his father another beer.

"We went out there already, didn't we?" he continued, as if still defending himself. "No sign of them."

Denis thought that with the arrival of the detective, the news of the missing family must finally break, sparking a huge investigation his father couldn't put off. But it was clear after Remy Gussie left that evening that his father had no intention of allowing such a thing to happen.

"You're not going to do *anything*?" Denis blurted out.

His father only stared at him, shaking his head.

"Nothing?" Denis said.

"I can't," his father said. "Can I now?" he added, turning to Denis's mother, as if it were her fault.

"You're as much a murderer as him if you don't investigate," his mother finally said, putting her fork down.

"Says the thief," his father muttered.

His mother's cheeks flushed red, but she didn't say another word.

"Your mother knows who's at fault here. She knows who's tied my hands."

"Chester . . . how can you think I . . ." His mother began to weep.

"Take that back." Denis was on his feet, shouting.

"Now look what you've started," his father yelled at his mother.

Denis lunged. Eye to eye, nose to nose, chest to chest. His father was not a violent man, and Denis had never before confronted him, had always been the most obedient of sons, but it seemed the sheriff had had enough of threats and bullshit. Afterward, his mother held a box of frozen pearl onions on his eye. His father concocted a radio call, a summons from the jail, and left for his office.

"He's just being careful, not raising a stink," his mother soothed, but her hands still shook. With anger or fear? Denis wasn't sure.

His father was not *careful*. His father was a do-nothing, it seemed, criminally negligent, Denis thought, like that fellow on Tremont Street who wouldn't tie up his vicious dog and looked the other way when it attacked children on their way to school. Now, Denis is struck anew by this evidence of his father's treachery, this blatantly cursory investigation that apparently even missed this massive clue: the Gussie family car parked not two miles from their property line.

"No one inside," Landon says.

He opens the passenger door. Keys in the ignition. Nothing else but an ashtray full of menthol butts and an empty baby cot in the backseat. A smell of sour milk, burnt wool, and pennies. Jaspar Goode pops the trunk, and all avert their eyes even as he shakes his head. The spare, that's all, and it's flat.

"If she ran away, she didn't take the car then, did she?" Helen Hubka is suddenly beside the Plymouth, her broad, curious face reflected in its windows, a set of clown mirrors that multiplies her and lengthens her features, exaggerating her mouth, which is open, always open. One town theory can be put to rest. She leans in to rattle off all the Gussie gossip: *airplane, fugitive bank robber, concrete pad, courthouse.*

"For chrissakes, Helen," Landon says, easing her away so he can shut the car door.

Caroline thinks Landon looks as if he has to stop himself from covering his ears or popping Helen Hubka one. Such blathering nonsense. She can't help observing, too, how Jaspar Goode circles the car. Is he looking for damage—dents and scrapes? How could anyone even notice under all that dust? But he must see something, because he motions everyone away from the vehicle.

"Leave it alone," he orders, and they all obey, except Denis, who can't seem to step away.

"My father should know about this," he blurts out. "And if not him," he adds, "the FBI."

In the light of day, Denis's black eye is pronounced, raw and painful looking, but he's no longer pretending to hide it. His cap is off, and he's his usual alert self. Warren is relieved. But, he thinks, If not *him*, the *FBI?* What's Denis on about?

"Ah, come on, son." The priest seems to agree, laying a hand on Denis's shoulder. "*The FBI?*" His chuckle is awkward and truncated, as if he's trying to defuse the situation without making a fool of the boy and his sudden passion.

The shame Denis feels throbbing along with the pain of his eye diminishes a little as he contemplates how he can raise the alarm on his own. He'll telephone from the first phone booth they reach. Law enforcement agencies didn't usually step on one another, but anyone could see his father hasn't been doing his job, that a young woman, a girl Denis remembers from the fairgrounds barn, had come to harm. She and the babies, gone. That man, Gussie, threatening his father, the sheriff, who should have told him to go to hell, who should have put justice first. Denis knew they'd been kids together, neighbors but not friends. What loyalty was owed? And what kind of debt would let a man like that get away with hurting his family? Because certainly, certainly he had. Everyone knew, thanks to old Helen Hubka. Denis can't help nodding in the Operator's direction, appreciating for once in his life the service she provided. Who would have thought?

THE OPERATOR

It's as if she crawls into the back of your mind or actually lives on the telephone table at the end of the hallway. Her voice is so familiar to them all, even newcomer Avis, who struggles to place it until talk turns to the big news in town: the dialup. Helen Hubka, Avis realizes then, is *the* Operator. What a shock it had been to discover upon moving to the opposite end of the country that, though the phone had a rotary dial, just like at home, it was of no real use. You couldn't simply dial a number like Avis's grandmother's—ME5–1207, memorized for an emergency—but must instead relay the desired number to the disembodied voice that lived in the receiver. You picked up the phone, and there she was, waiting for your first utterance.

"Operator," the voice would announce when she registered your presence.

Or . . . "Number, please."

And you had to talk! To say the number aloud. They weren't real phone numbers either. Depending upon where you lived in this very small town, you were assigned a letter, only one, followed by a mere three digits. Avis's was K359. Her mother made her repeat it again and again, as if remembering that impoverished series was an actual feat. Not everyone had a letter before their number, however. Doctors, for instance, couldn't wait around for an operator to connect them, neither could the police nor the ambulance nor the fire department, of course. And the very rich, like the mill owner, bought their way into a direct connection. Everyone else had to contend with the Operator, and most of the time, that meant not only talking to Helen Hubka but knowing that, unless she was very busy, scooting around on her swift black stool, swiping at the switchboards on all sides, she was likely a silent participant in any conversation she chose. "Stay off the phone," Avis's father warned, needlessly. Avis had no one to call. Neither did Teddy, but he was intrigued. Three party lines, a treasure trove of available gossip and news, a surfeit of puzzles and investigations.

No surprise then that Helen Hubka has come into the walk well-informed about the doings of Warren's family and Denis's parents and the drama over at the Gussie farm and, of course, the tragic stupidity of Jay Weller. She knows everything there is to know about the Solidarity girls, too, and was prepared to offer her own considerable advice about one or two things along the way. The Swenson family—Oren and Karl's clan—bore her to tears. They aren't from Humtown, and even if they were, they seem disinclined to speak even in person. Their phone conversations would be abrupt, near monosyllabic, inscrutable. Likewise, Landon only barks into the receiver to order supplies for the newspaper or his brother's farm. The Goodes—here, she smiles—now, the Goodes supply endless information, because she can always tell who's spending or losing money when a request comes in and a Goode is hired, but Helen Hubka knows little about this Jaspar, who's been away for some years. In the service, she surmises, but somewhere else, too. No one seems to be clear on the details or even mention him much. Helen doesn't even know how long he's been back or what exactly he's been doing. Something to do with the Coast Guard station, she thinks. He doesn't have a phone of his own, but uses a ship-to-shore radio, a device whose existence annoys her no end. The priest, too, mystifies her. She thoroughly enjoys the weighted calls to St. Anne's—and all the other churches, too—even though the Episcopalians have managed a nonletter number to bypass her and the party line. But she can't recall a single mention of new Father Dan.

Yes, the priest vexes Helen Hubka. Good-looking, funny, that singing voice. He must be the star of the parish. How has she not heard about him? Catholics and their secrets, she grumps to herself. An image of her President and his lovely wife with the square of lace pinned to her bouffant, taken as they were leaving a church, a *Catholic* church, crosses her mind as if to reprimand her. Her pique meekly evaporates. Mysteries, she decides, that's a pleasure she and her President share. His are of the holy sort, while hers, of course, are far more mundane. What an opportunity this priest could be for her. And, oh!—with a jealous pang, she remembers his greatest asset—*the confessional*. What stories he might share with her. Like any good detective, she begins with the simplest questions, but the priest won't play. All she can get out of him is that he's not from around here.

"And originally?" she tries.

"I love that word, 'original,'" the priest muses. "I shouldn't, of course. Its association with sin and all. But, golly, what a notion. Nothing like it— *original*. The beginning of all. Our road to redemption starting right there. How glorious that the sin leads to forgiveness leads to eternal glory. And all because of *original*. Sounds precisely like God, don't you agree?"

"Well . . . in my church . . ."

"The beginning of all, Helen. May I call you Helen? Vital. And yet, isn't where we end just as important?"

Round and round he goes. How does the President stand such nonsense? This *Danny* almost wears Helen Hubka out. She's not giving up. Oh, no, but when the swing of a coat catches her eye, she shifts course.

That girl, Avis. Helen is getting a bead on her, putting pieces into place. She can place the father now, the new engineer at the mill. She's heard him correct underlings on the phone and decline social events without a hint of a reasonable excuse. Blunt, Helen Hubka has decided, possibly rude. It's hard to tell with Easterners. A dark man, she's heard, but not inclined toward Portuguese Hill. An Italian, maybe. Look at that jet-black hair! And the rest of the family, well, Helen Hubka can't properly recall another one of their voices. The mother must be lonely, she thinks. Yet Letterbox Bob, the postman, has let slip the Mudge House address is deluged with mail.

Is someone in the family ill? Helen Hubka wonders. Unsociable? Why have they ventured so far from their home? Running away? From what?

Well, she'll find out, won't she? You can bet on that.

THE TRAIN CASE

The pause by the Gussie family car constitutes another break, to the Scouts'
obvious consternation. But the cocoa and water are catching up to all of
them, and perhaps it's dawned on at least a few of them that soon they'll be
out in the open, beside the bay and train tracks, with few chances for miles
to find cover. The walkers begin drifting off back into the woods to relieve
themselves. Even the Scouts give up. They are prepared, of course, tiny
trowels hanging from their packs, wrapped toilet tissue tucked inside. But
also determined to take the quickest piss against a tree and make up time
and distance with the even speed their Scoutmaster has taught them.

Caroline wishes she had to go. Or that Helen Hubka would be overcome
by the urge. Instead, the revived Operator has captured Caroline, outright
stupefied by her ignorance regarding the Gussie tragedy. *I mean, Caroline,
this has been going on for months!*

Here are the details Helen Hubka's gathered over the phone about Remy
Gussie, details she is happy to share:

Aileen and the girls supposedly drove away right before the storm, while
the roads were still clear, and everyone was trying to tack down their
belongings. Including (according to himself) Remy Gussie. He was so
busy he waited three days before he telephoned the sheriff. Didn't even
bother driving by his in-laws' house or telephoning one of her sisters. Of
course, they must have taken her in during the storm, he said. She and
the girls had probably ridden out the storm in her parents' basement.
He assumed she was okay, he said. They were okay. She was always running over there with the brats, he insisted. Her mother always tried to

61

get Aileen to stop by on Saturday morning. She planned to help Aileen with some sewing.

Early Thursday, the first clear day after the storm, Remy took his plane out. Not unusual, except he flew early in the morning, a time he'd normally be out in his fields. A neighbor and fellow pilot noticed. Later, he'd deny this, then say he'd flown over half the peninsula, hoping to spy the family car in what he called "all that carnage."

The week before, he'd borrowed butchering tools from another sheep farmer, even though he had his own knives and pen, and sheep butchering was many months away. He gave no excuse, and when he returned the tools, the other farmer noticed they were all sharpened and scrubbed clean as new, not an uncommon courtesy from any other man, but Remy Gussie was notorious for breaking or outright stealing anything he borrowed, then blaming it on the object's poor quality, its owner's cheapness. The other farmer had not expected to get anything back and had, in fact, lent Remy an old tool he no longer used.

The afternoon before Remy reported his wife and children missing, a fellow pilot stopped by and interrupted Remy hammering a rectangular frame into the dirt beyond the far side of his barn. For a concrete pad, Remy told him. Vaguely, he jutted his chin toward a wheelbarrow as if it were already full of wet concrete mix. For a plane hangar, the other pilot thought, to get the Cessna out of the old barn. He'd made one himself and would have told anyone else that the hole Remy dug was unnecessarily deep, but he knew better than to give that fellow advice.

Questions and theories abounded over Helen Hubka's thread on the party line.

Did he take his little family out over the Strait and fling them from his plane while everyone else was preoccupied?

Did he chop them up and bury the pieces on his property? Sealing them away under a new concrete pad?

*   *   *

"I didn't read anything about this in the paper," Caroline says.

"No, John was busy covering the storm, and he wouldn't print anything anyway. Family issue, he called it. Private matter."

Or he thought it was nonsense, Caroline doesn't dare to say.

"And you know the sheriff and Remy Gussie grew up practically next door."

"But Chester's a good ten years older than Gussie, isn't he? They're friends?"

Helen Hubka almost spits. "Remy Gussie doesn't have any friends," she says, definitively. "You don't know the fellow. Jay did, and he made sure you all stayed clear, that's for certain."

"Think about it, Caroline." Helen Hubka taps her own forehead before continuing. "Oh, Gussie has acquaintances—pilots, livestock herders, that gunsmith over in Spit Town. And, you remember, he used to race horses with little Bobby Shockley every Sunday at the fairgrounds. But those aren't friendships, my dear. More like transactions or . . ."

Helen Hubka almost can't help herself, all the gossip building up, but at least once she bites her tongue before she says the word: "blackmail."

"I can't imagine Chester looking the other way for a fellow like that."

"Our sheriff has his own back to watch. He doesn't want the Feds back in here, not after that fiasco at the port, smuggling sailors in his own town boatyard! And don't forget the time they raided his jail for an illegal still operation, right under his nose!"

"Not to mention not wanting any more eyes on Peggy's mess," Helen Hubka adds, raising an eyebrow. "Sticky fingers, methinks. Now, talk about deceit."

"Hush, Helen," Caroline says. "Denis is right over there."

While the others are preoccupied, Avis slips into the woods, climbing over damp ferns and vining, clutching plants until she's out of sight. She keeps the group in earshot. Miss Hubka's loud monologue, the priest's occasional song—these are threads that will carry her back to the group, even as she wades farther into a stand of cedars, into ferns so large that when she squats to pee, she all but disappears from view. Afterward, as she's hurriedly rearranging herself, she spots a tiny furry creature near her foot, and her hammering heart paralyzes her until she realizes she's looking at a stuffed animal, a tiny brown rabbit with long silky pink ears, soiled by the rain, missing one leg. She snatches it up and, almost without thinking, stuffs it into one of her raincoat's deep pockets. Something is not right. Not only the unfamiliar plants, the dim light, her shaking legs. What kind of place is this wood where a child's toy languishes? Being with Teddy has taught her to recognize mischief, or worse. There's more, she's sure of it. She crouches and surveys the space around her until it jumps out. The color blue. A scrap that should not be there. Impossible. And yet. Avis struggles to stand. Somewhere, not that far away, the tractor they heard in the fields stutters once more to a stop. And Avis begins to imagine a distant thrashing, as if her discovery has made the woods come alive. She will be too quick. No bear or cougar or raccoon or even a feral child pursuing the stuffed rabbit will appear before she reaches and scrapes away branches to uncover . . . yes . . . a pale blue overnight suitcase. Exactly like her own. Exactly like the one she hid away! The synchronicity spooks her. Teddy would do this. Trap her. Tease her. But he couldn't have known she'd be here. Couldn't have found her yet, could he? Not even Teddy possesses such dark magic. And yet, here it is: solid square, a miniature suitcase with a metal latch, but wait—Avis relaxes—the heavy handle isn't covered in the same blue fabric, but in bright yellow, a crude replacement. A bad repair, Avis guesses, imagining Teddy tearing the case out of her own hands, the handle breaking. Her mother had told her that stewardesses—all those glamour girls—carried cases exactly like hers, and Avis has the sudden, ridiculous notion that the suitcase tucked within the ferns belonged to one of those pretty gals in uniform, that it had slipped from a plane and plummeted into this forest like a stone into water. Gone, gone, gone.

But . . . not . . . because here it is, found again—by Avis.

"Excuse me," she says, interrupting one of Miss Hubka's stories. Avis seems to be addressing Caroline, but her eyes are on Warren and the Scouts. They've each finished their own calls to nature, returned to swig water from their canteens with relieved abandon, and now are antsy, ready to head off once more.

"Excuse me," she says again, the thin pipe of her voice rising. "I found something."

And because she's hardly spoken through the miles, because she is vibrating with purpose, the others gather around her.

It is exactly what Avis thought it was: a cosmetic bag, a tiny square suitcase, a "train case," and other than the yellow handle, it resembles hers in nearly every way, except that it is stained a brownish-red in one corner, and the latch is bent.

"Open it," Helen Hubka demands, and though Denis knows better, he says nothing.

One of the Scouts, Oren, offers to bash the latch with a rock. The priest suggests it might be locked, but easily picked with one of Helen Hubka's hairpins. Warren fumbles, but it's Avis who leans in and with one quick slide and flip, releases the bent latch.

Sprung open, the suitcase is jam-packed with what looks like doll clothes. Caroline reaches in to lift out a tiny green-and-blue-plaid dress, yellowed lace around the collar and the tiny puffed sleeves.

"How odd," she murmurs.

"What is it?" Jaspar Goode asks.

"It's just . . . well," she begins. "This looks exactly like one I made for Ginny."

She turns up the hem, and there too is a tiny red flower. Caroline had embroidered a little flower on every dress she'd made for her daughter. As she refolds the dress, her eye catches another familiar fabric, a tiny blue-and-white dress with a bright yellow pinafore and appliquéd sunflowers, a dress identical to one Jay's Swedish grandmother had also sewn for Ginny decades ago.

"So strange," she says while Jaspar Goode frowns beside her.

"It's got to be *theirs*, doesn't it?" Helen Hubka says, elbowing Caroline to one side.

"Should we go back and put it in the car?"

"Hide it somewhere else."

"Call the sheriff as soon as we can."

"I'll carry it," Avis says.

"We won't get to a pay phone for miles yet," Warren tells her.

"It's okay," Avis lies. "My bookbag isn't heavy."

"Well, let me take *that* at least," the priest says, and before Avis can stop him, he scoops up her plaid bookbag and opens his backpack. It's an old-time trekker's pack with a high frame that juts over his head. When Avis first saw it in the shadowed dark, she had the absurd notion that he might be carrying skis. Helen Hubka remarks upon its size, and then all of them wonder. What's he toting in there? Clothing? Food? The pack is well-worn, visibly patched in places, and the priest seems well acquainted with it. He acknowledges their glances with a laugh that confounds them.

"We take what we are given," he says to the Operator with a slight bow of humility, as if even camping equipment appears regularly in the weekly collection. "I've got plenty of room, that's for sure."

He offers Helen Hubka a scrap more. "You would make a very fine detective." He smiles.

His compliment takes her off-guard. She nearly blushes, and she misses the moment he settles Avis's bookbag easily within that monstrous back-pack. Fascinating how quickly he registers the bookbag's surprising weight and adjusts. He doesn't even shoot Avis a curious look.

"Let's get the heck out of here," Landon all but commands.

"Are you okay?" Caroline asks Avis, who can't take her eyes off the priest's pack.

"The handle is sticky."

"Oh, honey. Give it here." Caroline holds out her hand. "We can take turns."

But Avis is determined to hold on as long as she can, and she is relieved to pull away from Caroline when the Scouts remind her of her other respon-sibility. She rummages in her pocket for pencil and pad and consults her watch. With that, the Scouts are off again, pushing down the road toward Forgotten Bay, and as the group falls in line behind them, Avis is carrying the case filled to the brim with baby clothes with Helen Hubka hovering nearby, waiting, it seems, for a chance to snatch it away and begin her own renewed investigation. The priest is darn right she'd make a good detective. The Johanssons could have hired her instead of whatever lame gumshoe they found in the Seattle Yellow Pages. Ah, the clues she could offer. *Let's start*, she'd begin, *with that storm*. And she would have brought it up right then and there if she hadn't caught sight of Caroline's bent head. The woman was barely hanging on. In a rare moment of awareness, Helen Hubka bites her tongue. No, this wasn't the time to mention the storm.

STORM OF THE CENTURY

You *could* start with the storm. But what would that tell you about the world it blew up? No, first, maybe you'd need to know more about the Humtown boatyard, a region outside even the purview of Miss Helen Hubka. You'd need to know about the projects underway and the schemes whispered and about all the ways to subvert unnecessary regulations. You'd need to know who had only just arrived home from fishing up north and why someone, against the odds and the season, had plans to soon depart. You'd need to know at least a scrap about how important it is to trust not only each other when you're heading out to sea and trust, too, all the hands that repaired and readied the boat that will carry you, but also those who have visited you nightly in your dreams or stalked you through your shadows. You'd need to know who would treat you fairly and assure your safety should you venture off the map or who would blithely lead you to the edge of ruin. Most of all you'd need to know who, among the gossips that lived in nearly every man, woman, and child in Humtown, could keep your secret as if his own life depended upon it. You'd need to know Jay Weller.

He kept secrets even from her, Caroline knew. Now and then, presents for Jay would appear on their porch without explanation. Pies. Tools. A knitted blanket. She once arrived home from school to find a filthy man in overalls expertly stacking a new cord of exceptionally fine firewood—dry, split fir, madrona, and cherry—behind their garage, so dedicated to his task, he would only offer her a curt wave and, a moment later, something that resembled a bow. Another day, she found a teenager painting their back fence. His mother sent him, he grinned, to thank Jay.

For what? Caroline had asked.

The boy had only shrugged, as if to say *You know.*

But she didn't. Not always.

Every small town operates with a visible hierarchy—a city council, company bosses, the law. The deep-pocketed, relentless joiners of committees or boards, the entrenched, self-appointed directors. The ones who, at least superficially, make the rules. And, of course, the pattern persists in every social circle, right down to the high school with its athletes and brains, the prom king and queen, those Solidarity girls. If you were only half awake, you'd fully believe these types were the movers and shakers, the crème de la crème, the true hotshots.

But every small town, too, has its secret celebrities. Revered, but spoken about only in trusted company. If a newcomer to Humtown were to murmur about such a person (who might be a grandmother or a teenage stock clerk or a port mechanic), maybe boasting about their own special friendship, the others listening would not join in with their own tales. They would fall silent. A rare show of loyalty, but a natural response. No one would want to be the one to break the charm by making a fuss. Who knew what would happen if they did? Maybe that secret celebrity might go away and leave us all bereft. And then what would we do?

But let's say you had a real problem and were thought of kindly, well, then, eventually someone in Humtown might steer you to a particular destination in the boatyard. You'd have to go on foot, of course, past the dirt parking lot and the single-lane gravel track riddled with purslane that runs alongside the boat slips. Keep going, you'd be told, until you hear the slap of ice on a wooden ramp by the open cannery doors, head beyond the fuel dock and registration office, weaving between the occasional coveralled fellows on bicycles, carrying tools or sack lunches or a pot of varnish from one workshop to another. Edge behind the haul-out and the canvas-covered workshop beyond the cavernous Goode Building—you'll know you're there when you see sparks flying and hear hammers pounding, the scrape, scrape, scrape of chisels. Duck beside the narrow sail loft, where seamstresses are regularly blinded by bolts of white canvas. Don't pause, you'd be told, until you've made it all the way past the railroad tracks to the nondescript blue shed standing alone in the boatyard's far western corner.

You'd find no sign on Jay Weller's door. No stated hours of operation.

What was his business? He could have been a fabricator or a machinist. He had a lathe and a milling machine, didn't he? Or maybe he was a fisherman. He'd long been partnered with Charlie Beecher, who crabbed with a boat Jay seemed to own, though Jay himself hadn't gone up north for years. He might have been a welder or mechanic. A shipwright? He could fix or fashion anything, of course, but so could a number of men around town. A Humtown boy, born and raised, a nice-looking, regular fellow, maybe a little more wiry, a little taller and quicker, but yes, an ordinary fellow. Jay Weller was as able as the next man, but his great skill, the one for which he was most admired, lay in knowing what really needed to be repaired and being willing to do just that.

A sailboat might limp into the bay with a hairline crack on the engine block, fouled plugs, or a broken pump, and, sure, he'd suss that out in a wink. He'd haul and replace and fix—you bet he would—but not before he brought the exhausted couple onboard home to Caroline for dinner, offering them the guest room for a night or two, hot baths, whiskey. Or say a teenager went on a joyride and panicked once he got out too far from shore and waves began to roll. Wouldn't Jay be there in the nick of time with a rope ready to tow the wayward kid to safety? When the Port was about to impound an old-timer's ever-broken but treasured gillnetter on behalf of a heartless banker, "someone" had found a crane and a hauler, and the vessel had been moved to distant safety in the middle of the night. Yes, he'd save a marriage or counsel a teenager or foil a heartbreak. He'd find homes for dogs and dogs for homes. If you stopped by Jay's shop on any given afternoon, you might see him quietly working at his bench, while nearby, a crew of oddball visitors hovered—an elderly logger, a bank clerk, a young woman with a baby just beginning to fuss—all waiting for a chance to spill their separate, often secret, troubles or to "borrow" Jay, "just for a minute," to show him something. *Your opinion?* He wouldn't always offer that, but he would listen, and sometimes that was all that was needed.

So it wasn't all that unusual when, not long before the storm, Jay arrived at his shop early one morning, Charlie Beecher ambling beside him, to find a girl waiting for him. Jay told Caroline later how the child had a broom in hand and had apparently been busy for some time, because the paved area outside Jay's shed was unrecognizably pristine. She'd looked right past red-bearded Charlie Beecher to Jay's tall, stooped figure. She waited.

"You know this character?" Charlie Beecher had asked Jay, who squinted.

"Halde, isn't?" Jay said.

"Wait. Halde Bens?" Caroline interrupted Jay's story. "She was in my class only a few years ago, Jay. She can't be more than ten. Halde, sweeping?"

The girl had said nothing, Jay continued. Just kept her eyes on him.

"Okay, then." Charlie waved. And he left them alone.

"My father," the girl blurted as soon as Charlie was out of sight. "He's in trouble. My mother . . ." Her voice trailed off.

Jay took the broom from the girl's hand, ushering her inside.

Halde's father, Caroline knew, worked up in the paper mill's office, in one of those nebulous positions that involved carrying around a lot of files and looking busy. Doing Paperwork at the Paper Mill, a joke that extended to his nickname. He was called the Shuffler. The Shuffler seemed to think he was or should be important, and he seldom mingled with anyone who didn't wear a suit. Yet Jay had seen him not long ago wandering through the boatyard. The Shuffler had been talking to Cassidy, Humtown's answer to a yacht broker, about the Canadian sailboat anchored right beyond the breakwater. The Shuffler had been wondering a little too loudly if the boat might be for sale, if he could go onboard and have a look. When Cassidy told him the boat was not for sale, was in fact impounded by the Port, the man still pressed him to have a look. Halde's father, Jay said, had had that anxious look about him men got when they decided they desperately needed a particular possession.

"Fellow like the Shuffler should know better," Jay told Caroline. "No one *needs* the kind of boat he was eyeing. He had to know he'd be signing over a good bit of every paycheck until the day that boat sold." (The running joke: What are the two happiest days of a boat owner's life? The day he buys the boat and the day he sells it.)

Later, Charlie Beecher told Jay he'd seen the Shuffler in his brown suit arguing with the port manager, too.

"Guess he really wanted to get onboard," Caroline said.

"Bad timing then," Jay said.

Only a day later, that same impounded boat had somehow slipped its mooring in the night, drifted out into the bay, and supposedly run aground a mile down the beach. The Cravens had claimed it by midday, and rumor had it they'd already found a buyer in Seattle.

"Bad luck for Halde's father." Caroline smiled.

"Dodged a bullet," Jay said, shaking his head.

But when Halde turned up, Jay wondered.

"Is this about the boat?" he'd prompted the girl. "Your mother's worried?"

Halde looked confused. "No." She shook her head. "We don't have a boat. No."

Her father had been late again last night, she explained, dinner ready and waiting, so when they first heard the car, her mother, exasperated over the near-ruined supper, uncovered the plate of drying chops she'd been keeping warm over the pot of simmering water and forked them onto the plates, spooning corn and potatoes beside them. Halde poured milk. But her father didn't come into the house, and when her mother glanced through the curtains in the dusky light, she didn't recognize the car blocking the driveway. Nor could she fully see the man who leaned, almost slumped, against the driver's door. A cigarette glowed in his hand. A few strained minutes went by. The dinner began to get fully cold, but her mother stayed beside the window until the man tossed his cigarette into the dahlia bed and began to weave toward the house. Later, she couldn't say what her mother saw in the man that made her shout to Halde to go to her room. To close the door and sit with her back against it and not breathe a word until she came to get her. Halde heard the man knocking, a sound that was silenced by her mother's courage. She heard the murmur of her mother's voice, even-keeled and pleasant as always.

But then the man had yelled out for her father, Halde told Jay. He knew he was there, he hollered. The man might have been drunk.

Halde couldn't leave her mother alone. She raced down the stairs and startled the man, who was reaching out to grab her mother's arm. Halde's thundering arrival threw him off-balance, and her mother was able to shove him out the door and, breathless and shaking, lock it behind him. Oh, but the man kept shouting. He banged and rattled. He called her mother a witch. Halde thought he would break through the door.

"He called me a witch, too," Halde whispered.

"Poor Halde," Caroline breathed.

Finally, the man left. He slammed back into his car and drove off. Her mother tried to call the mill office, but the Operator wouldn't do it. Said she wouldn't get an answer. *Office has been closed since five,* the Operator said. *You know that.*

Halde and her mother huddled in the living room, with the phone right beside them, in case the man came back. They'd stayed there all night. Halde's father hadn't come home.

"Her mother *should* call the sheriff," Caroline said.

"Well, to be honest," Jay said, "I'm not sure he'd do a hell of lot of good."

Money, money, money. That's what Halde heard the man yell. Her father owed. Her father double-crossed. Her father better show up soon and live up to his part of the deal. Goddamned thief. The man would be coming back, he said. Every day until her father paid up.

"Mama says to tell you the man was Mick Craven. She says you'll know what to do."

"So, the Shuffler has something to do with the boat after all?" Caroline asked.

"Doubt it," Jay said. "The damn thing's anchored beyond the breakwater again, waiting to be transported down to Seattle. The Cravens are still dickering with the new owner over the price."

"We'll figure this out," Jay had told the shaking girl. "Your daddy's probably at work now. In the meantime, I know someone who will come and keep an eye on you and your mother. He's a real big fellow, even bigger than your daddy. He's even been to war. Your mother can count on him. And I'll talk to Mick Craven, okay?"

* * *

"But wait, how did Halde get to the boatyard from all the way out on Quarry Road?" Caroline asked.

"I wondered, too," Jay said. "I thought she might have come in with the milkman."

"No," Halde told Jay. "Mrs. Gussie."

Her mother had been planning to wave down Pete Wills when he delivered the paper, but before his old truck could rumble by on its early-morning run, Aileen Gussie's Plymouth appeared on Quarry Road. Aileen had her troubles—even Halde knew that, although the girl wasn't sure what exactly those troubles might be—and she was probably making her way to her own mother's house. Yet when Halde's mother flagged her down, Aileen stopped right away. She drove Halde to the boat haven and even waited with her for a while, her little girls sleeping in the backseat, as if she too would like an audience with Jay. But as the sun was rising and the port was coming back to life, the babies began to stir, and Aileen had to go.

"You'll be okay?" Aileen asked Halde, who managed to nod. In the rising light, the girl could see now the mottled handkerchief Aileen was holding against her cheek, the streaks of blood at the corner of her mouth.

"Well, my friend will drive you home," Jay told the girl. "Unless," he added, "you wanted to go on your broom."

The girl's breath hiccupped, but she'd smiled. "No," she said, "I'll go with him."

"And the Shuffler?" Caroline asked Jay. "Do you think he's really in trouble? Do you think he ran away?"

"Now what kind of a man would do that?" Jay asked her. "Leave his family just when all hell's breaking loose?"

That, Caroline knew, was his worst nightmare.

Certain dreams haunt men like Jay Weller, dreams of a man in midlife whose every waking moment is spent taking care of others. Dreams of distress: encroaching armies or creeping house fires or rabid animals snapping through open windows. Dreams of carrying a heavy bundle. Of running. Of trouble. In one recurring nightmare, he told Caroline, he must dash into eerie green waves, eyes tearing with grit, struggling to keep sight of a boat torn from the beach with—it seems—children inside. He can make out a flash of a red-and-yellow cap as the wind smacks him off-balance again and again. The sand beneath his feet begins to swirl, water seeping upward until he's mired in a swampy hole that grows by the minute. Beach logs, which moments before might have acted as the children's impenetrable and solid forts, are kicked up by the surf, and they too enter the fray, spinning and bucking toward the dreaming Jay Weller. Between the wind and the roaring surf and the sucking sand, he can barely move, and *then* the shore itself disappears beneath him. It drops straight away, and he knows he'll never reach them, never save them. When Jay would wake from this dream, his cheeks would still be burning, his hands would have gone numb, and he would struggle to hold the razor when he tried to shave the next morning. Throughout the day, he'd relive those dread filled moments, remembering how he screamed to a fellow who clung to the pier, sure that he too must see how the boat raced out of reach, see how it twisted wildly in the waves— and *oh god, do something!*—see how in a breath the wild bay simply swelled open and swallowed the children whole.

A dream, Caroline would soothe. *Just a bad dream.*

But even she knew, even then, it wasn't an impossible situation. Because, of course, Humtown was no stranger to storms. Name a season, and someone would have a story. Normal, until it wasn't.

The first indication that the Columbus Day storm would be out of the ordinary came from sailors well out in the Pacific who were watching barometric pressure plummet alarmingly. Radio calls to shore soon swarmed in. The storm approaching would not simply be a wild one; it would be monstrous. Forecasters scrambled to get the news out, and people around Humtown would remember the radio alerts much as they did Orson Welles's alien invasion announcement, *The War of the Worlds*, years before.

It didn't feel real, they'd tell one another afterward.

Where were you? they'd ask. *Where were you when the world was about to end?*

Turned out a good many people were at the Friday football game, holding tight as long as they could while the goalposts jumped out of place, hats went flying, and one little cheerleader soared halfway across the field while attempting a single flip. Soon the teams and fans scurried to make harrowing journeys home, trees cracking around them and anything not held down sailing through the air. All the while, the wind roaring.

Jay had slipped away to the boatyard in the early quieter hours of that morning, while Caroline had still been sleeping. A call had come in, he told her later. Someone needed a ride or a hand or an inspired solution. And of course Jay had been summoned. He'd spent the rest of the mostly uneventful day in his boatyard shed and arrived home well before the alerts began, in time to haul the patio furniture into the garage—a task he'd put off since the end of September. All the while, he seemed anxious.

"Something's going sideways," he told Caroline.

At the time, he'd made her smile, sniffing the air as if he could suss out trouble in a single long breath. Her husband, the nautical psychic. He decided to go back down to the port even as the sky darkened.

It seemed he'd only been gone ten minutes before Caroline heard the wind pick up. A caught breath more and the lights flickered and went out. Soon every window in the house began to rattle. Stew cooled on the stove, and Caroline waited. She could imagine how down at the boatyard Jay would be bent into the pounding wind, adding ropes to boats, tying and double-tying everything he could before he too must battle his way back to safety. *Hurry, Jay,* she murmured. *Hurry.*

The longest night. The town upended. She'd hear in the morning about how the wind peeled off the roof of the drugstore and carried it two blocks, right into the ballfield, how the storm had risen from the bay side, a fast-moving, pelting rain that surged into sheets of water, wave after wave. How an assault of winds screamed into town like a clutch of banshees, cranking on the alders and willows, the steadfast cedars of Humtown. She would hear about how antennas toppled off roofs, how tricycles had been propelled from backyards to be found later wedged into gutters blocks away, how, not far from town, a cluster of sheep flew into the air for two hundred yards, landing together in one horrid pile, how on the bluff overlooking downtown, the pines swayed as if rocked by a madman until, one by one, they thundered to the earth. Everybody was ready to relay those tales to her.

But only Charlie Beecher, arriving dead-eyed, wrecked, in the still-stormy early morning hours, could say what had happened to Jay.

They'd been down at the boatyard, he would tell her, all of them frenzied, trying to add lines, tie down as much as they could and get the hell out of there, just as she'd imagined. Only Jay, it seemed, was keeping an eye on the Canadian boat as it began to lose its anchorage. He hightailed it right down the dock, battling the wind and the surge of waves engulfing the wooden planks, and jumped into a ridiculously unsteady rowboat.

"None of it make senses," Charlie Beecher agonized. "We checked those lines. They were secure."

Yet they'd been loosened or cut, or the wily wind had slipped the knots.

Before anyone could try to intervene, Jay was already leaping out of the sinking rowboat and aboard the renegade boat. But why, oh why, instead of letting go of that vessel, already scarred by trouble, why had he tried so hard to save it? Why had he steered right into the maw of the storm, heading full on into that surge? Charlie Beecher was flummoxed. Heartsore and bewildered. *Jay doesn't make mistakes*, he kept saying.

I know that boat! Caroline insisted to Charlie Beecher. Or she'd heard of it. She was confused, but she was sure Jay had spoken about it, that he knew it well. *But what about the children?* Caroline kept asking, to Charlie Beecher's confusion. *What happened to the children?*

It was only much later, after a shaking Charlie had finally left, that Caroline realized she'd conflated Jay's worst nightmare with her own.

In the weeks after the storm, Caroline received a slew of cards and letters, a collection of celebratory Jay stories. She read each one with a combination of pride and fury. *Jay was the best of men.* But what had the best of men been thinking that night? What had been so important? Among them a carefully penned note from Halde's mother that simply said, *I'm sorry. So sorry.* Caroline hadn't thought about the little girl since Jay had told her about the visit to his shop, and now she realized she'd never found out what had happened to the Shuffler, if anything. Nothing, she supposed, because hadn't she seen him since the storm, driving by or going about his business in his familiar brown suit, looking like his usual squirrelly self? She couldn't imagine what a man like that would want with the impounded boat, a charlatan's vessel destined for heartache, a doomed boat, one she might try to set on fire herself if it hadn't already been destroyed, swept out to sea and shattered, yes, a goddamn thief of a boat that had stolen Jay Weller's life and hers along with it. Why couldn't the Shuffler have prevailed? Why couldn't he have been the one on the boat that night? Or better yet, sailed that damn boat away well before the storm took off, a runaway no one would be chasing?

HOBOS

MILE 10

There had been a time when industry in Humtown burned with purpose. A few cobbled fortunes out of that promise. No one would pretend a real boom was coming, reconciled as they were to the forever loss of a long-dreamed-of passenger train and true commerce, but the more mundane enterprises flourished. The paper mill invested in new equipment and a bigger plant, and after a deeper vein of a particularly attractive granite was discovered, the quarry, too, expanded. With those two businesses surging, heavy trucks became a scourge, hammering roads so that the common saying was that life on the peninsula had only two seasons: *Rain and Paving*. Then, in a wondrous development, government resources had been found to expand the industrial rail line so that the mill could bypass the unwieldy burden and expense of both ships and trucks. Roads would be saved, it was argued, and so more swiftly than anyone could believe, more tracks were installed with access roads, snaking along farmland and forest right down to a loading station by the bay. The newspaper printed progress reports, and jobs were steady even as the town proper remained undisturbed. Few people lived out by the quarry, and those close in to the mill were millworkers themselves and used to its smell and sounds.

But all signs of progress have thoroughly vanished by the time of the Big Walk, at least when it comes to the quarry. A scandal. Money, money, money. Money and lies. *What else is new?* Helen Hubka might say. Well, crumbling rock. The mill, too, only uses the train infrequently now. Trucks, it turns out, go *exactly* where you want them and with new commercial avenues opening overseas, the logistics of moving materials have become tricky. Sometimes, even a barge is a better bet.

Abandoned? Not quite. The train tracks are maintained for the sake of the once-a-month mill runs. But no workers, of course, are about when the walkers arrive. The Scouts reach Forgotten Bay Road first and cross that country lane with ease. Not a car in sight. Both examine the loading dock and train tracks as they approach, taking the measure, assessing danger. They've consulted the rough map Landon handed around and, used to hiking, could be much farther ahead, they reckon, but they are gentlemen-in-training, and as anxious as they are to plough through this walk with a resolute steadiness, they know they'll wait for the others at this juncture, at every crucial turn. Because no one can be left behind. No one can go unaccounted. If someone falls in need, Oren has a first aid box in his rucksack, and Karl is well-practiced in rescue techniques. He can tie a tourniquet or a bowline in seconds. Heck, he can tie practically any knot in their slim handbook.

A dog, patchy, black-and-white, sleeps on the empty loading dock platform, curled into a dry corner of concrete beside the old loading shed. He opens his eyes for the Scouts and Warren, raises his head as the women appear, but only rises and begins to howl at the sight of the priest, as if he recognizes the man and is warning the world.

"Shut up, Riddle," Landon growls, and the dog whimpers into silence, to Avis's relief. She wouldn't breathe a word to anyone, but dogs frighten her, especially dogs out on their own.

The air is brackish. They catch glimpses of the bay not all that far beyond the rails, the vista still weighted with morning fog. The access road they'll follow is nothing more than a dirt track running parallel to the rails on one side and a steep, forested stretch on the other. Oh, the walkers are so tired, here in the midmorning sling. Despite the unscheduled stops beside the found car and train case, a few of them would not complain if they could rest once more here beside the loading dock. Yet forbearance seems to be a shared quality within this group, varied as they are. They eye the loading dock, the gray pebbled beach along the bay, imagine the ease of a morning nap even beneath mist, yet not one even hints at another break. They move on. Not far off, a truck engine revs under a heavy foot, its muffler complaining, and rumbles toward them on Forgotten Bay Road. The truck slows, idles loudly. Riddle, the dog, begins barking again, endlessly. But only one or two of the walkers register the confluence of sounds, so outside their endeavor.

Surprisingly, it's Landon who keeps hustling them forward, away from the road, away from easy visibility. That uncharacteristic hurry for the old man gets them all going again without a single remark. You'd think he'd hollered, *Move 'em on out!* and cracked a whip like one of the rawhides in *Wagon Train*.

Avis recognizes so little around her, such an alien landscape: thick mud as gray as the sky, endless evergreens, paths wind-strewn with the reddish-brown debris of fallen cedar berries and more of those fat slugs, which turn out to be yellow. She is grateful when occasional raindrops tap on the hood of her coat, when wind tickles her face. Those she knows. She has fallen back to walk closer to Landon and Denis, the little blue suitcase banging against her shin from time to time. Helen Hubka seems to avoid the stringy old man with his constant brown cigarette, and her avoidance makes him an appealing companion to Avis. She hasn't wanted to leave Caroline's side, not only because the teacher is always looking out for her, but also because Caroline has fallen in beside the priest who carries Avis's weighted bookbag into his overlarge rucksack. But Helen Hubka keeps eyeing the train case, so Avis slows and easily lets the older woman outpace her until they are spread well apart, almost out of sight from each other.

It's hard not to look at Denis's left eye. His is a new bruise, Avis knows, still blue and purple and angry. She's well-acquainted with the stages. She has several of her own at the moment, both livid and fading, the worst on her upper left arm. Although she avoids overusing that arm, a mere glance at Denis's eye sets off a throbbing within her, her own pain resurfacing in recognition. Unlike Helen Hubka, who's already asked and received a pure lie, Avis doesn't want to know how Denis got his shiner. She can guess from Warren's surprise and reticence that the injury had nothing to do with sports or fights with other boys. It's a home thing. She knows that, and since she's also learned that Denis is an only child, she guesses the how. But why? She wonders, too, if Denis will guess about her, if he'll notice the visible scars by her mouth and along the side of her right wrist. She has her usual new excuse ready for Helen Hubka (bicycle accident), but thinks that if Denis—or Caroline—asks, she might just stay quiet for a while and see if they figure it out. The farther she gets from Teddy, the more she realizes that if she does what she's come to do, she can't go home again. If she does, he'll kill her. At least then, she figures, with a growing sense of resignation, she'll be released. Once more, she thinks of the young mother and her two baby girls, the toy rabbit and all those tiny dresses she carries for them and wonders where they are, wonders if they've really broken free.

In full daylight, still walking, Caroline feels herself tearing loose from town. Even the constant gabbling from Helen Hubka can't hold her. The drama of the found car and the train case behind them, she concentrates on the act of moving forward. The walking itself is different among others. Or she is. Her attention is less bound by association, and despite herself, despite her determination to let this world go, she feels as if she is waking up to its beauty, its incessant demands, suddenly attentive to each slight variation in the landscape, each corresponding reaction within her own body. Her right knee complains occasionally, but she is used to that. All those years of crouching down beside five-year-olds have taken their toll. There have been mornings when she woke with one knee or the other announcing itself with such throbbing fury that she'd wonder how she'd get out of bed, and many nights, too, when Jay mixed her a bracing cocktail well past the usual hour to help quell the ache enough to sleep. A kind of magical relief appeared for a while after Jay died, as if the pain taking up residence in her knee recognized its inferior power and acquiesced to the far more intense, the near-unbearable torments coursing through every other part of her. The cure for pain is greater pain, apparently. Too soon, though, aches reappeared. Walking doesn't silence that distress, but it dulls it, gives it brief respite, and up until now, her knees have cooperated and allowed her that momentary peace. Although she'd slipped a bottle of aspirin in her big pockets before she headed out and has managed to down a couple in the ten miles or so they've covered so far, all it takes is a glance at lumbering Helen Hubka or that relentless old Landon to steel her determination.

And too, as they descend the sloping gravel road from the loading dock to the flat rail access trail, Caroline feels a tremendous shift, a nagging recognition unlike the layered memories that assault her as she paces around town. Maybe this is one true step in letting go, a sliver of true perception, but as far as she knows, she's never been on this trail before. Yet she's sure she recognizes the long line of wild rugosa roses fighting for space with cloudberry bushes. She knows with visceral certainty this particular view of Forgotten Bay over the train tracks. High above, an eagle circles, hounded by a shrieking ring of crows. The moment of *déjà vu* is so strong, so powerful that she finds herself whipping around to see how far Jay is behind them. She stops herself only a moment before she calls out to him, letting others pass, before she pivots into pretending an urgent question to Landon.

"Has this trail been here a long time?" she manages.

What she wants to know is if this was a place Jay knew well, if by leaving town and her haunts, she's happened on one of his own beloved landscapes. A secret harbor against a storm. Why hadn't she thought of that? Jay often took a Saturday hike or got up at dawn to go fishing in one of his hidden spots.

"I guess it has," Landon says, "but it's not a common way."

"You wouldn't come out here to fish then?"

"Nah, better spots near Gold Egg Beach, where you don't have to deal with the tracks, and . . ." He glances up, tips his head, ". . . you won't encounter strangers."

Caroline can see then, ahead of them, three men sitting on a wood-plank bench not far from the gulley that separates the trail from the raised train track. Raggedy men, used to avoiding townspeople. As they catch sight of the walkers, two rise, pick up their bindles, and climb into the woods above, disappearing almost at once onto a thin parallel dirt path she's only now noticed. One is limping badly, but doesn't seem cowed. He shoots the walkers a look of fierce assessment that makes even Helen Hubka hesitate a moment before proceeding. This last hobo stays still, doesn't even blink, it seems, until they are nearly upon him. In moments he is walking among them, slowing them down.

"Oh, boy," Denis says, under his breath.

Above them, shadows seem to be keeping a steady pace that matches their own, and though Caroline knows the walkers carry nothing of value, she feels uneasy with the intrusion.

"Where you heading so early, folks?" the raggedy man is saying. "Going on a trip, are you?"

His eyes skitter over the Scouts to land on Avis and the train case, which seems to jump a little in Avis's hand, as if the man had called out to it in recognition. Warren begins to explain, even as the man maneuvers closer to Caroline.

"The President, you say!" the man exclaims. "All of you, walking fifty miles! The ladies, too!"

He reels in feigned wonder beside Caroline. He is, Avis thinks, the dirtiest man she's ever seen. Even out here, the animal stink of him—a urine-soaked moss, tobacco breath—announces itself. Helen Hubka marches back to push Caroline to the other side of her, as if the teacher might be pounced upon, but the hobo seems too skinny and weak to hurt anyone. Indeed, the women also prove too fast for him.

"*Ask not,*" the hobo intones with real solemnity as they leave him behind, "*What your country . . .*"

He nods at Jaspar Goode and Denis, recoils slightly at the sight of Landon, then perks up when he spies the priest.

"Professor!" he says, then noticing the collar, corrects himself: "Ah, no. 'Scuse me! *Father.*" His laugh is gruff and full of surprised delight.

The priest tries a sharp nod, a quickened step, but the raggedy man—perhaps he is not as old as he first appears—chugs right along beside him.

"Don't you remember me . . . your . . . Holiness?" the hobo grins.

"Should I?" the priest asks.

"You might," the hobo says. "You might even recall we had a slight misunderstanding last time we met."

The priest tips his head to one side. "No," he says, "I think not."

"Good, good," the hobo says. "Glad to clear that up. Forgiveness, that's your act, yeah?"

The other walkers are all pushing forward. Even Landon and Denis have left the priest and hobo behind, but Avis senses a familiar danger in the air, one that signals the confusion of a sparking wire, a sudden, incoming stab or angry push—a disruption arriving seemingly out of nowhere. That feeling should send her running, but Teddy's not here. How could the trouble be meant for her? She ignores Helen Hubka's backward scowl and slows and slows until she is only steps ahead of the men.

"So, you're taking a long walk, you say?" The hobo's tone incredulous. "For the young Prince Kennedy?"

"What other reason would bring us out here? Out into the wilderness?" Avis can hear the smile in the priest's voice.

"Oh, you never know. We get all sorts out here lately." The hobo's jocular tone has vanished.

"Do you?" The priest's voice, too, has tightened. Gone is the sweetness of the singing "Danny." A warning is in the air, an offering.

"You know, *Father*, some men were just put on earth to cause suffering."

"A sad truth," the priest says. "You know this man, you say?"

"Not personally," the hobo says, "but you might. Being in the business and all," he adds, as if mocking the priest's collar.

"A traveling man?"

"Not unless you count a tractor or a truck, which I decidedly do not."

"Or an old car?"

"A jalopy?" The hobo seems to reflect, before shaking his head.

"Group like this might find it easier to walk along a main road, I'd think," the hobo goes on. "Plain sight and all."

"Not the best idea," the priest says.

"Well, then."

The men pause, and Avis does as well, bending to fiddle with her shoe-laces. With her head down, she can't help but notice the hobo scuffing the toe of his broken boot in the dusty trail. Both men are making marks in the dust as if their feet are having a conversation of their own. The hobo's boot seems to be drawing stars beside the priest's well-worn shoes, swirls and arcs, a series of marks that reminded Avis of an inky drawing of a constellation she struggles to place. Is it a map? A clue? She is startled out of this puzzle as other boots appear beside her own.

"You all right?" Jaspar Goode asks.

It happens so quickly, but as she stands, she catches a flicker of fear in the hobo's face as he takes in the muscular fisherman in his head-to-toe camouflage, his sharp, swift glance at the ground beside the hobo's foot. The priest bows his head again in thought or maybe in a kind of blessing, she thinks, and resumes his walk without another word, and Avis is blown before the men, almost skipping as she scurries to catch up with the others.

"God bless America," the recovered hobo hoots to their backs. "And all its good people."

Avis imagines he will remain behind, continuing his dusty diagram. She is certain, too, that she hears a scattering of gravel behind them, but when she glances back a moment later, the hobo is gone, and she has to squint to see the faint outline of his ragged figure moving along with the others on the ghost trail in the woods well above them.

GUESSING GAMES

"It's the accent, I bet," Helen Hubka is telling Caroline, "that Midwestern twang." She's been trying to place the priest's origins since she first heard him speak. (She's guessing Michigan or one of those farm states all jumbled in together in the middle of the country.) "These bums are all from far away. They hear someone sounds like them, off they go, imagining they've found kin." Her laugh is a hissing simper, a sound that could be attributed to background noise—a teakettle, a radiator—acquired to obscure her presence on the phone. Still, she can't resist the lure of being the first in town with this news of a friendship between the new priest and the hobo population. She's been puffing, struggling a bit, but this fresh crumb of information seems to have given her a second wind.

"What will you do now, Helen?" Caroline tries to divert, as Avis sidles beside them. "Now that the dialup's come in, I mean?"

"What do you mean? I've got a job with the phone company, you know. People still need to call the Operator."

"Good lord, the questions I get," she goes on. *How do I get lumps out of my gravy? How can I get this baby to take the bottle? When is the frost coming?* You'd think I was the Oracle of Delphi."

But the sadness in her voice gives her away. Her real job is over. The party line is no more. People will dial the Time Lady and the Weather Man directly, tell their secrets without a single outsider listening in. They will make assignations with lovers and bad companions and shady business people without anyone, without *Helen*, to sound an alarm, however muted. It's tragic.

For miles, she hasn't managed to be quiet. If it's not gossip she's spewing, it's complaints about the weather, the path, the ever-lingering stench of the paper mill, her painful feet (or "dogs" as she sometimes confusingly calls them), the priest's enormous pack, which blocks her view, the sun in her eyes (or the lack of sun), the uselessness of the near-abandoned train tracks, even the faint smoke from Landon's brown cigarette. But somewhere around Mile 16, Helen Hubka shifts. She begins a game with anyone in earshot. She seems to have decided that she's become their social director, which should come as no shock. What does surprise Caroline is how easily everyone falls in line. Not even her most eager kindergartners take to a game as quickly as this group has. An adult version of I Spy. It's perhaps meant to be a simple contest of identification, but Helen Hubka's inscrutable clues don't help at all.

"It's the exact shade," she'll say, "of Gert Eckles's original hair color."

"Fat," she'll add, "like you-know-who's alligator wallet."

Helen Hubka looks to Caroline first, as if certain the teacher in her will be eager, but Caroline is almost as good as the priest and Avis at deflecting. Caroline is also pretty sure that Helen Hubka is not as interested in playing as she is in instigating conversation. It clearly pains her that she can't get on the horn straightaway and spread the Gussie revelations, but Caroline guesses that if the Operator is going to wear herself out on what she's starting obliviously to call "this death march," she wants to get as much as she can out of it.

"Is it a kind of bug?" Caroline tries. "Denis was always very good with bugs."

She offers the boy a smile over her shoulder. One he returns, along with a memory of his five-year-old self displaying a potato bug on his outstretched palm.

"Now it's cars," Warren says. "If we play a game about cars and engines, Denis will murder us all." He, too, glances back at his friend, but at the word *murder* Denis's head jerks up, and he has no smiles to offer Warren.

"Maybe," old Landon says. "Maybe not."

"You spent quite a bit a'time on the Quarter Mile, didn't you?" he says to Jaspar Goode, referring to the long straight stretch of Churchill Road used for Sunday evening drag racing.

"Who hasn't?" Jaspar Goode parries. "You old boys were out there, too, if I remember right."

Humtown tradition. Boys in Paradise, that stretch. Whole underground clubs had been formed, not for the matching shirts and jackets, but for the exchange of car parts and tools and expertise. There was a saying in town, Caroline remembers now. Her daughter used it to persuade Jay to teach her to drive. *Boys ride horses until they can drive. Girls stay at the barn.* Drove Jay nuts, the idea of his daughter stuck and diminished. Or maybe it was the fairgrounds barn itself that bothered Jay.

Caroline remembers now where she's seen that fellow Remy Gussie. He was one of the men who raced horses every Sunday at the fairgrounds. The Wiry Weasel, Jay called him. Look at him ogling the teenage girls, look at how he preened before them, ordered them around. And yet the girls were charmed. She guessed that from a certain angle (that of a yearning teenage girl), Remy Gussie could be viewed as handsome. He had a crooked smile and muscled arms and, at least at the fairgrounds, practiced the manly squint of a cowboy in a spaghetti western. He hassled the girls with barbed words, withholding attention, until he abruptly chose a favorite. His way of flirting. Diminish, ignore, engulf. It was a wonder to watch the way even the stron gest girls succumbed, if just a little, to his not-so-jocular battering, the sudden way he'd turn, the shock of his hands boldly adjusting the hips, the legs, the seat of a girl on her horse. How they marveled at what they took to be his expertise, the "old man" of thirty still riding at the fairgrounds. A bachelor, his widowed mother recently deceased, he raised sheep and indulged himself in hobbies: an airplane, the horses, high school girls. Half the Sunday race audience cringed at the sight of him, but the girls . . . No wonder Jay had fallen swiftly to Ginny's ploy for driving lessons.

That weaselly fellow had gone and married one of the last crop of horse girls, she'd heard. A girl who turned seventeen on her wedding day, when she was already four months gone. "Damn crime," Jay had said then. He looked as if he'd like to rouse Charlie Beecher and a few men from the Port and go rescue the girl-wife, who was clearly in for a bad time, and Caroline vaguely remembers Jay driving over to have a fierce word with the girl's parents, who, at that stage at least, seemed more intent on avoiding shame, to Jay's great disappointment. The girl was too old to have been one of her students, but Caroline knows the family, half remembers the swift, hushed wedding. Johanssons. Yes, Aileen Johansson, tall and shy with an abundance of reddish-brown curls escaping from a thick braid, utterly oblivious about the impression she made on the world.

Aileen Johansson was a few years younger than Ginny, but Ginny had been a big fan, cajoling Caroline and Jay into coming to the fairgrounds to watch the horse girls, to watch Aileen. Before she lost interest in horses, Ginny wanted to ride like Aileen Johansson, who came alive on a horse, her long lean body surging with a beautifully precise energy that matched the animal's. Her love for the horse was so raw and visible, and everyone observing fell in love, too, with both of them. With a shock, Caroline realizes that the captivating child on the horse must be the missing young mother. A girl with two little girls. Where could she have gone? No money, toting along two near babies? The girl had never left town before. Aileen Johansson was her mother's girl, wasn't she? Why had she not gone home? Waited out the storm with her true family? Maybe she had, and they'd hid her, found a way to send her and the little ones away? Caroline feels a breath of relief imagining that possibility. But each time she'd gone home before, they'd sent her back. That was marriage, they'd said. And now, according to Helen Hubka, her family is still desperately looking for her, too.

Or so they claim. Maybe (more imagined relief) her family is hiding her and feigning worry. (All these months, though?)

Or the unthinkable, the monstrous: the probable horror of Remy Gussie.

Ahead, the yellow-handled blue train case with all those little girl dresses (so like her own daughter's) and footed pajamas and folded diapers bobs up and down with Avis, and despite her aversion to Helen Hubka's gossip, Caroline can't believe that no one searched for the missing mother and her two little girls. Helen Hubka appears to know every detail of their lives, down to middle names and pet chickens. Yet Denis seems absolutely certain no investigation was or is underway.

If so, Caroline—still reconciling the multitude of details Helen Hubka has given her with her own memories—can imagine how even the damning discovery of the car might play out: The sheriff's office will retrieve the car, keep it for a few hours, then drive it back to the Gussie farm, leaving it half in the scrub, not wanting to block Gussie's tractor. Her family still left desperately hoping Aileen had fled with the children. Her mother might spend every free moment hovering near the phone. Her brothers might continue to visit the old haunts: the fairground stables, Gold Egg Beach, High School Hill, and the tiny near-hidden playground on Dilly Street. Her father and brother might even go to the house, ignoring for once Remy Gussie's long-stated command to keep her family away. That Remy is as wily as he is mean, apparently, and even if he is out into the fields, he will surely spot them from a distance as they stalk around the barn where he keeps his plane, and though he couldn't manage to get to his wife and children before the family car supposedly left the driveway, he will thunder onto the kitchen stoop before Aileen's father and brother can turn a doorknob. Will he barrage them with curses straightaway, or will he let them in reluctantly, truculently, only long enough for them to confirm the babies' toys are still in the playpen, her winter coat on the hook, tiny rubber boots in a jumble? Her father will move heavily, in a daze, but Aileen's brother might notice a hole in the wall, another dent next to the stove, a stain in one corner, and over all, a peculiar scent—peppermint over bleach. His finger might reach out to touch a bit of pinkish-brown fur under the high chair, startled to recognize the dismembered leg of Cheryl Anne's stuffed rabbit, the one she called Bummy, the one she could not be without. He might succeed in sweeping the leg up and into his pocket, but not likely. Gussie will surely not miss a move and will stop him with a crude word or a raised hand about to strike. Yes, Gussie might have been wired shut up until then, displaying a version of his best behavior, but his silence is a bad nerve that, once pressed, would open a stream of venom, threats so vile neither her father nor brother would understand them at first.

What was wrong with the sheriff? And why is Helen Hubka the only one still willing to spread the word, to roil up attention? Shouldn't the whole town have been out combing fields and woods, beaches and byways? Jay would go batty over this "family matter" nonsense. Privacy becoming another word for the containment of violence and razored secrets. Helen Hubka says that the family even tried talking to Aileen's cousin and former best friend, Karin Johansson, who had still been riding at the fairground stable at twenty, an "old girl" now, so sharp-tongued and pinch-faced she's left alone most of the time. Karin, who used to ride woodenly in Aileen's shadow. Karin, who alone of all the relatives and lost friends, mingled with

Remy Gussie, keeping company with him at the fairground barn while Aileen was "stuck with her brats." Karin might know something, Aileen's mother pleaded, remembering how the girls were inseparable at the stable until Gussie took advantage. Aileen's older sister tried with the cousin, too, according to Helen Hubka, but all that came from that was a blunt reminder that Karin and Aileen had fallen out, that the cousin believes Aileen does not deserve her husband, that the children are being raised badly, spoiled babies, that Aileen was a slut who would probably run off (*had* probably run off) with some other fellow who promised her better. A workman, a transient— who knows? *Consider her past behavior*, the green-eyed cousin declared with feigned primness, ending the conversation there. She'd said enough.

"She could have run off," Helen Hubka says at one point. "Maybe one of her brothers tucked them all up in a logging truck and spirited them away. Maybe the family's play-acting to get Gussie off the scent. Maybe," Helen concludes, "a Good Samaritan came along, and she saw her chance and ran."

Although Helen Hubka is talking to Caroline, nearly all the walkers are privy to the conversation, and nearly all, too, keep their heads down, their faces blank, and all are silent when she says, "I sure as heck would. Wouldn't you?"

Among the walkers floats the young mother in that dusty green Plymouth, her babies lulled into open-mouthed sleep by its boatlike sway as she pulls onto the abandoned road. Who would be there to meet her, to gently take them from her arms? Who would be brave enough to spirit mother and children away from that monstrous man and never say a word? Caroline glances at Jaspar Goode, and for the briefest moment, she believes in the possibility of a rescue.

"Could have happened," Helen Hubka says.

Is it then that the crows, one so broad-winged and cocky it might be a raven, begins to harass them—dive-bombing around and between their heads to tweak the green feather on Helen Hubka's brown hat—then that Caroline is jolted into the night after the dog died? Jay's dog, of course; all their pets fell under his spell. That night, she was tidying the kitchen, Jay tinkering in the living room, and a knocking began on the windows. First one, then another, *rap, rap, rap*, the cats going mad, racing from room to room. When she flicked on the porch light, they all peered out windows to see a black-chinned hummingbird, out of season, frantically circling as if trying to find a way in. After a moment, Jay reached past Caroline to turn out the light.

He needs to know, he told her gently, *that he has to move on.*

The dog had been a breed of its own, perhaps part Rottweiler, part Lab or maybe part St. Bernard. So large, she joked that having him around was like having another couch in the room. But the dog seemed to have no clear notion of his size and, observing the cats curling up on the end of the bed or in Jay's lap, tried once or twice to do the same, to be enfolded by Jay. Of course, he couldn't leave this earth without trying again.

The crow/raven circles and dives once, twice, three times and finally manages to snatch Helen Hubka's bright feather, knocking off her hat and scratching her temple in the process. The Operator, of course, exclaims, yet no one else seems unduly startled, only relieved that the conversation can shift away, the woman's list of her current and past injuries.

"Get away, you devils," she cries, swatting the air.

"Oh please, allow me." The priest intervenes, raising a hand. "My job."

Helen Hubka shoots him an irritated look. Is he making fun of her?

Far back in the line, someone—Landon or that fisherman—snickers.

Maybe they did run away, Avis is thinking. She tries to imagine a young mother and her little girls, babies really, and at first can only conjure up an image of the President's beautiful young wife and her own two royal children, huddled together in a storm-torn wood. The First Lady becomes a lisping farm girl, slipping away with toddler Caroline and baby John-John. A crazy picture. Gradually, Avis adjusts. She sees Aileen Gussie's oldest girl, curly-headed, climbing back and forth over the car's bench seat as her mother drives, the mother admonishing her to stay put. And the other little girl, hardly more than a baby, sleeping in that infant cot on the wide backseat.

The young mother and girls appear so clearly to Avis, but when she conjures the husband, Remy Gussie, she only sees Teddy. Hears only Teddy. Teddy as Remy Gussie subjecting his young wife to a conversation Avis knows well, a daily escalation of grievances, insults, and threats. Normality.

She is stupid.

She is ugly. A milk sow.

She is only still alive because he allows her to be.

No one can protect her.

He could kill them all if he wanted.

If he says it enough, it becomes true.

Avis's dream mother says in her ear, *If that's the case, darling, wouldn't it also be true that if you ignore him, if his words evaporate even as they leave his mouth, they mean absolutely nothing?*

Go deaf, she instructs. *Turn blind.*

Learn to weep without making a noise.

But where do you put pain?

Open a drawer and whisper?

Breathe into the night air?

Sob as quietly as can be into a cup of water, then surreptitiously spill the water near a neighbor's doorstep?

It nearly worked. One last early morning in the Philadelphia house, Mrs. MacDougall, that blessedly determined neighbor, tapping on the kitchen door. She had *something to say*, she told Avis's mother. But Avis's parents can't acknowledge a universe where Teddy, *their boy*, would knowingly hurt his sister.

Who'd asked her to meddle in their private family business, to make insinuations? Avis's mother complained afterward.

"Almost as bad as your mother," Avis's father said. "Watching too many soap operas, always ready to stir up trouble with her own starring role."

Of course, Avis had tried, early on, gulping out baby words through tears, words Teddy translated. Accidents, clumsiness, intentional mess. *Oh, Avis.* And even when her parents witnessed the gentler assaults of shoves and pinches, they would only prod Teddy for soft faked apologies that left everyone unsatisfied and infuriated Teddy: *Tell your sister you're sorry.*

The burn marks on Avis's arm sing out. The long red scar on the side of her hand where she broke through a glass window once, when she still thought she could escape. Her never-quite-healed ribs. The thinned hair on the crown of her head. Bruises and scrapes. The constant dance of cringe and flinch.

Stay out of his way

Don't antagonize him.

Avis is such a daydreamer, her mother tells everyone. *A magnet for little disasters.*

You know better, her mother insists to Avis, unaware how neatly her words echo Teddy's.

Avis can imagine how the young mother might have left. The middle of the night—her own solution—would be too hard. No matter how tired the farmer was, he'd stop them. He owned his house, owned them. She would have had to wait for a busy morning, an emergency—sheep giving birth, a windblown fence line. Avis knows almost nothing about farms, but she's seen enough episodes of *Bonanza* to imagine the problems that might arise. A fire would be too dramatic, too much of a risk. Who could count on a tornado that would rival Dorothy's and might land them all in another land where justice was equally capricious? The young mother would have to be ready, always ready. She wouldn't be able to pick the day herself, but when the moment did appear, she would recognize it. And then the storm did come. The Storm of the Century, Avis has heard it called. A storm just for her, and she'd run. One baby crooked in the broken fold of her arm, the other twined within her skirts, holding on for dear life. The day arriving much as this March day had, rain sheets razor-sharp, sudden and swift, hammering on a night roof or slicing through a day graced with yellow light—light that would have been shining on the pots of dahlias her mother gave her to brighten up the yard: gold and orange and fuchsia. The mother might have left them on the side of the house where he wouldn't have seen them straight away, but the storm would find them and do his job anyway. Ruined, she thought. She might have sobbed, but she'd grown used to senseless destruction. Avis could list all her own broken treasures. But she knew, too, as the young mother must have known, that blossoms, crushed, must push back slowly, determinedly, or die, and she had done that as well. Daily. But that day, the rain didn't stop, and the wind plowed across the farm, upending a shed, throwing the sheep into disarray, even lifting one or two off their feet and sending them into the fields, head over tail. And Remy would have had no time for her. He'd be out in the barn, desperately trying to contain the damage, tying down everything he could as if he were at sea and battling one rogue wave after another. He would be furious when he finally came back inside the house, and she would be captive, too, to the storm. She saw her chance. Her only chance. The little girls calling her, she gathered her strength. Of course, she could not, would not, leave without them. They would go together. Or they would die.

This fellow Remy Gussie, this version of Teddy—if his family did get away, Avis knows he must follow them. Maybe not right away, but he'd come after them. He wouldn't brook defeat, insubordination, lack of control. Yes, he'd track them. He'd find every scrap of them. Unless, Avis thinks . . . unless someone helped them. The baby's stuffed rabbit is well-hidden deep in her coat pocket. She strokes a satiny ear and decides she'll keep it. And when it's clear they are safe again, when *she* is safe again, she'll find a way to them, she thinks, and restore this loved object, a child's bit of comfort.

THEORIES OF TIME

Words flow between, across, beside them. The walkers catch them as they please, enter and leave conversations as if picking up a refrain from a song—a lullaby, a march. They keep their eyes down even as the words circle, eyes on feet or the sway of a coat hem ahead. Every now and then, with effort, one might look up to consider the landscape, the path ahead. Every now and then, Warren tries to energize the group, using the Kennedy Walk battle cry he and Denis practiced: "Onward," he'd call out. "*Vigah!*" The silly imitation of the President's Boston accent never fails to make most of them smile, but no one quickens the pace. The pattern is assumed and ingrained so naturally it seems they've been hiking together all their lives.

"Is it still the same day?" Caroline asks the air around her. "I feel as if we've fallen out of time."

Jaspar Goode nods. "It happens on a boat, too," he says over his shoulder.

Caroline knows. She's heard Jay talk about the difference between time on land and time on the water. *The sea doesn't care about you*, Jay would say. *Forget the romantics who read swelling waves as anger, calm waters as acceptance. The sea is its own entity, with its own set of rules, including time. Even the sunrise and sunset don't affect it much.*

The moon, okay; the stars, perhaps, Jay would say. *Not us, nope.*

The land around them does seem as oblivious to their endeavor as the sea must be to that of a fishing boat. They tramp across its surface, a cursory passage, hardly awake, hardly present at all. Caroline, for instance, is only a little aware that the so-called access road they've been following has narrowed, become a rocky footpath, one that they are now gently climbing. If she glanced toward the bay, Caroline might note another alteration in the landscape, a low cloud farther out, the water turning to steel, but her

97

attention is riveted on the dance her feet perform, the rhythm involved in selecting the clearest, most even spot of earth for this footfall, then that, and on and on.

Time is a steady drum.

Time is a heartbeat.

Time is a constant push forward.

But wait, here is the priest's voice behind her, singsong and jolly.

"What is time but a made-up thing?" he calls out.

Mind reader.

"How can you say that?" Caroline manages after a pause.

This is something else that's entered the walk, this pause, these slight gaps within conversation, as if they all need that space to catch the words, hold and examine, before they can respond.

"Well," the priest says, "someone decided the format of hours and days, and there have been many different calendars: Ptolemaic, Julian, Coptic, Florentine, Hebrew. Probably hundreds more before we got to the one we agree upon now."

"*What!*" Avis's shock is profound.

"The sun rises, the sun sets," Helen Hubka grumbles. "Can't disagree with that, can you?"

"But is each hour or day equal to another?" the priest persists.

The other three push up the ridge and ponder as they do. The fisherman might be recalling endless days waiting, followed by the exhilarating rush when they hit the fish run, and too how different that same pattern felt in Korea—a long stretch of intense boredom, followed by frantic ritual and pure panic. Avis feels the aching watchfulness that comes with living with Teddy, the never-knowing, time upended as she crouched in her closet throughout the night. Caroline is hit anew by the way time fractured when Jay died, that splintering moment that refuses to let go and surfaces without warning, again and again, re-creating heartache with stunning accuracy.

"Of course, they aren't," the priest continues gently, as if to console them all. "That's why we need clocks and calendars, a pretend frame of time. So time won't meander. It did once, you know."

He tells them about the origins of the Gregorian calendar, about how it was necessary to reset the calendar, which had drifted away from the connection with the seasons. That sunset and sunrise, too, he adds, nodding toward the fisherman. It was in 1582, and what was decided was that to get time back on track, the calendar would skip ten days, from October 5 to October 15.

"Ten days?" Caroline says. "Ten missing days?"

Avis can't help herself. "How?" she blurts out. "Didn't anyone notice?"

What she wants to ask is what would happen if your birthday was October 7, as hers was. When would you consider yourself a year older?

"It was the beginning of the Middle Ages, Avis. Not many people actually kept track of the days in a calendar. Just the general idea, I suspect," the priest says.

"How do you know this?" Caroline asks.

"He's a priest, isn't he?" Helen Hubka snaps. "And he's talking about the Middle Ages."

She's baiting him, Caroline thinks. Getting ready to spew some nonsense about the priest she's heard over the wires.

But Caroline is wrong. Helen Hubka is only curious. Her President is a believer. Her President listens to priests, she'd like to tell Caroline. Of course, they must know a great deal.

"The Middle Ages must be like yesterday to a priest," Helen Hubka continues.

"Or today," the unperturbed priest says. "Or tomorrow."

The ten missing days are all Avis can think about for the next several miles. If she could take a few days out of the calendar, she has a good idea what those might be.

FALLOUT

The idea must have come to Teddy during Thanksgiving weekend. They'd gone to their grandparents' house. An all-day event beginning that morning with the Gimbels Parade blaring on her grandparents' television. Avis's family arrived late. Not even her father would miss the Mummers Day Parade on New Year's but Gimbels' offering was an optional diversion, one they'd watch at home if they so desired, thank you very much. "Too much together time," her father grumbled. Her mother's brothers and their families packed as much as they could into the holiday. Before Avis's family arrived, they also would have indulged in a round of touch football in the nearby elementary school's playing fields, another reason her family arrived later.

"Who do they think they are?" her father liked to complain. "The Kennedys?"

And what a crowd they were! The eleven cousins (thirteen counting Avis and Teddy). Always a baby to pass around. A gang of little boys racing slot cars in the basement. Annette in a corner with a book. Avis managed to stay in the kitchen with her grandmother until the last cousin, Eileen, got it in her head to help, too, bungling tasks and snacking underfoot, and the aunts shooed them both away. The living room full of roaring, joking men watching football, her father on his own, chain-smoking in a corner armchair, full ashtray beside him. A blue-skied, shatteringly cold day, the neighborhood stilled, all the families inside, deaf, dumb, and blind to anything beyond. Eileen wanted to play a grownup game, like canasta or pinochle, but decided she'd have to settle for Go Fish with a reluctant Annette. She was rummaging through bedroom drawers, lifting girdles, shifting scarves. "For a deck of cards," she explained to the uncle coming out of the upstairs bathroom, who nevertheless proceeded to lecture her about the indecency of going through other people's things. From the bottom of the stairs Avis heard him ask, "Did your grandmother say you could?" even as she felt Teddy arrive beside her.

"Cal, get down here!" Another uncle's voice roared from the living room. "They're getting massacred. Karras sacked Starr again!"

Eileen was off the hook. Their uncle thundered down the stairs so fast he tripped over the last step and only saved himself by catching Avis's arm. She'd planted herself, anticipating a push from Teddy that never arrived. Instead, beer-soaked Uncle Cal almost brought her down. Teddy's snicker was meant to be heard, and Uncle Cal was clearly nonplussed as he lumbered to his feet and realized his nephew, this sly boy he'd warned his own kids to avoid, was as tall as he was. A slender, *pretty* boy-man. None of the aunts could yet believe tales told about Teddy. Gosh, those long lashes, those eyes. The uncle saw right away, though, and unlike the aunts, he didn't give Teddy (or Avis) any slack.

"You again. You put her up to it, didn't you?" he huffed into Teddy's face. "Stealing. You're going to find yourself locked away if you keep this up, boy."

Locked away! What an idea! Teddy in a box. Avis cringed. She couldn't move, but she closed her eyes and turned her face away. It would be worse if Teddy remembered her watching. Eileen had no such worries. She tittered from the landing, out of the uncle's sight, but right where Teddy could see. Annette joined her, giggling. The two of them soon in hysterics over the joke that was Teddy. Avis knew what was coming. She could have stopped it, could have corralled the little girls in her own game, in plain sight, but she hadn't, had she?

The two girls whispered together during dessert. A secret. Pitch dark by then and all the adults getting soused. Pretty much all the men could talk about was football, Vince Lombardi's undefeated Packers trounced by the Lions. *The Wizard of Oz* had taken over the television, the other cousins flattening the carpet the moment Danny Kaye began his introduction and a house carried one girl away and landed upon another, the grownups' voices rising in the dining room as the conversation rattled toward politics. A thrill of a Thanksgiving, but one also suffused with relief. The President had reached a deal with Khrushchev mere days before. No more hiding under desks. "No more digging bomb shelters in the backyard," one of the aunt's said. Teddy blinked the tiniest bit at that last comment, and that was how Avis knew. That was why, hours later, as the others searched and searched for Eileen and Annette, as the aunts became more frantic, as her grandfather broke out every flashlight and sent the uncles into the neighborhood, that was why, alone beside her mother, Avis managed to whisper "bomb shelter," as if it were a shy conjecture.

"Oh, Avis," her mother said too loudly, with too much clear resignation, and to Teddy's dismay, the girls were rescued. Who could blame Teddy? He'd sat amongst the adults in the dining room. He'd lounged on the couch, cheering on the winged monkeys. He'd made a turkey sandwich while the others were beginning to gather their sleeping children. And the girls, hiccupping through tears, didn't mention Teddy—or Avis. They were following clues, they said, notes written on a chalkboard and an etch-a-sketch. Clues that had vanished, of course. A special game, leading them to the attic, the basement, out the storm cellar door (like Dorothy!) and on to the shelter. But that last door closed and locked behind them. The shelter had never been left unlocked, their grandfather declared, pulling keys from his coat pocket. Yet someone had been in the shelter before them, the girls swore. A stub of a candle lit inside.

"But *then*," hiccupped Annette, "it blew out."

Vagrants, thieves, neighborhood kids. Only their grandmother truly guessed, but she also knew the violence that might erupt if the uncles learned the truth. So Avis endured the disgusted looks from her purse-mouthed aunts and weary, beer-tuckered uncles and the even more disappointed one from Teddy. Her mother, not surprisingly, did nothing to disturb the perception that Avis either tricked her cousins or abandoned them to a dangerous game.

"Blessed are the peacemakers," she reminded Avis as she prodded her toward the car.

Some peace, because, of course, Teddy's imagination had been piqued. How many bomb shelters had been built throughout their own neighborhood? And who would care about these backyard saviors now that the threat of fallout had ended? Even Avis overheard conversations.

We'll plant roses around it in the spring.

I'll have Al dig it up. An eyesore.

Don't jump the gun now.

If not the Soviets, the Chinese . . .

But the truth was, fears of the bomb were easing away. The shelters languished. Unimproved, unused, blips in the landscape.

Everyone looking. No one seeing.

Another truth, a quiet, necessary-to-Avis one: Teddy could be really fun. On those long afternoons when she and her brother were on their own, sent out to play, it was Teddy who came up with the best games, who challenged Avis (to "make her brave"), who found the narrow winding cave beside a nearby stream, the opening only big enough for Avis to crawl through; Teddy, who instructed Avis step by step until she could climb the tallest tree in their own backyard, then travel across one backyard after another without ever touching the ground or showing herself; Teddy, who invented the wiliest neighborhood competitions like Card Games with Consequences that included dangerous feats (*walk a tightrope, leap from a garage roof into a pile of leaves, explore an abandoned house*); Teddy, who devised initiations for short-lived secret clubs (one memorable challenge demanded glass be shattered from great distances, using homemade slingshots: eyeglasses smashed on a sidewalk, martini glasses in the crook of an elm tree, attic windows and, okay, the MacDougalls' car windshield). Teddy was extraordinarily good at all this. Because of Teddy's fleeting interest in magic tricks, too, Avis learned a little rudimentary magic. Teddy soon grew bored, but Avis persevered, embracing misdirection and sleight of hand. She knew how swiftly a turn in one of Teddy's games might appear, but she like all the others fell under his spell and glittered when he included her, treated her as a true playmate. Even the nuns, the ones who might have suspected Teddy of misdeeds, often could not help but find him charming, and most of them decided that Avis, so quiet, Avis, so problematically unforthcoming, was the sly one. Only her grandmother never doubted. *She* never blamed Avis, not once. She had Teddy's number, she'd say. *Street angel, house devil,* she called him.

"Avis fell again?" she'd say to Avis's mother. "Down the stairs? Off her bike? Through a window?" *I Don't Think So.*

"Where was Teddy when this happened?" Her grandmother would want to know, interrogating Avis's father. "Where were *you?*"

"I do have to work sometimes, Maureen," her father would say drily. "They're kids. Accidents happen."

It was none of her business. No one's business. What would people think, her mother wondered, if her own mother went around telling horrible tales on Teddy like that. Avis was fine. Just ask her.

"Is that true, Avis?" her grandmother would finally ask, already knowing the answer. Because Avis would stick to whatever story her parents or Teddy concocted. Insist on her clumsiness. Did she have a choice? And with each capitulation, Teddy's power increased.

"Come on, Avis," he'd all but whistle, and she would trot behind him, Teddy's dog.

Of course, Teddy had been intrigued by the bomb shelters that had been constructed in the last year. He'd always been consumed by buried treasure, she realized. As the crisis lifted, the preoccupation with stocking up supplies and practicing for fallout waned. First, Teddy would only scavenge from less-visited shelters, lifting curious foodstuffs or radio equipment off a concrete shelf. Easy pickings. Who noticed the loss of tins of Spam or a never-used radio antenna? He soon discovered that more than one neighbor also used a shelter as a family safe, storing important papers and—surprise—jewelry. Teddy's own private stash grew. Too easy. He needed another challenge, didn't he? That's where her classmates, the nearest she had to friends, would come in. A trio of girls rendered silly by the sudden good looks of Avis's dangerous brother. It had only been a matter of time before someone else would follow Teddy. Only a matter of time before Avis would get in the way and, for once, be unable to lie for him. Her fault, all her fault. *If you'd only done your job,* Teddy would say later, *no one would have been hurt.*

THE BLIND CAT

The Scouts are the first to spot the coins. A penny here. A dime there. Soon, a cache of dirty nickels. Avis plucks one up.

"An Indian Head," she says, causing the Scouts to stop and confirm. As much as they hate to lose momentum, a pinch of envy slows them, especially Oren, who's been working on his Numismatic Badge, studying currencies. His present collection is so meager, consisting only of a few Mexican pesos, a Canadian dollar, and two Franklin half-dollar coins his sister gave him for his birthday last year. Soon Oren and Karl, too, are bending down, gathering, examining, hoping for their own piece of good luck.

"Well, look at that, will ya," the priest says. "Someone's piggy bank tried to run away."

He has shrugged off his big pack and is already crouched on the ground, expertly pinching up the loose change.

"But these must belong to someone," Denis says, a statement that seems to give the Scouts pause. Denis, of course, wants to collect the coins and hand them over to the next county's sheriff when they deliver the train case.

"You think someone accidentally lost all this change?" Helen Hubka says, cackling. She's managed more than a few dimes, even a quarter, herself, and jingles them in her fist while she talks. "And they'll go to the sheriff's lost-and-found to see if it's been turned in? *Excuse me, officer, I want to report lost money.*" A silence tells her that's exactly what the Scouts might think and exactly what Denis, roiled by any suggestion of mystery or missed clues, would do.

"Leave 'em alone," Landon barks, causing another kind of pained look to crease the priest's face. "Let's just stay out of whatever little mess this is. We're not far from the highway. Let's keep moving."

With that, the Scouts reluctantly release their bounty back onto the trail, and to Warren's obvious relief, the rest of the walkers straighten up and begin again, too, but not before Helen Hubka surprises the priest by offering him her palmful of coins.

"For your collection plate," she tells him with a wink.

What would they do without Helen Hubka? Even when she declares she's fading—which is frequently—she's ready to spring back with another bout of tattling. Information, she calls it. If an early bear is cruising nearby, even famished from his winter's fast, he'll surely avoid whatever area these walkers inhabit. It's as if we're all wearing cowbells, Caroline thinks.

"Oh, lordy, wouldn't I like to hop into a hot bath right now," the Operator says. She's barely caught her breath after the last slight incline, but no one else seems alarmed, save by the image of Helen Hubka in a bath, so after a single loud exhale, she barrels back into position beside a resigned Caroline, who is now certain that Helen must have been listening and storing up for months, and with the coming dialup, decided they might be her last audience for all her bits and bobs of overheard conversation. By the time this walk is over, Caroline surmises, every secret in town will have been spilled—even hers. She wants to cover Avis's ears, especially when Helen Hubka veers into whispered affairs up at the mill and the fugitive bank robber who supposedly slinks around town, sweet-talking housewives by day and, at night, rummaging through the outbuildings of big old houses "like the Mudge House." (*Oh, yes, that's your house now, isn't it, Avis?*) Helen has mean-spirited whispers and old wives' tales and flat-out lies to spare. Caroline wishes she hadn't tucked away her map somewhere. Right about now she'd like to know how far they have to go before the next break, how long before she can slip away from the Operator's side. She almost interrupts Helen Hubka midsentence to ask aloud, but stops herself, imagining the plaintive tone she'd sound, like a child on a car trip: *Are we there yet? Please, dear God, are we there yet? How much farther?*

Karl could tell her, if he and Oren weren't so far ahead again. He keeps a careful watch on his pedometer and nudges Oren as the miles inch toward Highway 27. All along, the Scouts have spotted the rough ends of deer paths leading upward. They've also become aware of a half-hidden trail, parallel to this access road, much like the one the hobos slipped onto earlier. Their Scoutmaster has pointed out such "ghost trails" on their troop hikes, shown them how the routes are blazed by what he calls "shy travelers." Of course, Oren and Karl think only of Davy Crockett and the Indians who could move through a forest without ever being seen, and they can't help feeling watched, even tracked, themselves.

"Close to here, the old fellow said," Oren says.

"Landon," Karl says. "His name is Landon." Karl's learned all the names. He has to nearly shout. The wind flogging the bay again. "Okay, we'll wait." He pulls out his stopwatch. "I'll time the break."

"For the girl who's keeping the log," Oren adds as if Karl won't remember.

"Avis," Karl says. "Her name is Avis."

Of course, Karl's been paying attention, and though he and Oren have kept to the head of the line, he's also overheard plenty from Helen Hubka. He is particularly struck by all she seems to know about Avis's house, the *Mudge House*.

On a camping trip last summer, their Scoutmaster gathered them before bedtime for tales of the uncanny. These were generally terrifying (grotesque faces floating in the dark, claws slashing through a pup tent), told, Oren had decided, to toughen up the Scouts. Routine danger, he told Karl, would be small beans in comparison. Okay, but Karl wouldn't sleep at all until he was home again and could slowly relay every story to his sister, who would go through each detail, revealing impossibilities until all the horror was pushed out into a laughable light. Silly jokes, she'd conclude, like in Abbott and Costello, and Karl could dream again without the intrusion of monsters—real or imagined.

The story last summer . . . well, that story was different. For one thing, it took place not far from home. In Humtown. In a long-gone time when the harbor was thick with sloops and galleons, frigates and brigantines. Men and boys ("just like you") were regularly shanghaied, caught in the night and transported via tunnels to ships that were well out into open water before those conscripts woke from a drugged stupor. Sailors, you see, were in constant demand. Pretty much disposable. Those massive sailing ships, the Scoutmaster told his young audience, might be grand-looking, but the journeys were perilous, everyone at the mercy of storms and the infamous rogue waves along the Strait. The work was harsh, the food nearly inedible and scarce, and perhaps worst of all, the ships were horribly overrun by rats.

Those infestations infuriated Humtown's famous Captain Mudge, especially when he found a legion of rats rummaging through the drawers in his private quarters. So before he set sail again, he sent out three of his sailors to collect cats, which they did, stuffing the creatures into two big gunny sacks they tossed into the ship's hold, setting off a massacre below deck, a constant scuttling and screaming that drove more than a few sailors purely mad, especially when the horrific sounds began to act as a kind of siren and the rats began to swarm over the decks in plain sight, even onto the open stern, where deckhands themselves went wild with killing, battering and shoveling off rats in droves. Days, it seemed, this went on, until finally, mercifully, all began to quiet. If a single rat remained aboard, it had learned to become part of the woodwork. What a relief! Yet pretty soon another sound reached the ears of the sailors in their bunks, a feline keening that grew and grew and never seemed to end. Ah, the noise, the noise, that persistent noise! The cats were hungry, locked down below. Still, the captain refused to feed them. Starving cats, Mudge continued to declare, made the best hunters.

Constant and pervasive, the mewling seemed to creep inside each sailor as if summoned by their own unvoiced wailings, until finally, a desperate pair of deckhands dared to disobey. They crept into the hold with a bucket of fish heads, ready to fend off the starving cats and whatever litters they'd surely had by then, but were shocked to discover only a single cat left alive. Ravenous, near skeletal, the creature left off its crying and inhaled what they'd brought in mere seconds, nipping off a fingertip in the process. Before the sound could commence once more, one of the deckhands wrapped the cat in his shirt and carried her up on deck, only to see her stumble and fall again and again. It didn't take long to realize the cat had gone blind in the black hold. Still, that mangy, blind cat—the ultimate survivor—soon become a darling of the crew, some of whom, it must be admitted, also felt equally hard-done-by.

The captain was having none of it. What use was a blind cat? One morning, striding the deck, he nearly tripped on the animal and, almost without thought, scooped the creature up and tossed her over the side, an act he'd soon regret, not least because by the time the ship reached Humtown again, an army of rats would have regrouped. No one saw the captain's deed, and he certainly never admitted it to his idiotically besotted crew. An inevitable accident. The cat's blindness had doomed it. Yet the crew knew. They did. More than one sailor cursed Captain Mudge daily. Piles of curses. Curses as regular as daily prayers. Maybe that was why, upon arriving home, snug in his own bed at last, the captain once more began to hear the cat's distinctive cries.

"But wait," one Scout interrupted. "The cat was drowned."

"Exactly," the Scoutmaster said.

Night after night, Captain Mudge would startle awake, sounds of the cat's agony crawling behind the plaster walls. He had the enormous cellar scoured. Holes punched into a dozen walls and a ceiling undone without any sight of the creature. Of course, he couldn't find the cat. No one could. They could only hear her. *For years.*

As soon as he could, Captain Mudge fled back to sea, but his luck on the water had soured, too. The ship, source of that great local fortune, was lost—in a storm, of course—though rumors circulated about a mutiny gone wrong. His widow repaired the walls, avoided the cellars, but it's said that, even now, anyone who stays a night in the Mudge House will be awakened by a clawing in the walls, an endless mewling. Anyone, that is, who has something to hide.

When Karl finally brought the cat-haunting story to his sister, she explained that as far as she could tell, the Scoutmaster hadn't been telling a ghost story at all but a kind of morality tale, like the Aesop's Fables Karl heard way back in kindergarten. It wasn't so much that the cat was otherworldly, she told him, as that it was a kind of symbol of how bad acts or secrets might hound you all your life, become a part of your proverbial house. Karl wasn't sure he completely understood his sister, but her soothing voice put him at ease. Now though, as he waits with Oren, battered by the wind, Karl imagines himself onboard that sorry ship, indentured to a cruel master, and he feels a well of sorrow rising for this girl Avis, who must live surrounded by the evidence of someone else's rotten decisions. How, he wonders, does she keep from going crazy herself?

ACCIDENT?

Other than the Scouts, whose unflagging energy keeps them in the lead, the positions of the walkers shift—slipping, adjusting—as they continue. As if they are bits of flotsam in a rapid stream, Caroline thinks in a fanciful moment. One pauses to tie a shoelace. Another falls off to heed the call of nature. A sip of water from a canteen is needed. A cigarette (Jaspar Goode, the priest, Landon) needs to be produced and lit. Warren, who keeps an eye out over the entire walking line, feels an enormous satisfaction. He doesn't see them as flotsam at all—loose and vulnerable—but as a kind of miraculous machine, gears reversing, advancing, turning. An engine that is everything the President might wish. Their rude health and determination are the definition of patriotism. It's true that if the walk had followed Warren's original plan—a more or less straight shot along the main county highway—the route would have been clearly defined, and no one would need to wait for another. The Scouts would no doubt accomplish the record time they'd hoped for. But the convoluted route requires the walkers to move as a unit, albeit a loose-limbed one, and Warren finds he's grateful. The President would approve. Warren feels sure of that.

Soon, with their backs to the train tracks and glimmers of the bay, the group embarks upon the long switchback upward toward the highway. The priest, most likely trying to avoid another hour of Helen Hubka's interrogation, slips past Caroline and Avis, and now he and Warren are a pair, steadily pulling ahead behind Denis and the intrepid Scouts, who are well out of sight. To Avis's extreme discomfort, Helen Hubka's reveries have turned to the box newly found on Gold Egg Beach.

"It wasn't even a bottle of old port, you know, only a half-empty pint of common whiskey. Someone's idea of a joke. Of course, the whole setup is a con, don't you know? There never was a box of gold eggs found on the beach."

"What do you mean?" Caroline can't help saying. "Of course there was."

Avis would like to chime in, set them both straight. *Not gold eggs, but yes, a box of treasure.* She doesn't dare.

"Nope," Helen Hubka insists. "Never was a box that washed up. Not on its own. It was in a boat."

A boat!

Both Caroline and Avis are rapt, despite themselves.

"And that's not all. Two little children inside, as well. Must have been others put in that lifeboat, but only those two children survived that storm. The children were taken up to what was the hospital, and a few weeks passed before they were restored to health, even longer before relatives were found to claim them. Meanwhile, whatever else was on that boat with them was supposedly kept safe. Who really knows if there had been more than that single metal box, a locked box, with those gold objects?"

"Eggs," Caroline says, nodding.

"No, dear," Helen Hubka corrects (how she loves correcting). "Not eggs, some kind of 'art.' Religious art. Might be gold, might not be."

"There's no gold egg in the town museum?" Caroline finds herself filing away this fascinating news to tell Jay.

"Not an egg, no," Helen Hubka repeats. "A kind of a talisman, put on board to keep the kiddies safe."

"Talisman?" Avis asks.

"Magic," Caroline explains.

"Not an egg," Helen Hubka repeats. "And *magic*? Silliness more like it," she scoffs.

"But the children," Avis goes on. "They were safe, weren't they? So maybe it *was* magic."

"Good luck, I guess, although . . ." Here Helen Hubka grows thoughtful. ". . . now that I think about it, well, the museum was the only downtown building spared any storm damage, wasn't it?"

If only she'd known, Caroline is thinking. If only someone had told her earlier. She would have swiped that treasure and sewn it inside Jay's coat, made him carry it everywhere. She pauses, ducks her head to one side to hide fresh tears. Helen Hubka reads her hesitation as another kind of need.

"You gotta go?" she asks, and Caroline discovers she does, urgently.

When a less scrubby patch of woods appears, she decides she can wait no longer. Avis and Helen Hubka slow down, and the Operator waves on the fisherman and a reluctant Landon before they can see Caroline "undoing her drawers" among the trees. Avis takes the opportunity to set down the little suitcase. She wasn't lying earlier. The case isn't heavy, but the miles have made it so, and her palm is reddened and sore, her fingers a little numb. She shakes out her hand to regain some feeling. Vaguely, she is aware of Caroline returning to the trail, and she reaches out for the train case, ready to resume, but Helen Hubka has beat her to it, grabbing the yellow handle.

"Let me take a turn with that, dear," Helen Hubka says, and before Avis can protest, the older woman has grabbed the yellow handle and swooped up the train case.

"But . . ."

"Go on, girl."

Helen Hubka is making a mistake. What can Avis do? Only hurry, she guesses. Once at the next rest stop, she'll reclaim the responsibility of the case. Years of switchboard experience may have given Helen Hubka swift fingers, but Avis has had more practice darting in, leaping away, even holding on, than anyone might guess. Helen Hubka is no match for her. Of that, she feels sure. Lightened, Avis takes the lead for the first time. A challenge, even though Caroline, too, is experiencing renewed vigor, relieved in several ways. She can sense Helen Hubka falling behind a bit, but believes Warren and Landon are still far behind them all and worries not at all. Caroline's right knee has been complaining since the last big hill that brought them up from the bay. She's been determined to ignore it. If nothing else, she's become very good at disregarding her body these past months, and though she does feel vastly eased after her moment in the woods, she has to acknowledge that squatting has aggravated the stiffness in her knee. Even as she jauntily matches Avis's newly energized gait, every now and then a tiny stabbing pain lands. One surprises her so much she nearly cries out and actually thinks she must have. A yelp hits the air. *Sorry*, she starts to say, before realizing the sound did not come from her.

* * *

As the path winds upward into a forested stretch, the wind ripping off Forgotten Bay seems far away, and the priest is reveling in a familiar silence that comes within the haven of trees. In the calm, the repetitive steps, the switchback rhythm, the priest begins a lulling tune. As if in rebuke of his song, an interruption comes in the form of an unnervingly shrill whistle. Had the wind sheared a weakened tree? When no fallen limb immediately thrashes to earth, the priest freezes, waiting. But . . . *nothing*, no other sound, except, oh dear lord, here she goes, the horn that is Miss Helen Hubka. Warren, too, hesitates, hoping, but as the sound intensifies, even the nearby birds take flight, and soon he is on the move, running downhill. The priest, however, only briefly halts, suppressing the urge to cover his ears. He won't even look back. He congratulates himself for that as he continues his own walk. Equanimity will save him, as it always has.

The blows have come out of nowhere—a weight, a twisting pinch, a hammer hit. Helen Hubka loses her balance. A searing burn. Is that hissing coming from her? Who has struck her? Another woman might have been stunned into silence, but Helen Hubka has never had time for mute shock. She howls. The bone-chilling noise that assaulted Warren and the priest even almost reaches the Scouts, who hear not a woman's cry, but that of a gull in distress. A mimicking raven. Not far ahead of them, Denis assumes the faintly irritating sound comes from the highway not far above, a logging truck's jake brake seizing after the descent from the mountain roads. Warren and the other men hesitate, but it's not until they hear three sharp whistles that they double back to find Caroline and Landon kneeling beside Helen Hubka, her howls tapering to pained yips.

"I've been bitten," she manages with a strangled gulp.

"No snakes around here," Landon says. "A weasel, maybe."

"Or nettles?" Warren conjectures, still hoping for the least possible problem.

"I don't think so," Caroline says, noting the blood oozing through the lower edge of Helen Hubka's trousers. "We should sit you down somewhere and have a good look."

"Are *you* okay?" Jaspar Goode asks Caroline, who nods quickly, hardly registering his concern.

Out of habit, Helen Hubka raises a hand to adjust her hat, which shifted sideways as the woman collapsed. Avis is the first to notice the other wound, a gash by her temple. Already a thin line of the Operator's gray hair has gone dark with blood.

"Her head." Avis points.

"She's been hit," Caroline says.

"By what? By who?" Warren asks, looking around. "We haven't seen anyone for hours."

The high bluffs to the south of the walkers are mostly forested, but one long open green stretch catches his attention. He can make out a slumped roof, a suggestion of wood smoke.

"Oh, hell," Landon says. The old man is suddenly all wire and sinew, his arms out as if he could tighten the group and manhandle them forward.

"Wait," Jaspar Goode says, and he motions to Caroline.

"Please," he says, and she understands, her pretty bluebird scarf flying off her neck into his hands.

"It's not the best tourniquet," he says as he ties it around Helen Hubka's leg, "but it should keep the bleeding down."

"What do you want to do with that?" Caroline asks Landon, who has been scouring the ground and is inexplicably holding up a fallen branch, as if blocking the path behind them.

No, the view from *above*, she realizes. He's hiding us. But why?

She's about to ask when Landon notices the little blue train case beside Helen Hubka.

"Can you run with this?" he asks Avis in a low voice.

She nods.

"Good girl. Get up that path and under the trees as fast as you can. If a fellow shows up and tries to stop you, you just throw that case at him and keep running."

"A fellow?" Caroline interrupts.

But Avis has scooped up the train case and is flying up the trail, even as Caroline tries to make sense of Landon's instructions. The Scouts, Denis, and the priest are well out of sight. At any other time, she'd stay beside Helen Hubka, but her training kicks in. *Stay with the child. Keep the child safe.* Wincing, Caroline runs toward the woods behind Avis, who has leapt into her task as if she were made for it. Meanwhile, Jaspar Goode and Warren get on either side of Miss Hubka, draping her arms around their shoulders.

If Helen Hubka had been in a better state, she would certainly have reveled in the proximity of the high school cross country star and the muscular fisherman. Sure, she would ruin the moment, complaining about jostling, their sweat, the chafing of Jaspar Goode's bristled cheek as it falls against her own. Oh, she would love it! But no one speaks as they rush toward the highway, least of all Helen Hubka, which is a darn shame, because finally she has everyone's full attention.

RESCUE MISSION

MILE 20

What a shock to reach the highway. It's not a true highway, of course, only a main country road linking two towns miles apart. As the walkers stumble out onto the road's shoulder, every muscle burning, one car whizzes by, then another, blank faces gaping, the sweet-sick linger of gas exhaust on the tongue. Just those two cars, then nothing. The road quiets. With relief, the emerging walkers see the Scouts and Denis in front of the café, a mere hundred yards ahead. Denis's red-and-white varsity jacket is off, thrown over an anchor that serves as a base for the café's sign. The Scouts' khaki packs droop beside their feet, even as Avis runs toward them, Caroline limping behind her, but when the Scouts see Warren and Jaspar struggling with Helen Hubka, young Oren snatches up and unbuckles his pack so fast that Denis jumps back.

"The first aid kit," Karl explains.

The Scouts know this place well. They lead Warren and Jaspar Goode behind the café to a picnic table, damp and puddled and marked with bird crap. Helen Hubka is eased down, and the Scouts all but elbow the others away. They have been training for an emergency for months. Caroline's scarf is soaked through, unrecognizable, and Helen Hubka is pale and, unnervingly, wordlessly mumbling, but Oren doesn't hesitate. He unties the ruined scarf, pulls up the lady's trouser leg, and presses what looks like a clean bandage against the wound. He's supposed to apply pressure, but he can't help wondering for how long. Until the bleeding stops, the booklet said. How long is that?

A waitress comes out of the back door, summoned by Karl.

"You're doing swell, Oren," the waitress, his sister, tells him, peering over his shoulder. The slim bandage is already drenched with blood. She sends Karl back inside for hot water and clean dish towels, soaks and folds two, and passes them to Oren, who cleans and presses even harder against the wound. Helen Hubka shudders quick breaths.

"Easy, kiddo," the sister says.

"A doctor," Oren says, reciting the script in his head. "That's the next step. *Stop the bleeding. Seek medical aid.*"

He keeps his hand tightly on Helen Hubka's shin, but motions to Karl, who snaps open the first aid kit for him again. Soon, he's ripping tape and bandages with his teeth, winding and rolling until it looks as if Helen Hubka is wearing a splotchy plaster cast.

"Her head," Avis points out, and Oren resumes his frenzy. The cut at the temple is smaller but deep. The dishtowel he uses to clean the wound first comes back with blood and what looks like bits of gravel.

Meanwhile his sister has slipped back into the café, returning with an older man in a rumpled suit, still wiping his mouth with a napkin.

"This is Raymond," she says, mostly to the boys.

"What happened here?" the man, Raymond, asks.

Guesses abound.

A fall

A bite

Nettles

"She's been hit by rocks, hasn't she?" Denis says, surprising everyone. He's dropped his pack and is now squatting down beside Oren.

"Rocks?" Warren says.

"Rocks?" Caroline repeats.

"Yes," Landon says, after a pause. He holds up a rock, size of a child's fist, one sharp angle stained with blood. "A hobo on the higher trail could have dislodged them, eh?"

Landon's the last to arrive but hasn't missed a beat. If anything, he appears more alert than ever before, scanning the parking lot and highway.

"That's a lot of blood for fallen rocks," Caroline says.

"Could have been a local kid with a slingshot or even a twenty-two, practicing at what he thought was a deer," Jaspar Goode weighs in. "I mean, look at her. Didn't even think not to dress like a target."

They each turn to take in Helen Hubka, clothed from head to toe in shades of brown. Her brown hat, so somber without its jaunty green feather, beside her on the picnic table.

"She's out of season," Denis says without thinking, and despite herself, Caroline might have laughed outright at that if she hadn't caught the look of fear on the boy's face.

The Scouts' sister makes a mental note to remind them both to keep their red kerchiefs on, even as she registers Helen Hubka's more than slight shivering.

"Karl," she says, "Storeroom. Get that blanket over the freezer."

Of course, Oren thinks, irritated at himself. Soon the two boys have the shivering Helen Hubka wrapped tightly in musty plaid wool.

"You need to get her to the hospital, Raymond," the sister says. "Now."

"Me?"

"No one else has a car but me, and I have to stay here."

"You all got here without a car?" Raymond is incredulous. "Nancy, you can't be serious. And why me? You got that old couple inside. Don't tell me they walked here, too."

"C'mon, Raymond, you know they're not heading toward town. Plus, they can barely toddle themselves."

"The bus will be by soon."

"Raymond, the lady's been hurt! She's probably in shock. You want her to wait for a bus!"

"I don't like this," the man says. "No, I don't like this. Not one bit."

He recoils as the walkers gather around him, but soon is cajoled into leading Warren and Denis as they carry Helen Hubka to a shiny Buick in the front parking lot, Landon and Avis following. Jaspar Goode pulls Denis to the side, the boy nodding vehemently.

"Yeah, I'd better go with her," Denis is saying. "I'll take that—" He tilts his chin toward the train case Avis still clutches. "—and tell someone about the car, too."

"You could use the pay phone inside," Warren says. "Call your dad. Send the case along to the hospital and have him pick it up there. You don't have to leave the walk, do you?"

There's a quaver in Warren's voice that only Caroline seems to hear.

Warren catches himself when she tilts her head, hoping she won't intervene. There's so much more he wants to say to Denis, quotations from President Kennedy, reminders of their own vows to follow his lead. The immediate danger may have been skirted, but the Cold War continues, no matter what anyone says, and their generation has to ready themselves to lead into the New Frontier, and that begins right now, with the challenge of the Big Walk. In his head, Warren has already written the article he wishes his father would publish, the one in which he and Denis provide the lede.

It's up to us, Denis, Warren wants to remind him.

But Denis won't be listening. Denis is shaking his head. Warren hardly recognizes his closest friend. Any other time, Denis under pressure might simply shift a lollipop from one cheek to another, pass Warren one sharp glance, then shrug, offering up his open palms as if to say, "No problem." Only now does Warren realize how much he's counted on Denis to always agree with him, always go along. The fellow before him might be a stranger; his voice is low, steady, determinedly opposed to Warren's need. An adult, Warren thinks with a start.

"Thing is, Miss Hubka was hurt in this county," Denis says. "The sheriff here is involved now."

"The sheriff!" Raymond interjects. "Some rocks fall on a lady, and you gotta call the sheriff!"

Warren, too, is surprised, even more so when Jason Goode chimes in to agree.

"Wouldn't hurt," he says, "to get rid of that suitcase."

And, Denis decides he'll say, they couldn't be sure, could they, where exactly the county line was? Perhaps the train case also had been left in this other jurisdiction. Of course, Denis knows exactly where their discovery had been made and knows, too, no other sheriff need be involved because of that. But Avis doesn't, and they'll want to talk to her since she found the case, won't they?

A relief. Still, Denis imagines his father's face when he learns that his own son has been the one who handed another agency key evidence, when he learns that Denis doesn't trust him and when he realizes, too, that whatever courthouse blackmail Remy Gussie is trying against him and Denis's mother can't be held back. The car will have to be examined. The news of that at least will get out. No matter what theories float around town, the one that claims Aileen drove off with the girls is shot to hell.

"I'll call my father from the hospital," Denis says, reaching out for the train case's yellow handle.

What he means is, I'll call him after the other sheriff is on board.

It clearly hasn't escaped Raymond that he's mixed up in a mess. Might be an innocent accident, a rock falling out one of them high spots or a nut of a fellow out there trying to hunt with a slingshot full of rocks. But it's fifteen miles to the hospital. Fifteen miles with this troublesome woman. He wants to be relieved that he'll have Denis's company, but the kid's broken face is giving him even more pause.

"Is someone chasing you folks?" He wants to know from Landon.

"Doubt it," the old man says. "A dumbass hunter, maybe. He might not have dreamed anybody would be out on that trail today. In any case, I'd bet he hightailed home as soon as he heard the screaming. I sure would have."

"I don't want any trouble," Raymond says.

"What if she dies on me?" he whispers to Landon.

"I wouldn't worry," Landon says. "That boy there did everything but operate on her. Just get the lady to the doctor so they can fix her up proper."

"But *that* boy . . ." He cocks his head toward Denis. "He's talking about the sheriff."

For the first time along the walk, Landon looks weary. He pats Raymond's shoulder and, without another word, heads inside. He'll take a breath and find a booth, light a brown cigarette, wait for coffee, and hope they get back on the road as soon as possible.

Raymond has no choice, it seems. As Denis settles Helen Hubka in the backseat of Raymond's pristine Buick, a stack of kitchen towels beneath her blanketed, bandaged leg to protect his precious upholstery, and Caroline leans in to press Helen Hubka's hand and offer one last scrap of reassurance, they can hear the man lamenting, haranguing the Queen of Questions with one of his own: *Lady, what the heck did you do to get someone so riled up at you?*

But Helen Hubka is, for once, utterly silent, having fainted a good five minutes earlier.

THE CAFÉ

While the others are still fussing with Helen Hubka in the parking lot, the priest wrestles his backpack into the café's narrow restroom. He replaces his long black raincoat with a heavy, ribbed navy-blue sweater. The wool sweater is well-worn, pilled along the sleeves, and all but covers his collar. He dons a cap, navy-blue again, with a bit of braid along the inner rim of its wide brim. He's quite used to that old enormous sled of a pack and barely disturbs its contents even in that tight space. He does remove Avis's book-bag and is struck again by that surprising weight. He'd felt it as he walked. Like the princess sensitive to a single pea under her bed, he possesses an unerring sense for items that aren't where they should be. What can the girl be carrying that is so heavy the strap is close to snapping? His fingers, light and clever, can't resist.

"Oh, ho," he says, as he lifts out the sock roll and unfurls treasure.

"Oh, ho," he says again, stunned not as much by the rich reward of his good deed, but the surprising deviousness of a little girl. He says a prayer for her, then one for himself as he performs a particularly satisfying sleight of hand. He is, he tells himself, relieving the child of what must certainly be a true burden. Most riches are, aren't they?

Avis wouldn't argue. It's only when she lets go of the yellow handle, relinquishing the train case to Denis, that she sees the blood—Helen Hubka's blood—splashed on the side and sees too the stain on her own hand. Yet even within all the tumult, Avis does not neglect her duty. She doesn't even hurry to the café bathroom to scrub her sticky palm. As Denis and Raymond drive away, she pulls her assignment notepad from her coat pocket and checks her Timex while Oren, his own hands a terrible mess, arrives beside her shoulder to clarify for her the exact time he and Karl halted their walk.

The notebook is stained by her efforts, the blood, a not-unfamiliar sight that jars Avis and finally sends her hurrying inside to find the priest. What a relief it is to see him emerge from the restroom, holding her bookbag lightly in hand as if it weighs nothing at all.

With Raymond, the reluctant Good Samaritan, gone, the only other customers in the café are an elderly couple who finish up quickly as the walkers stream in and collapse into booths. The couple is neither laudatory nor amused when Warren tells them that the group is on a patriotic mission, that the President told them to walk.

"Did he now?" the husband asks. "He says 'jump,' you all say 'how high?' Didn't even do the walk himself, did he? Made his little brother take the pain."

"Don't mind him," the wife says. "He's still mad at Roosevelt."

As soon as the couple leaves, the walkers can't help themselves; they loosen laces, slip their damp stockinged feet from their tight shoes. Good lord, do they stink, the waitress thinks, the lot of 'em. The stench brings tears to her eyes, and with them another realization: She'd expected her brothers' companions on this walk would be high school kids, and only now notices her brothers are nearly the only children on the walk. Should she be relieved? Or should she worry?

But oh, what a stoic bunch they are and have been, blisters blooming so that even the slight touch of a wool sock becomes a knife edge, piercing again and again. Caroline's calves are knotted up, and one foot is cramping painfully. Avis hands around her Band-Aid box. The Boy Scouts offer moleskin and splashes of Bactine. The priest offers Caroline a "miracle liniment" for her knee, which she gratefully tries. They bandage and repair, and no one talks of quitting.

Warren has not planned for long breaks. Breathers. Momentary rests. Left on his own, he would have taken off with only a sack lunch, eaten it on the fly. Of course, he would have held to the main road, too. His ideal walk would have been straightforward, just like Bobby Kennedy's, only regrettably without the trailing station wagon full of Secret Service men, fresh socks, and thermoses of hot chicken soup and sugared black coffee. In one of the regional papers his father considered a rival, Warren had read about a boy in Anacortes who did the walk all on his own and would have made perfect time, too, except he curled up in a ditch on the side of the road and slept for a couple hours. That fellow had been a paperboy, and *his* paper had lauded him with a splashy article called PAPERBOY'S DAY OFF. Warren was impressed, as much by the attention the other boy earned as by his feat. Warren would be lucky if his father mentioned his achievement at their own dinner table, and he doubts this group will break a single record, but even so he is as anxious as the Scouts to keep moving, to make the best time they can. To do their best.

Still, they've all had a shock, haven't they? Even Warren can't quite shake the image of the dark stain spreading across Helen Hubka's trouser leg or the nickel smell of her bloodied temple, a stink that has invaded his own skin, even though he's scrubbed his face well in the café bathroom. He's mad at himself for not somehow preventing an apparently random event. Who could have guessed that Helen Hubka, always in the middle of everyone's business, would drift away from the pack and dawdle into trouble? How, Warren reasoned, could he have stopped that? Landon seems a touch undone, too, his eyes continually jumping toward the door. Yes, they've all had a shock. Even the Scouts seem willing to take this break. Oren reorganizes his first aid kit, while Karl, his arms crossed on the red Formica counter, is clearly fighting the urge to rest his head, close his eyes. Meanwhile their waitress sister and the cook slap frankfurters and hamburgers and buttered buns on the grill in a frenzy. The giant percolator nearly empties, and the Scouts' sister sets up for refills. She lets Oren pull out bottles of pop from the glass cooler, ignoring the cook's glances. She'll settle up later, she declares to no one in particular. Caroline intended to eat her pocket apples but is seduced by the smell of fried onions and charred meat, a greasy paper boat filled with French fries. She is surprised to find her wallet at the bottom of one of her deep pockets. A reflex, she tells herself, bringing that along. She pays for hamburgers for everyone but the Scouts, who sit at the counter, inhaling all their sister puts in front of them. The rest of them methodically work through their own plates. They don't hurry, but no one lingers either.

Each rest stop recasts all the walkers, it seems, if only temporarily. The Scouts, for instance, mere towheaded children at the walk's start, have matured considerably in everyone's eyes. The other walkers can now tell them apart, too. Oren is the elder brother, his hair the whitest shade of blond, his eyes a deeper gray, the wary color of a washed March sky. Karl, the younger, is taller and only a touch awkward, like a colt who doesn't yet trust his ungainly limbs. Although he mimics Oren in his steady demeanor, his is the more ready smile, and he isn't above nudging his brother with his shoulder to share a joke or subtly point out a curiosity in the landscape. If you ask their sister, Oren is determined and Karl is eager. Anyone can see she is the hardworking model for them both. She might have come straight in off a farm, with her braided hair, her strong arms, and constant energy.

Caroline eyes the sister's braid with unnecessary envy. Her own scarf is gone, of course, yet at least for now, her hair remains neat. Out of habit, she's reapplied lipstick and sits among them, a lady walker. Warren, disappointed by Denis's decision to leave, sits uneasily in a booth with Landon and Jaspar Goode. Beside those men, he appears more a boy than ever. He's propped the map in front of him again and brushes his hand over his crewcut anxiously, only stopping when the food arrives.

In contrast, without his collar evident, the priest has grown older, tougher. He is, the others are beginning to realize, something of a quick-change artist. He started out as Danny, the lighthearted singer propelling them out of the night, out from the still and shadowed town streets, with pop tunes and television commercial jingles and Robert Preston's "Chicken Fat" song, cheery melodies that seduced them all, not simply the limping Solidarity girls, into humming or even singing along.

That goofy fellow began to slip away at the first rest stop, transforming shockingly into Father Dan, the inscrutable cleric with the kindly manners, who listened patiently to Helen Hubka and trudged tirelessly as if he were on a clear mission. Not long after the discovery of the Gussies' car, another version emerged, a rougher sort, one quick to offer up random bits of philosophical observation, a ruminating chatterbox who sweated profusely and rummaged often for a cigarette, revealing his own chain-smoking habit. Like Jaspar Goode, he carried not only a canteen, but a flask. It soon was evident to anyone with eyes that his enormous pack was not half empty, that the priest was well-provisioned, as if anticipating a much longer journey.

His willingness to accommodate (or tease?) Helen Hubka vanished right about then, too.

The café gives them yet another incarnation: watchful, introspective Daniel. Vertical lines are now visible on his face, and in the hours since they've begun walking, he's also become in need of a shave. His black hair, slicked back by the rain earlier, is shockingly long, almost down to his ears, and the gentleness they've all heard in his singing voice and rambling philosophical theories is absent, replaced by a rigid solemnity in this more public place. Priestlike, Caroline guesses. She attends St. Luke's, the Methodist church, and has an ingrained belief that her ministers are more gentlemanly and distant, yet also more clearly affectionate, than Catholic priests with their draconian rules. This harshly contemplative side of the priest fits. In another man, the priest's newly private expression might be taken as one of quiet scheming, but Caroline imagines the tender thoughts of this man of God, how they must arrive with the unabashed glee of the singer ("Call me Danny"), only to be burned and battered, judged and argued, funneled into acceptable liturgical shape, and the brooding reverend seems, oh, not conniving, not at all, but suddenly acutely aware of the stringent demands of his holy trade. A real priest, in other words.

Avis, however, wonders. No priest she's ever met would even know who Ricky Nelson was, let alone the lyrics to all his songs. She notices his hands, too. Rough, even grubby, so unlike the milky cleanliness of the priests back home. But maybe this, too, she reasons, is another difference between Philadelphia and the Pacific Northwest. The priests here are less coddled. This one probably spends his days chopping wood and working on the rectory or parishioners' houses. Likely that's where he heard the latest songs playing on a transistor radio, or learned how to cobble unusual repairs, like the one he makes for the broken strap on Avis's bookbag as he hands it back to her with a wink. Later, when the strap comes undone again, and Jaspar Goode repairs it by splicing and knotting an intricate braid, he will laugh at her, believing she, not the priest, tried to hold the strap together with what appears to be chewing gum and a shoelace.

A clear eye would have to reconsider Avis, too. The bone-thin girl, the waif, so worrisomely fragile at the walk's start, has not flinched once—not at the blood-speckled suitcase or the hobo, not at Helen Hubka's blood. She's taken on the role of timekeeper without discussion and kept up with all of them. When Warren expressed relief that Landon had a whistle with him to call for help, Landon had scoffed. "Sure, I got a whistle, but I never got a chance to pull it out. That one," he pointed to Avis, "just let loose. Good pipes." No one has heard her complain or brag or celebrate or even talk much at all. A closer look, and despite the trouble they've encountered and the punishing hours of walking through dark and rain and mud and wind, the girl is relaxing.

But how easy it is to make jarring notes fit when the alternative might shatter the world altogether.

The waitress, for instance, thinks Jaspar Goode and Landon could be two men returning from an early morning fishing outing or a hunting trip, tired but also invigorated by the hours in open air, the success of navigating silent hours on the water or in the woods. In his camouflage outfit, Jaspar sure fits right in at the highway café. A working man, but something else, too. A volunteer firefighter maybe? She likes the look of him, and when he catches her staring, he raises an eyebrow and gives her a smile that seems to say he likes the look of her as well, as if maybe he already knows her. Interesting, she thinks. The Scouts' sister wonders if he's been in the café before. The priest, as well. She feels as if she's seen him more than once.

"You recognize that fellow in the cap?" she mutters to the cook.

The cook squints.

"Yeah, sure," he tells her. "He fixed the furnace last December, didn't he?" He squints again. "Or maybe," he qualifies, "he was the fellow came by selling yo-yos last spring."

"My brothers say he's a priest."

The cook actually guffaws, as if she's finally managed a decent joke.

"That's a good one," he says.

So, she thinks, he's moving on. Not unlike a good many who've come through the café door.

Truly, only Caroline, the lady walker, seems out of place with her lipstick and pretty blue sweater under that wool car coat. The waitress doesn't even notice Avis, a fact that would cheer the girl considerably.

Almost the moment the walkers finish eating, the group begins to re-assemble. The break has been only a little more than a half hour. Now they are eight, and Warren checks in with each walker. It's his job, he reckons, to assess their comfort, their viability. At least, he's taken it on. Landon doesn't care. He was clear about that early on.

"I'm no babysitter," he spat when Warren first asked his opinion about scheduled breaks. "I'll bring the maps, and they can walk or not."

"If anyone needs to leave now," Warren announces, "there's a bus coming in fifteen minutes, heading back to town."

"And one going the other way 'bout the same time," the cook jokes from the back. "In case any of you want to get to the finish line faster."

"Or keep out of trouble," he adds.

The Scouts look appalled. Their tidy rucksacks are already on their backs, straps tightened. Their shoelaces are retied. Canteens refilled. Their sister has wrapped up pieces of blackberry pie and a stack of oatmeal cookies. They are more than ready to go.

Outside, maps are pulled out once more, but not really necessary, even though Landon has proposed a slight alteration. He points to the next trail they'll follow, across the old highway, jabbing a finger at the map to illustrate and dragging it along an invisible line.

"Couple of twists, but it'll get us to the state park all right, keep us off the main road."

Okay, okay, the trail is obvious to anyone with eyes, the Scouts think. Yet Karl obligingly retrieves his copy of the map, which has been stuffed in a pocket with his official Boy Scout kerchief, and spreads both out on the bench by the café's entrance. He even finds a good rock to hold it down. But he's not really listening to Landon's few revisions and soon turns his back on the map. Although he and Oren memorized the original route over lunch, they are nothing if not adaptable. Avis passes him what's left of her roll of Life Savers. He pinches out one piece of candy to Oren, takes one himself, and puts the quarter-roll down beside the rock. The Life Savers briefly distract the boys as Warren explains again that their route will shift now away from the water. They'll climb up that trail to a dirt logging road cut across the hillside. That will eventually intersect with another long-unused byway, a forest service trail that parallels the two-lane highway for the next ten miles. The service trail will lead straight into a state park and their next scheduled rest stop near a pay phone. A brief one, he emphasizes.

"Anyone need more time?" Warren asks, but by now the Scouts are practically pawing at the ground. Oren sends a meaningful glance to Avis, who obediently opens her notebook and scribbles numbers. Then Oren springs off, waving at his sister as Karl, head down, runs along behind him.

THE PRECISE LOCATION
OF THE SOUL

In retrospect, that early afternoon stretch between the café and the state park will seem the loveliest time for all of them, tiring as it is. As a group, they are quieter, more peaceful. Avis feels comfortable enough to leave Caroline's side. For a mile or so, she keeps company with the priest, who's lightened up considerably since they left the café and is almost jolly. He's taken an interest in the girl, offering to teach her the words to a popular song. He's instructing her in harmonies when she interrupts him.

"Father, can I ask you a question?"

What she really wants to say is, *Can I tell you something?*

But, of course, she can't. Still, it's dawned on her that this is a rare opportunity to ask a question that's whirled within her for years. What she wants to know is where exactly the soul is located. About the time she first learned she had a soul, she'd been in kindergarten, and a classmate, child of a doctor, brought a model of the human heart in for show-and-tell. As the classmate stammered through a description of the four sections, segueing into a garbled vision of internal organs, somehow Avis came away with the image of a kind of Aladdin's cave within her, separate chambers designated for rubies, sapphires, gold nuggets the size of duck eggs, and one glowing room claimed entirely by her soul. Avis's soul appeared to her as a shimmery lady, plain and good and patient, always ready to scrub off black marks of sin while Avis, post confession, performed her litany of Hail Marys and the long, absolving Act of Contrition, almost all in repentance for the multitude of lies Teddy required.

Avis hasn't entirely shaken the image of her lady soul, but after one incident at school, when she'd taken the blame for Teddy—a rock thrown at the head of a child who'd annoyed him, the nun shaking her, saying again and again, "There is no excuse for such behavior. You *know* better! You *know* better"—after that, Avis's lady soul seemed to turn her back at the girl's stupidity, her complicity, and Avis began to imagine the soul floating somewhere in her head, in that unfathomable entity called her brain, past a region called "common sense," to which neither Avis nor her lady soul could claim access.

Brain. Joseph Deppi carved the label on the back of her desk, bitter at her constant achievement, but who wouldn't get good grades if all they did out of school was hide in the back of a closet and do homework with a flashlight beneath the swinging cloth of wool coats, or read the encyclopedia propped between tumbled boots? Clearly, Avis was no brain, only a coward, and if that were true, maybe her soul, too, was a shrunken thing with no real place to reside. A painful conclusion. Unless she was wrong and the soul had a different home within her, one that existed not unlike this forest—a secret marvel within the ordinary world.

"Where does the soul live?" the priest repeats. "Where does the soul live?"

"In what way d'you mean?" he asks.

"What part of me?" Avis persists. "Inside me, that is? Where, inside?"

Normally, she'd be blushing and stammering with the effort of talking directly to a priest (and about her body, too!), certain he'd read her sins on her face and call her out immediately, the way a visiting priest once did from the confessional. But this priest is not much like any she's known. She's watched him smoke cigarettes and steal French fries and change his tattered socks in public. He's carried her bookbag and eaten half her Life Savers without asking permission.

"Where, *exactly*?" she says.

She waits and waits.

"Some believe the soul to be a great mystery," the priest hedges.

"Like God," Avis says. She wants to add, *I know, I know.* But it's not the mystery of the Holy Trinity she wants to explore right now.

"Well, yeah," the priest says while Avis waits some more for a real answer.

He adjusts his pack, shifting it from side to side as if reallocating weight.

"It's a particular sin that worries you, is it?" he asks.

He seems, Avis thinks, genuinely curious, but no, sin isn't a subject she'd like to address right now. What she wants to know, she says again, is the actual location of her soul, a question that now seems to stir the priest, who offers up a string of theories and names.

"The Egyptians believed," he says, "the soul lived in the heart, that you could tell a good man by the weight of his heart—the size of his soul, you see."

"Of course, you'd have to kill the bugger to figure that one out," he adds with a laugh.

Avis doesn't crack a smile, forcing the priest to grow thoughtful again.

"You know Plato?" he asks. "Aristotle? Well, they had ideas about the soul's home, too. Personally, I'd vote for the lungs. The breath of life and all that. I'm guessing the Buddha would sign on to that theory. But what about Descartes? You know Descartes?"

Is he teasing me? Avis thinks as she shakes her head again and again.

Her ignorance seems to please the priest, who is nodding confusingly, as if they've both agreed on a vital principle.

"Yes, indeed," he says. "Who's to say the soul resides in one single place? Or in the body at all?"

"God?" Avis tries. "*God* says, Father." She's been well-schooled. There are unbending rules. She won't fall into that trap.

"And who is God?" the priest goes on, oblivious to Avis's growing unease. Does he expect her to recite the catechism?

"*God is the creator of heaven and earth, and of all things,*" she obliges.

"Okay, sure," the priest says, as if that's an acceptable guess, not the Catechism's One and True Answer.

Caroline has been listening. You bet she has. I can tell you exactly where the soul lives, she'd like to tell Avis. She wants to point to her own midsection, to her gut, to the center of her being. *Right here,* she'll say. When Jay died, her soul must have flown partway with him, because for a time she was hollowed out and could not eat, could not sleep, could barely straighten and walk. Certainly she was barely alive, hardly a person, soulless. Where does the soul live? Right here! Her hand creeps protectively over her abdomen as she listens to the priest's twaddle. She, the sometime Methodist, can barely contain herself and is about to contradict a priest when he stops on the trail, pointing. The interruption couldn't be timelier. Jaspar Goode nearly runs into Caroline. *He* hasn't overheard the conversation—at least she can't imagine he has—but he's quick to see what the priest wants to point out.

"Well, look there," Jaspar Goode murmurs, "God's rays."

Avis takes in the slanting beams of gold light cutting through the forest's dimness, beams so singular, so selective. She follows the light as it illuminates moss and fern and tiny shoots of white flowers (early trilliums, Jaspar Goode informs her), and the priest doesn't have to tell her; she gets it. She knows right away that, yes, this is where her lady soul would live, given a clear choice, in a cloistered forest, among the trilliums, only visible within the momentary brilliance of "God's rays."

The Baltimore Catechism could use illustrations, Avis thinks.

Yes, a perfect answer, yet she can't help wondering about this priest who circumvented the catechism, offering not a prepared answer but a clever serendipity. What kind of a priest are you? she thinks. Not the Philadelphia kind, that's for sure, steeped in rules and punishments. Father Donohue would have immediately censured her ignorance, pummeling her with questions until she managed a mangled version of the catechism answers, the ones that clarify nothing.

She thinks of other words she struggles to define, words she might have asked about long ago if the nuns and Father Donohue hadn't been so terrifying. Mouth-pleasing, mind-twirling words like *liturgy, dogma, ecumenical, salvation.* Avis imagines the fanciful spin this priest might provide for each and feels a pleasing tingle of alarm as she imagines Father Donohue's volcanic reaction. *God's rays, indeed!* Would that be *sacrilege?* (Another confusing word.) Not for the first time, Avis struggles to imagine this traveling priest at her church. They'd once had an assistant pastor who played basketball during recess sometimes, and Father Donohue drank whiskey sours at her uncle's wake, but neither one would have stood for a whiff of dissent. Even a priest would be in trouble if he didn't toe the line.

Maybe, she thinks, this priest, too, is in trouble.

"Chiclets?" the priest offers when he catches her staring at him.

"I don't think he's a real priest," Avis says to Caroline when they are walking together again, the priest well ahead, out of sight.

"No?" Caroline can't help feeling amused. He certainly doesn't fit her image of a priest, but what does she know?

"He thinks the Pope's name is Jerome," Avis continues.

Caroline laughs. Even she knows better.

"But he's joking, isn't he?" Caroline says.

Avis is aghast. "A priest wouldn't joke about the Pope."

"And," she goes on, "he says he hasn't heard about Vatican II." (*Do tell* was his actual comment.) "Said that the news hasn't reached here yet."

Caroline looks blank.

"It's a big deal. My grandparents are all upset about it. Two of my great-aunts are nuns. One is excited, but the other might even leave the convent because of the changes to the Latin mass. Ask him what he thinks. Go ahead. I don't even think he knows any Latin."

"And," Avis says, adding the final point, "I've never, ever seen him at the church."

In all the hours they've walked together, Caroline hasn't heard the girl say so much. "But why pretend to be a priest, of all things?"

Avis shrugs, opens her mouth, closes it. She's been thinking about this, mulling over the advantages of being a priest, almost all of which, to her mind, have to do with living more or less alone. He baffles her. She shrugs, but Caroline's question sets her conjecturing anew. Even as the enormous pack comes back into view ahead of them, Avis reaches a conclusion.

A priest, of course, cannot go unnoticed. But a man posing as a priest vanishes into the image. What will anyone remember? A black-haired man with a four o'clock shadow? A singer? A philosopher? A tramp? Perhaps. But Avis feels sure that, if asked, their description of the man will be far more general, even as they believe it baldly specific. *A priest*, they'll say. *He was a priest.* And that simple word will contain and safeguard him, will make him invisible, even as it sets him free.

Avis couldn't be more envious.

ESSENTIALS

Earlier, outside the café bathroom, when Avis reclaimed her bookbag, she managed to tuck in the little stuffed rabbit she'd been carrying in her pocket. She would have liked to repack everything, but old Landon waited at the door, and she only had time to squirrel her hand down to the bookbag's corner to feel the rounded shape within the sock. Fleetingly, she had allowed herself to imagine its absence. Would she have felt relief? Or worry that somehow the treasure would find its way back to town, to an investigation, to Teddy, to Avis's own bookbag? Avis is sure that even though the sheriff can apparently overlook the disappearance of a mother and her children, he won't look the other way for gold thievery. As she hurries to join the others on the new trail, she thinks the train case must have been heavier than she realized, because she notices how light her plaid bookbag feels, how thoroughly inconsequential, nothing to hint at the weight she must carry. The bookbag is an illusion in any case, a pretense that she has prepared for more than a walk, for a journey. A worry flits. What *should* she have brought along? Does she ask that aloud?

The Scouts, she learns, carry what they call The Ten Essentials:

Pocketknife
First Aid kit
Water
Trail food
Rain gear
Hat
Matches

Flashlight
Map/Compass
Extra clothing

They recite them for Avis, not to lord it over her, even though they are certain she carries none of these, but to reassure her.

Avis still has a roll of Life Savers in one pocket and her much-flattened sandwiches in her bookbag. She also has two objects, she believes, of entirely no use to this walk—one stolen, one found. She wishes she had at least one more item, one that would take her far away at the end of the walk. A bus ticket, maybe, back to her grandmother's house. He'd find her there, of course, but at least she would have more time to be alive, to try to explain herself.

Caroline has brought along two pocketsful of tiny apples from her root cellar. They are sweet and possibly magical, because when she pulls the apples out from her deep pockets and offers them around, whoever accepts finds that a single bite refreshes and energizes. She did fill Jay's canteen and even strapped it across her in exactly the same way the Scouts have theirs, only hers lies under her coat, next to her heart. What else? A mostly empty bottle of aspirin. A favorite lipstick. Her wallet, apparently. She left her keys (house and car) on the hall table, next to her letter to Ginny and her long list of bequests. She's wearing her favorite sweater, pale blue and part of a twin cashmere set Jay gave her for Christmas a year ago. Not hiking wear at all, but this one, she thought, she'd take with her. Not enough, she thinks, for the long haul, perhaps, but plenty for what she has planned.

Landon carries his pocketknife, a flashlight, multiple packs of thin cigars, a lighter *and* matches, several large clean white handkerchiefs, a whistle, and his wallet.

Extra copies of the map—modified by Landon—are in Warren's jacket pocket. Like the Scouts, he carries two canteens (three now with Denis's added), a compass, a flashlight, and a Band-Aid tin. Like Landon, he has a whistle. He also carries a bag of jelly beans and his mother's coin purse stuffed with nickels and dimes for a pay phone.

Jaspar Goode seems not to be burdened with anything extra, but like any Goode, he is prepared with more than the usual tools (knife, flashlight, compass: these are child's play). No, his supplies are those of a soldier, sent forward to scout, all his needs secreted away in various pockets, inner and outer. Rope and water and extra food (real rations), a more curated first aid kit and an identification badge and, too, his own gun, buttoned and strapped away. To the casual observer, Jaspar Goode appears woefully unprepared, but he is more than ready.

The priest—oh my, what doesn't he carry in that pack of his? More than a few changes of clothing, including (among others) wool hats, a folded gray fedora, and a second borrowed cassock. A *half-dozen* billfolds. A tiny transistor radio in a brown leather case. A woman's linen handkerchief still faintly redolent with a lilac scent. A slingshot. (He did leave town with a worn baseball, but that's found another home.) He, too, has rations that might look not unlike those of the hobo they encountered—tins of sardines, corned beef, Spam, and condensed milk, three boiled eggs, candy, gum. A knife to pry open the cans. He has enough supplies (*essentials*, he thinks, grinning to himself) to take him halfway across the country, if necessary. He's done it before. Oh, sure, he can do it again. He's all set, ready and able to fulfill the tasks ahead, barring any real interference, that is.

BACK AT THE CAFÉ

The walkers have barely gone, the Scouts' sister still clearing their tables when she hears the bus stop outside. This one will be coming from Humtown, and she doesn't expect anyone will get off here. When it comes to the bus, this outpost of a café is used as a drop-off or pick-up spot during the work-week, but no one is waiting today. She's about to go out and wave the bus driver on when she hears footsteps coming up the café ramp and thinks she notices the mere outline of a face peering in. She hurries to clean up.

"We're open," she calls out. "Come right in."

But moments later, after depositing the dish tray in the kitchen, she returns with her bleach-dampened rag to wipe the tables, and no new customer is waiting. Again, she glances out the window. The bus is gone. A mistake, she thinks, brooding.

"Someone out there?" the cook asks, coming up beside her. He points toward the trail. "Someone forget something?"

One of her brothers' bandanas had been left under a rock on the arm of the front bench. The waitress had noticed it not long after the walkers left. But as careful as they were, they wouldn't come back for that. They would trust her to bring it to them later.

"Something's moving at a pretty good clip," the cook squints. "Might be the tail end of a deer family."

"Boy," the waitress says, "I hope they don't run into my brothers. Both of them are dying for that hunting badge. They've been training, though I bet the boys will be more careful with their slingshots after what happened to that lady."

The cook is still gazing into the woods beyond.

An hour later, and only a handful of customers: a couple of truckers filling up on coffee and pie, a local coming down from the hills for his hamburger plate. Too early in the season for tourists and campers. The Scouts' sister and the cook refill and restock and prep and sweep and scrub. Apple pies cool on a rack. Meatloaf is in the oven, hours ahead of the dinner special, which they may end up eating themselves. The cook and the waitress play gin rummy. She is thinking about the drive she'll take after closing, all the way to the Big Walk's end. She's piled blankets in her car, two pillows. The boys can sleep all the way home, celebrate the next day. She'll stop at home first and reassure her mother, not saying a word about the woman with the torn leg. Was it a slingshot? How outlandish that sounds now. More likely, the woman fell into something. Hysterical. But look how calm her brothers were! How strong! Oren not even flinching at the blood, the white-faced woman, the crowd around him. For the first time since the Big Walk began, she relaxes.

And then the Spetle County sheriff's car rolls up.

"How's the lady?" the waitress wants to know.

"Ah, she's fine. Mostly shock from the blood loss. From being attacked."

Whoa, she thought, old Raymond was right. That could have been her little brothers that got hit. Did the sheriff know who or why?

"We're working on it," the sheriff told her, before repeating that fisherman's line: "Probably a kid hunting out of season."

Denis is with the sheriff. He looks a wreck with his purpled eye, his haggard stance. He took a wild pitch in the eye, he's explained. A wayward ball, he told the Spetle County sheriff. He might take another one once he gets home, he thinks. This sheriff has called his father, and they will meet at the Gussie farm, but the train case will stay in this county's evidence room, all those little dresses and footed pajamas catalogued and bagged. Most of the blood on the case is fresh (poor Helen Hubka), but the sheriff's deputy could plainly see another stain under the yellow handle and make out a similar but tiny brown mark on the interior pocket. Tests would be underway. If those stains belonged to a human as well, they'll find the blood group soon enough, maybe narrow things down. But the sheriff wants to talk with all the walkers, especially Landon and Avis. Denis doesn't know Avis's last name. All he knows is the route they are taking. He'll show them the map, he tells them. It's in his jacket pocket.

When Denis doesn't see his jacket by the sign where he left it, he leads a deputy back inside. The Scouts' sister and the cook can't help. She remembers the scrum of walkers around the picnic bench out back, that moaning woman. She remembers noting Denis's damaged eye and being glad he was off the walk. She hadn't registered then what a boy he was. A jacket? No, she hasn't seen that. Everyone had dropped their coats and even shoes all over the place during that rest. At the same time, she can't help but note that the bandana, too, is gone from the bench.

"The bus was by," she tells them.

"Anyone get off?" the deputy asks.

She's about to shake her head when she remembers the flush of deer, the running figure on the trail beyond.

"Yes?" he prods. "Yes?"

Not a half hour later, another customer. A sinewy man in his thirties. Not half-bad looking, the waitress thinks, but holy cow, he couldn't care less, could he? Stained clothes, filthy hands, stinking of livestock. Farmers don't frequent this café unless they're part of a group—men fishing together early in the morning; ham radio buffs having a face-to-face; families returning from a solemn occasion, like a court date. Even then, they begrudge the dimes spent on a cup of coffee. This fellow enters slowly, walks bowlegged, like he's just climbed off a horse instead of out of a truck headed for a dump run, its bed piled high with what looks like broken furniture. He casts his eyes around the empty café, ducks down the hall to the bathroom, peers inside. He even steps into the kitchen, earning a scowl from the cook.

"Can I get you something?" the waitress says.

The fellow eyes her up, and for the first time that day, she feels real fear. He's sulfur; he's rusted metal. She can feel the raw and rotten edge of him.

But why? But . . . no. She's still on edge from the sheriff's visit. This fellow is only a smelly farmer.

"Gimme a coffee," he says, lighting on a stool. His head tilts to peer out the back window. It's as if he's chewing up the place.

"Where'd your crowd get off to?" he spits out.

She can't help herself. She almost snorts with laughter.

"Our crowd? Do we look like we had a rush?"

"He means the kids, the walkers," the cook interjects, a tightness in his voice.

"Do you?" she says, brightening. "You know about the Big Walk? Pretty exciting, isn't it?"

"*Big Walk?*"

Is he sneering? Pride assaults her, and the waitress can't help herself. She explains, extols the President, his challenge, her young brothers, *fifty miles*! He's not impressed.

"Sure, they'll walk fifty miles today," he snorts.

"Oh, they'll make it all right." Her back is up. "Nothing's going to stop them. Not even an accident."

She can't help herself. She goes on and tells him about the bloodied lady, the hospital run, her well-trained brothers.

"Serves them right. They should stick to the road instead of plowing through private property," the fellow says.

She starts to answer before she fully realizes he wasn't asking a question.

"Where they gonna turn around then?" he interrupts. "Coming back on the highway?"

"Nah," the waitress says. She can't keep the pride out of her voice. Her two little brothers walking the long northern line of the peninsula.

"Nah," she says, again, "they're heading straight through Spit Town to the coast, that viewpoint. What do they call that?" she asks the cook.

"End of the World," he says, his voice suddenly quieter.

"Trespassed right across my land, too," the fellow is bitching.

"Your land?

"Yeah," he says. "Right at dawn, like a bunch of thieves."

"Thieves! C'mon, they're on a walk!"

"Look at those damn tramps," the fellow snapped. "They'd stuff a lamb in one of those big packs they carry if I didn't keep a twenty-two handy."

"Sure, buddy, the Boy Scouts brought their knapsacks along on a fifty-mile hike so's they could steal from you." The cook can't help himself. He smirks.

"And that little girl with her tiny blue suitcase." The waitress is laughing at him, too. Dumb farmer.

"A suitcase? They're walking with luggage?"

"Gosh, no." She's still laughing, but she can hear now how odd it sounds. She hurries to clarify. "No, not a real suitcase. She had one of those boxy little cases, like stewardesses carry, you know. Only hers was just a kid's, decked out with a yellow handle."

"A boxy *blue* case?" the fellow repeats, his voice rising. "With a *yellow* handle?"

"Goddamn," he is yelling as he grabs at the waitress's wrist. "I knew it! That's mine! I put that handle on myself."

"Oh, get out of here," she protests, pulling away. He might be ridiculous, but the man's almost left a mark. "You're . . ." She's about to say "nuts," but stops herself. This fellow is definitely off.

"I'll find them," he says.

"Anyone could," the cook says, coming to stand by the waitress, their shared mirth vanished. "They're not hiding." His voice is even and low now, as if he's placating a snarling dog.

Thinking about her brothers, the waitress adds, "If any of them picked up something of yours, you know, it wasn't meant as theft. Plenty of pay phones along the way. If they found anything important, you bet they'd call the sheriff."

"The sheriff? Who the hell needs the sheriff?" he says. "I'll find them."

She is about to tell the man to stop at the café tomorrow midmorning. She'll ask her brothers, she'll say, hunt down whatever this farmer thinks he's lost, but the cook clears his throat, a signal between them, and so she only fiddles needlessly with silverware, putting an end to the conversation. She tries not to look as the farmer empties most of the cream pitcher into his cup and gulps down what's left of his coffee. Finally, grudgingly, he puts a dime next to his spoon. No tip, of course. Only after the door closes behind him and a truck's engine screeches into a rumble does the waitress realize she's been wiping the same metal edge of the Formica counter, holding her breath.

"A piece of work," she says, whisking the coffee cup into a dishpan. "A real crank."

"More than that maybe," the cook says. "Used to see that fellow out at the county airport. Has a Cessna, but had run-ins with so many other pilots that I heard he carved his own runway out of his fields in town, so he could take that plane up anytime he pleased. Seen him by the railroad tracks, too.

"And . . . a couple of times, up in the hills." The cook is frowning.

"You still have that sheriff's card with the number?" he asks.

THE FIVE TENETS

A walk untangles the mind, Caroline's learned. A long walk accelerates the process. A long walk with others concentrates a relationship to the bone. Within mere hours, less than a day, they've moved from strangers to acquaintances. And now, midday, they are approaching something close to relatives. How easy it is, Caroline's discovered, to talk when you don't have to look at someone else, when you're batting off swarming clouds of gnats or avoiding ruts and roots and the snag of brambles, when your voice in the open air sounds almost exactly like the one in your head, but clearer, more honest, when you only say what you need to say and are surprised by what that might be. With each mile, the world she knows recedes, as she hoped. The surprise is that, temporarily at least, she's walking into another one, peopled by more than agreeable companions. Since Jay died, she's become a stranger to herself, as if, without the mirror of his attention, she's lost all notions of how to be. But now old habits resurge, and she finds herself making gentle conversation, much the same way she would with her kindergartners or their young parents. Unlike Helen Hubka's interrogations, which root and pry, Caroline's queries float and settle and stir. *Who are you? Tell me, please. How interesting.* And who doesn't want to try for her?

Jaspar Goode, perhaps. Caroline has heard him exchange a word or two with Landon, and he may have offered advice to the Scouts or Avis along the way, but so far he's been closemouthed around Caroline. She's not deterred or offended. Caroline's met more than a few men in Humtown who don't waste words on predictable conversations. They don't mean to be rude or secretive. They just don't see the point of gabbing out their every thought. *Watch me and you'll know me*, Jay once said, explaining the sort to Caroline. She does know that Jaspar is one of a large family, without whom the town would likely fall apart. The Goodes are the plumbers, electricians, mechanics, masons, carpenters, and nurses of town. Jay used to joke that his dearest hope was that Ginny would marry a Goode.

"We'd be in clover," he'd said with a grin. "I could retire and fish all week."

Ginny did, in fact, briefly date Cyril Goode in high school. A steady boy who swept his eyes around Caroline's kitchen (and Caroline and Jay, even Ginny, too) as if seeking out their many defects and developing a repair schedule. Jay laughed when she told him, but the boy's attention worried her. Up until recently, she'd always liked a little mess in her life.

"Cyril is my cousin's kid," Jaspar tells her when she asks. "Married now, baby on the way. I tried to get him on a boat crew, but he's setting stone for his father. Hates the water, he says. They all do," he adds.

Jaspar, Caroline surmises, is an anomaly in the Goode family: a sometime fisherman, a traveler, an outlier. He must be set to scoot back up to Alaska with a boat in a matter of weeks. Jay declared any willing soul with a strong back and half a brain could make a bucket of money crabbing. But Jaspar Goode mentions none of this. He's not chatty in the superficial tradesman way of the Goodes, many of whom call her not Caroline or Mrs. Weller but Mrs. Jay, as if they're all playing characters: The Wife, The Husband, The Plumber. Jaspar's different. Maybe, Caroline thinks, it's all that time on the boat. Fishermen are nothing if not good at waiting and musing. He's not shy or even particularly quiet, but his conversation is thoughtful. He listens before he speaks. And Jaspar seems to share his cousin Cyril's focus. More than once, she's glanced up to glimpse an intent expression on the fisherman's face, as if he's calculating or inventing or maybe simply arguing with himself.

When their pace shifts, and a noticeable gap appears between the pair of them and the other walkers, Jaspar Goode leans in and almost knocks Caroline sideways when he says, "I heard about Jay."

He's sorry for her loss, he goes on.

Did he know Jay? Well, of course, if he's been working in the boatyard, he must have, yet Caroline can't remember Jay mentioning him. What a boon that would have seemed—a Goode in the boatyard. Maybe Jay, too, hadn't connected this unlikely fisherman to the famously water-averse Goodes. Hadn't breathed a word of him.

Caroline thanks the fisherman, her head down (of course, of course). Such a strange custom, thanking someone for acknowledging your great grief, and yet she's grateful, always grateful, even more so that he held off his condolences until this point in the journey, but still . . . she feels the now familiar welling-up, her chest tightening, her breath stopped. Cratering. The little death that comes with each reminder of the Big Death. If only, she thinks, if only she could amplify that moment and drift away. If only each condolence snipped away another thread that kept her tethered to this stupid life. She manages to change the subject, points awkwardly at his outfit.

"What do you hunt?" she asks.

He shakes his head. Not a hunter. He's been in the service, he explains, overseas.

She has stopped reading the news. She doesn't miss the nightly half hour, and her radio, when on, plays only music, but she's glimpsed photographs in magazines, young men like Jaspar Goode, broiling under a foreign sun in their camouflage. Why wear it once you were home again? She wonders aloud if he misses the army.

"No," he snorts. "Not at all."

"Jay's war was different, I guess," she says.

"Do you think?" he says after a long pause. "Probably no war is all that different from any other, at least in one sense."

"What's that?" Caroline asks.

Again, Jaspar Goode takes so long to respond, she's almost sure he hasn't heard her. Finally, his answer floats across to her, his tone softened as if he wants to whisper the words.

"It's never really over, I guess," he says.

And now Caroline can see what Jay and this young fisherman might have had in common. The sense of a secret life. Jay's was partly in his past, too, a wartime role that he didn't care to talk about, but she believed (fancifully, perhaps) he'd been heroic in that old-timey sense of quiet, selfless actions. In Humtown, Jay seemed to court trouble, but more likely the war had simply heightened his sense of possible disasters. Despite his readiness, he always seemed to see a better light coming, and that, she guessed, mostly kept him calm. But then there were other times, like with that boat the Cravens pulled off the beach, when he could not stop brooding, anticipating dire complications no one else seemed to see. Jay had looked the boat over and been puzzled by the whole affair. Structurally, he told Caroline, the boat didn't seem hardly damaged, and nothing indicated it had been torn from its moorings either.

"I don't know how that boat ran aground or how the Cravens got to it so quickly or why anyone thinks it's a great idea to keep it anchored beyond the breakwater again, but they need to get it the hell out of Humtown," he told her.

At the time, she'd thought Jay meant the Cravens were lining themselves up for another court case. Wouldn't be the first time they'd be accused of stealing a vessel they supposedly rescued. Later, she would believe Jay had been telling her something else altogether, and she'd been too dense to understand. The port was full of comings and goings, though, wasn't it?

"It'll sail away before you know it," she'd tried. "Someone's got a plan, I bet."

Ridiculous, that reassurance coming from her. But she could see that boat had got to Jay somehow, and that nonsense with the Shuffler and little Halde Bens hadn't helped.

She knows so little and has no way of separating fact from rumor. Charlie Beecher had only stared at her when she'd mentioned the strange boat the Port tried to impound, the one the Cravens had rushed to rescue and claim. Now she tries a rumor on Jaspar Goode, hoping he'll enlarge or correct her information, most of it gleaned from Helen Hubka this very day.

Helen Hubka had been on a rant about some supposed fugitive on the run and federal agents and a whole lot of other nonsense. Caroline should know better than to give too much credence to Helen Hubka's information bank, but her attention had been caught when the Operator mentioned another investigation entangling those Cravens and their uncanny ability to interfere with impounded vessels.

"Smugglers, were they?" Caroline asks Jaspar Goode. "The ones who first had the boat?"

Jaspar Goode isn't biting.

She tries again.

"Do you think Mick Craven was involved?"

Another long pause. Jaspar Goode is suddenly flustered. Caroline waits.

"We'll never know, I guess," he says, finally.

"Why not?" Caroline asks.

"Well, the boat's gone now, isn't it?" he says, his voice so gentle and anguished Caroline suddenly understands, she knows immediately what Charlie Beecher couldn't tell her, that the boat Jay had tried to save, the one he'd jumped aboard and sailed right into the storm, had been the same cursed vessel the Cravens had tried to claim, the same one the Shuffler had tried to buy.

Caroline is surprised by how angry she feels. A fury she's been tamping down for months is beginning to surge. She grabs Jaspar Goode's arm.

"Why," she demands. "Why would he turn the boat into the storm?"

Jaspar Goode shakes his head. "I don't know. I don't know."

In his voice, Caroline hears her own bewilderment, and her anger begins to seep away. Of course, Jay wouldn't hurt her or any of his friends on purpose. She's about to apologize to Jaspar Goode when he continues, rattling out words as if they hurt.

"No, I don't know, but maybe he thought the boat was too close to shore, that the wind would slam it right into the breakwater or onto the beach, maybe he thought it would be broken up immediately if he didn't do something and that by taking it out, he could maneuver into open water and ride out the storm. Not a bad idea if you're trying to save a crew. Sailors do that, you know, Caroline."

She can tell that even he doesn't really believe that.

And who was aboard, she wants to know, what crew had been on the boat that night, and how had Jay known?

"On the boat?" Jaspar Goode seems surprised when she asks. "That's the thing. No one was on that boat. No one could have been. No one but Jay."

Caroline wants to know more, of course. How can he be so sure? How could Jay have got it so wrong, then? But Jaspar Goode only shakes his head. Unlike the priest, who will enter any discussion and take it for a ride, sprawling past the original conversation with conjecture and declarations, Jaspar Goode draws lines, stays inside. This is all I know, he seems to say, leaving Caroline to puzzle out the pieces of this mystery along with the fragmented selves he's offering—fisherman, soldier, Goode, known acquaintance of her beloved Jay—none of which seem to present a true picture of the man. He doesn't wear a wedding ring, hasn't mentioned children. How does he fit in town? It's as if he's taken an oath, vowed secrecy. Secrecy to what? To whom? Their conversation ebbs away as the priest and Avis amble up. Jaspar Goode falls back, accommodating as the newcomers shift into place between them. In his easily reclaimed silence, Jaspar Goode resembles Avis—one reason, Caroline reckons, she is most comfortable with both of them. They can stay quiet and present for ages, eyes on their shoes, walking, walking.

But this priest, Father Dan, Danny—now, strangely, *Daniel*—is another story. He is a rambler, a minor philosopher. As, she concedes, a priest should be. As, come to think of it, the President himself is. Jay liked Jack Kennedy, liked Bobby even more, and might have liked this priest, too. Still mulling over Jaspar Goode's connection to Jay, Caroline can't help wondering if Jay and the priest had met as well, if the priest ever heard any of Jay's theories, what he jokingly called his Five Tenets, as if Jay Weller were an institution in and of himself. Jay's Five Tenets weren't always the same five. He adjusted, fine-tuned.

The last five she can recall circle in her mind:

1. Not enough people know when enough is enough.
2. There's no perfection except in nature.
3. You can ruin anything with a bad enough attitude.
4. A good theory starts with a strong statistical correlation.
5. There's no justice on the face of the earth.

She almost recites these to the priest, almost tells him about the greatness of Jay, but a new worry stops her, one having nothing to do with the truth of the priest. She worries that in drawing Jay for a stranger, she'll mythologize him, make him less and less real. She needs him, even in shade form, to be real. At Jay's funeral, one of his extended family, a little cousin who'd visited a few times and gone fishing with Jay, asked Caroline if she got a headache when she cried, if others got headaches when they cried, because she did every time, so that she had to close her eyes and sit in a quiet room. That seven-year-old was the first one Caroline wanted to tell about how she erased herself as she moved around the house without Jay.

How she hurried to smooth out the bedclothes, scour every dish, scrub the sink. She filled boxes with knickknacks and her old clothes, but nothing of Jay's. No, she wanted to hang on to every scrap of him. Truth is, the best part of her had gone with Jay, and what remains . . . well, that shadowy version of herself has no place any longer.

The priest claims her attention, pointing uphill where, beyond one scrim of trees, a surreal scene is becoming visible. A whole other forest, it seems, but this one has been flattened and ravaged, a Broken Forest. One giant cedar appears fully uprooted, as if a furious god had a temper tantrum. The sight dizzies Caroline. It so closely resembles the boatyard that dawn after the Columbus Day storm, boats upended, thrown halfway uphill—sailboats, gillnetters, a wooden tug—by that vicious, unrelenting wind. A miracle only one person perished. A tragedy that that one was the great Jay Weller. Caroline stares at the field of broken trees jabbing across the landscape like so many snapped masts, the ache within her growing, drowning out most of what the priest is nattering on about. She hears, not "burn pile," but "pyre" and chokes a little at the smells of blackened wood, damp smoke.

"Where will the animals go?" a stunned Avis ventures.

"*There is no justice on the face of the earth,*" a voice sings out from behind them.

Caroline whips around, but Jaspar Goode has all but vanished. She struggles to separate his camouflage from the surrounding woods, to see how he's paired up with Landon once more, to watch him gradually return to focus in her landscape. As she does, the priest murmurs his way into . . . well . . . not a lecture, not a rant, but a mournful humming, followed by a melancholy lullaby, one with a seemingly endless refrain that will carry them through this latest region of devastation.

THE PAIN THAT CANNOT BE ACKNOWLEDGED

Feet, you betcha. Hot, swelling, squeezed tight

Pinched calves, strained muscles

Sore knees

Ah, geez, shoulders

Blistered heel

Neck: tension, stiffness, one crazy pain lighting up the back of the head

Shins

Burning toe

Nipping bite? Sting? Rash? Itches under an armpit?

Headache, a crabbed point between the eyes from squinting into the sun

A stitch right below a rib, insistent

Shooting pain in hip

Twitchy eye

Thigh muscle, cramped, pulsing

Lower back, aching

Tingling fingers

Anxious knot

A tender spot just below the chest, in the center of all, as if a punch has landed, as if the heart has been hollowed out and replaced, emptied of all but flecks, piercing shards, splinters of memories

Drift your thoughts in the wrong direction, and oh, boy, hurt, hurt, hurt.

THE COUSIN AND
THE HITCHHIKER

On any given Saturday in March, the main road from Humtown to Spit Town might see spurts of traffic. A football team returning home on a yellow school bus. A family on a shoe-shopping outing in a dusty Studebaker, all of them yammering over the sound of a rattling muffler. A mother and daughter in a brand-spanking-new Rambler, hypnotized by an excursion to pick up ribbon and rickrack and notions for an Easter hat. And, as dusk approached, the occasional fellow hitching to keep a date with a sweetheart. Karin Johansson normally wouldn't have stopped for any of those thumb-waving dopes, playacting their weekend love and putting others on the spot. The bus ran between the towns, didn't it? Two or three times a day. A dummy could figure out a schedule, couldn't he? No, Karin, who has scraped together enough to buy her brother's old Chevy (a few tiny dents, a flickering headlight), usually has no sympathy for a besotted hitchhiker. Her heart has resided in a caged box, a stifling chamber so suffused with envy and venom it's a wonder it could beat at all, a wonder she hadn't driven over at least one of those young bucks in the past as they flagrantly flung themselves from town to town for some dumb gal. Karin's mouth usually tightened whenever young love exhibited itself in her presence. *Wise up*, she's wanted to hiss. But, oh ho, how that's changed! Justice has arrived for Karin, bad decisions rightfully upended, and she has been embraced by her own secret sweetheart, her own heady inevitable romance, and her sour meanness is swiftly mellowing into a less-constant disapproval. She is, if not indulgent, much less offended by teenage romance these days. Even a few months ago, she wouldn't have stopped for the boy. But she is on her way to Spit Town to meet the man she loves, *in public* for the first time, albeit, she acknowledges, well away from the prying eyes of Humtown: a cocktail (or two) at the Spit Town Lanes Lounge after the task ahead.

If she listens closely, she can hear the boxes he placed in the trunk of her car shifting around, an occasional thump. She'll only have to live with that inconvenience until later this evening when they'll meet on the spur that leads to the Spit Town dump. He'll deal with all that. She doesn't even know how many boxes are in the trunk, only that they're heavy and full of *their* crap and that he didn't want her help. "Stay in the car," he'd ordered that night. And she'd been happy to get out of the cold, dark damp and sit with the radio playing love songs that made sense to her now. Now that she's won.

The rain that has plagued most of the day is easing, scraps of brilliant late-afternoon sun breaking through. She'd flicked on her headlights, but now muses that she might even see an evening rainbow, which she will surely take as a sign. Though no one could accuse Karin of harboring a poetic soul—pure pap, all that sentimental crap—after years of being second-best, she's been singled out—*courted*—by the man who should have chosen her first long ago, who has finally seen the error of his ways and corrected the situation.

"I'll fix it," he told her as he grasped onto her, his fingers leaving actual marks on her arms, witness to his passion.

"I'll fix it," he said, and her tight, mean heart surged with triumph.

Only a few years earlier, her wily cousin, the pretend innocent, had seduced him, blinded him with her slutty ways. When Karin had stumbled over them in the barn, she couldn't believe her eyes. She hadn't, in fact, and her cousin, who'd spent a whole summer warning Karin against him and openly snubbing him as he tried to help her take real command of her horse or teased her by tossing hay (or dung) on her head, that cousin, that fake, had fed Karin a cock-and-bull story about him grabbing her. *Him* grabbing *her*! Against her instincts, Karin—what a dope she'd been—had believed her cousin's lies, even as her own crush deepened, but after a memorable bout in the girls' room at school, her pale cousin upchucking throughout first period, she could see the trap that had been laid. Some goddamn innocent! And by then, Remy and Karin had even shared one sweet, ravaging kiss. But what could he do? He had to marry the cousin. How was that supposed to go? Only months later, it seemed, he was saddled with a passive milk-cow of a wife, with babies screaming day and night. What kind of a life was that? Meanwhile, Karin, trim and clean and undemanding, waited. One year, then another. Karin, who kept her mouth shut, groomed her horse and clucked in sympathy as he complained. Karin, who despised children, swore *she* would never have even one ankle-biter, reassured him he'd been wronged and rode the swell of indignation right along with him. Karin became his Everything.

Her cousin thought she was some kind of a princess, didn't she? Thought she had him locked tight and could run his household, his life! Ruin it, more like. Always running off to that family of hers. *Let her stay with them,* Karin wanted to tell him, but she knew he'd steam. Despite his desire to get shed of the lot, he wasn't about to let his wife take the upper hand, shame him. And then all those years he'd have to work to support the brats, no matter where they lived.

"I'll fix it," he'd said, and Karin didn't ask a thing, only imagined herself in the farmhouse, all the milk-and-diaper stink bleached away, every scrap of her cousin and the brats scrubbed out.

"I'll fix it," he said as he and Karin lay twined together in the barn. Or maybe he said, "I'll fix *her*." Did it matter? He wanted (he *wants*) Karin, not her malicious fake of a cousin, a houseful of wailing. And now, it seems, finally, he is free—they are *gone, miraculously gone!*—and Karin is feeling uncharacteristically generous, so much so that she doesn't even mind that the hitchhiking boy is wearing a red-and-white Humtown High School varsity jacket. She's only been out of school a couple of years herself, but she still feels resentment when she sees this emblem of popularity. Sure enough, when the boy slips into the car beside her and tilts his head toward her, she can tell he thinks he's a prince. He's got that Kennedy grin. How Karin hates that clan. Show-offs, do-gooders—Karin doesn't trust any of them, not the photogenic President, the cultured, girlish wife with her wisp of a voice and camera-ready tots, especially not the righteous brother with his floppy hair and toothy grin. Karin can spot a phony a mile away. She doesn't need to wait for a gossip like that Helen Hubka to confirm the horny details. She may not recognize this boy with the striking good looks, the glossy hair just this side of too long, an unnerving blue stare—"black Irish" pops into her head—but she knows he is not what he's pretending to be, and that makes her attempt at goodwill a sham as well. *Screw 'em*, as Remy would say. When the boy's eyes drift to her pocketbook, she risks taking a hand off her juddering steering wheel to loft her purse into the backseat.

"Spit Town?" she says. "What is it? Bowling or a sweetheart?"

The boy says nothing. He's playing that popular-boy game, pretending to consider or, worse, not to hear her. In her own damn car. He keeps that up, she decides, she'll put him back on the curb lickety-split.

"Or both?" she asks.

These questions from another girl might come across as flirtatious teasing. Karin sounds more like a school principal. *I've got your number, young man. Don't try any funny business.* And yet the boy remains unaffected by the sarcasm in her voice.

"Those are my only options?" he finally murmurs, tilting that blue gaze on her.

Whoo, she thinks. Aren't you the playboy?

"Unless you've got others," she says. "Must be important, giving up your Saturday night."

"Well, it is, *Karin*," he says, reading her name off the old graduation tassels on her rearview mirror. "It is important. My sister's missing."

The kid's words mimic almost word for word the call she received earlier that week. *If you know anything, Karin! Anything at all!*

"Oh, she's probably found a fellow, run off for fun." Karin can't help shaking her head, pursing her carefully painted lips.

The boy plays with her car's cigarette lighter, eventually punching it in before he responds.

"She ran away, all right," he says. "But not with a boyfriend. Avis is only fourteen. My little sister."

"She won't get far," he adds. "I'll find her. Before she gets into trouble. Again."

Tough guy, she thinks and would have mocked him to his face, but as she glances sideways, she is nearly burnt by the venom coming off the kid. She recognizes the heightened vibration, a vicious determination that she finds violently attractive in her own lover's rough edges. The boy is certainly prettier than her man, smoother in every mistrustful way, and she should be dismissive. She should pull over and tell the boy *to get out and get bent* the way Remy would. (Who is she kidding? Remy would have smacked the kid into a ditch by now.) But Karin's mouth can't help curving upward into an approving smirk. This kid's no Kennedy clone, she sees that now. He doesn't care a whit about pleasing her or anyone else.

"Well, good for you . . . ," she begins.

"Teddy, Karin," the boy says. "I'm Teddy."

Oh, geez, like the President's brother, the youngest, most slippery one. Yup, she despises that family, the way they charm the simpleminded into believing the country is one big happy family like theirs, each willing to pull his weight for the betterment of all. Baloney! Bet if you crossed a Kennedy, you'd find out what kind of helping hand you'd get. Them and their kiddies, that endless touch-football-team of a family. Bunch of competitive phonies.

The lighter pops out; the boy punches it back in again. Is he trying to irritate her?

"Your folks couldn't give you a lift?" she snaps. "I bet you've got teammates, maybe, coming to the rescue, like a bunch of Kennedy Musketeers: *All for one, one for all.*"

The boy scorches her again with a look so steeped in disdain, Karin nearly smiles.

"That *your* motto?" he asks.

"Fat chance." Karin snickers. "My motto? *Trust is for suckers*, more like. You got one?"

"A motto? Sure," he says without a beat of hesitation. "How about *Every man for himself.*"

Her lips purse and twist approvingly, and when the lighter pops back out again, its coil ignited. Karin flicks open her pack of Salems on the dash, holds it toward the boy.

"And yet you're out looking for your sister," she says. It's as much question as statement, but the boy doesn't seem inclined to answer.

In the closeness of the car, she can feel the heat coming off the lighter's red coil as the boy bends it near his face. He lights up and takes one long drag, exhaling slowly. As she reaches out through a veil of smoke, he actually steadies her hand and, instead of handing her the lighter, places the lit cigarette between her fingers. She is pleasantly shocked by this intimacy.

"What about you, Karin?" he says. "Got a hot date in Spit Town?"

She almost tells him. *Trust is for suckers,* she'd said, her guiding principle for years, but Karin's luck has turned—look at her almost flirting!—and why shouldn't that shift bring along a kindred spirit at the precise moment she is aching to shout out her news? Remy is free, and he is hers! *You bet I've got a hot date, kid,* she wants to crow. She wants to spill her romantic trials and triumph, tell this charmer everything and witness his amazement at what she's wrought.

For the briefest moment, Karin wonders if Teddy might be useful, if she and he might strike a deal. She'll drop him at the bowling alley, because that's where all the kids end up in Spit Town on a Saturday night. This pretty boy in his Humtown letter jacket . . . who wouldn't want to chat him up? Share gossip.

Remy, that's who. Remy, who's fixed everything for her. Remy, who trusts no one. No one but her, that is.

She taps her ash, remembers.

One final act, their shared endeavor. This pretty boy, no matter how fierce he might pretend to be, would never be so clever or courageous as her man. This one—he's just plain trouble. Karin shakes her head, unrolls her window, throws her cigarette butt into the wind.

"Just an errand," she tells Teddy. "A simple errand for a very close friend."

And then, she wants to add, *a brand-new life, one for the whole damn town to see.*

AVIS, THE INVISIBLE

What a world they've entered! During the earlier stretch of the walk, Avis clung to the familiar—lapping water, the weedy gravel between railroad tracks, grass and mud and rocks, the tough, torn bark of trees. Even the occasional jarring note in the landscape—a sodden striped sock, a flattened tire, cigarette butts and littered newspaper scraps far from any house or road—reassured her. At least she recognized them. But the Broken Forest made it clear that *this region* is unlike any she has known or could imagine. And now they've entered a much denser forest, one she gathers the other walkers view as intact, normal, and Avis is utterly at sea. After a while, she wonders aloud about a plant with purple berries, then a scrawny bush that looks as if it's dotted with drooping pearls. Soon the priest and Jaspar Goode are tossing out names: *Salal. Snowberry. Red Alder.* More follow: *Oregon Grape. Orford Cedar. Rhody. Broom. Himalayan Blackberry. Nettle.* Even Landon gruffly introduces her to *Devil's Claw,* as if the spiky, sprawling plant is a relative of his.

Caroline pulls wisps of gray-green moss from low branches to sweep across Avis's palm. "Witches' Hair," she says, causing a chill to race through the girl. "And look at this," Caroline says with a laugh, pointing out a plant whose leaves look to Avis like little families—each dark green leaf bearing a brighter green miniature of itself, as if it's wearing one of Avis's grandmother's brooches. "Youth on Age, this one's called," Caroline says. When a fallen tree blocks their way, they climb over without a word, Avis's old school shoes slipping on the slick lichen and moss, and afterward Caroline explains nurse logs, how once fallen, the heavy limbs begin to decay, creating new habitats for other plants and creatures. Nothing goes to waste in this forest world. Not even disasters.

When Avis hustles into their range, the Scouts prove even better at identification. A clacking begins above them, and Oren pauses only a moment before he spies the eagle, perched on a high branch and looking to Avis like the very picture of a cartoon vulture, despite the white markings, the golden beak. The boys seem to know every creature's name (private and public) and habits. (In that, the Scouts remind Avis a little of Helen Hubka.) Avis, they discover, doesn't know anything. Not of the woods or the animals or the people in town. All she knows is Teddy, and she can't share that. The Scouts show her how to make marks along the way to indicate the path they're taking.

"In case we get lost?" she asks.

The boys look at her as if she's crazy, but Karl says, "Sure, okay."

If they suddenly came upon water, Avis is sure these two would make them all a boat and fashion life rings, too, out of bull kelp and shoelaces. They tell her about the merit badges they have, and although they are modest, she is impressed. Archery, Camping, Canoeing, and Fishing: these are exactly the activities she might imagine for a Boy Scout. But Cooking, Astronomy, Metalwork, Woodwork, Geology, Leatherwork, and . . . Horsemanship?

"You ride horses?" she asks. "Real horses?"

Both boys nod.

But the merit badges they most desire, they tell her, have to do with leadership and citizenship.

"Not just because we'll move up the ranks," Oren insists.

"But because," Karl finishes, "we'll be better men."

Teddy would sneer at the pair of them, Avis thinks.

This walk, Karl is explaining, will bring them closer to a Citizenship-in-the-Nation badge. After all, the President has asked; they are answering.

"Our duty," Karl says to Avis.

"And yours," Oren adds—a little pompously, Avis thinks.

The Scouts are working toward even more merit badges: First Aid, Weather, Insects, Indian Lore, and Numismatics—which Oren must explain to her.

"Like your Indian Head nickel," he says with gentle longing.

(Yes, how Teddy would despise them.)

When Avis swears she hears a cat meow and peers into the underbrush, the Scouts point upward to an enormous blackbird, three times the size of a crow.

"Raven," they pronounce as one.

"Meowing?" she asks.

A raven can imitate almost anything, they tell her. Cats and police sirens, airplanes and wind, her own voice if they hear it enough.

What a skill that would be, Avis thinks.

As they walk, the Scouts test each other, throwing out questions, making more complicated identifications. Karl decides to help Avis keep a list of the wildlife they'll encounter this day. (If there was a badge for Generosity, Karl would have earned that long ago.) Mostly birds, racoons, squirrels, moles, rabbits, coyotes, but he suspects, also, elk, black bear, cougar. If their Scoutmaster had come along, he might have reined in the boys, observing, for instance, that the scat they attribute to a black bear is likely that of a raccoon or, even more disappointingly, is only a desiccated pinecone. But the Scoutmaster is not here, and the Scouts call out animal tracks in offhand tones that startle Avis. *Right there*, they'll say as they point to ridges in the mud that might be the mark of an alien hand, three fingers around a broad pad. They warn her of elk thunder, how the ground might tremble, and if it does, how she must find the nearest tree and hug it tightly until the herd gallops past. And there is more. Avis has never imagined a walk where one might worry about being trampled by elk or stalked by a coyote or surprised by a winter-starved bear lumbering into spring. The boys show her how to hold her arms up straight to make herself look bigger as she walks backward. They caution her against running *ever*. Worst case, they tell her, if a bear is too close, roll into a ball, play dead. Now *that* Avis understands. She reckons she's spent half her life in the fetal position, readying for a blow from Teddy.

Yes, what a confounding place the forest is. Not at all what she's imagined. When, for one scant quarter-mile, the logging road closely parallels the main road, the rush of a passing truck on that other road slaps diesel on the tongue, assaults them all with a manufactured surge of wind, and how relieved Avis is when the logging road turns upward again, when they tramp back within the trees and she breathes in the spicy scents of cedar and pine, the damp mosses, as if they are creatures traveling beside her, unwashed and rich with themselves. It's the trees, she decides, that make her feel safest. Their wildness is like her oddness, kin. She's learned to watch for what she thinks of as ground branches. Great knuckled limbs growing under and even right above the forest floor, connecting one tree, it seemed, to all the others in a way she cannot comprehend, a way that nonetheless feels powerful and true and completely right. When the talk between the walkers eases, as it does again and again, when exhaustion begins to push at her, that tedious gravity, when the wondrous terror of what she's done and what she still needs to do and what will come after, when all that threatens to overwhelm her, knock her to her knees, Avis keeps her eyes on the ground, on those roots, the endless conversation between the trees and all they contain. She wonders, If I stay here, could I be part of that?

"Look!" Karl says, pointing out scratch marks on a tree trunk. The boys examine and declare with certainty that cougars are nearby.

"But we'll probably never see them," Oren says with clear disappointment.

Cougars, you see, the Scouts inform her, are "the ghosts of the forests." Most of the time you'd never know they were there.

"Don't scare the girl," Caroline says, coming closer.

"Don't worry," one Scout tells Avis.

"We'll take care of you," says the other.

Boys. Mere children, who have no clue that, even as they earnestly warn of cougars and the art of concealment, Avis is growing less fearful and more certain she belongs here.

The places Avis has known best are not places at all, but textures and scents: the heavy wool next to her face—tobacco, mint, sweat—as she hid in the downstairs coat closet; the nubby safety of her chenille bedspread, wrapped around her in an icy corner of the sleeping porch; the cool painted basement floor, her head swimming with the stench of heating oil; dust and plaster walls; mud and gravel, dirt and the penny taste of blood, all because of a single paragraph she'd come across in a library book on magic and one vital trick, in particular, the *art of invisibility*.

Once you are invisible, she'd read, *the world around you also falls into pitch black*. It's a circumstance most people aren't prepared for, apparently, no matter how much they think they know about disappearing, about slinking unseen behind enemy lines, or slipping into a villain's den to record his plotting. If you're not practiced, you'll surely give yourself away, banging into walls, tripping over the vast lots of rubbish that surround evildoers. Seeing in the dark, Avis learned, is a key step to successful invisibility. She'd been practicing all that time, courting vision in the depths of closets and dim cellar corners, under a neighbor's back porch. At night, she would wrap herself in a black overcoat, a mothballed wool monstrosity that her grandfather had worn during a winter war. Her grandmother had intended to donate the coat to the Salvation Army bin, but Avis claimed it and took it into the night. She'd roll under bushes and even fall asleep there. At first, it seemed those outings only left her stiff and sheepish, sneaking back into the house while her mother made coffee in the kitchen. But soon enough, Teddy came looking. More than once, he'd crept around the garden, his flashlight darting and circling. She waited for the yank, the blows, but nothing came. Up to that point, her only defenses had been weak: to never show pain, to keep her mouth shut. Her invisibility lessons gave her an edge for the first time. Because it's true that when people don't see you, they take it for granted that you can't see them either. So Avis was able to learn from Teddy, to follow him in not a few of his nocturnal wanderings, and for all his cleverness, Teddy's not yet noticed that Avis is fearless and surefooted in the night, that she is expert at moving in his shadow, that her best trait, her clearest talent, is her ability to absorb everything and forget absolutely nothing.

THE WEATHER WITHIN

By midafternoon, they've worked their way out of the deep woods, skirted the highway once again, with Landon's guidance, to land on a high coastal path, well above another bay. Trails of backlit clouds across a glassy sky. In only a few hours, they'll be in dusk. For now, the walkers seem to tread a line through thinning light between two mirrored worlds. To one side, the vague outline of high mountain tops still crowned with snow. On the other, the far-off Strait stippled with white foam. For a good mile, the new wind that swirls around them on this open path mimics the distant waves, pummeling the walkers from the front and side, pushing from the rear. Packs go askew, weight shifts painfully. All of them keep their heads down, resisting as best they can. Caroline's shoulders are so tight and sore, she's surprised she can move her neck at all. Avis's eyes stream as she lifts her gaze to peer toward the distant chopping waves. Before today, she kept away from the beaches in town, which bear almost no resemblance to the summer-burnt, sandy Atlantic shore of her real home, and had taken only the slightest notice of the equally foreign wind, which seemed a singular thing, like a wild animal, a steadfast winter howling. The walk is changing her. From the graveled access road beside Forgotten Bay, through the mauled woods littered with fallen limbs and creaking overhead boughs, along the gentle forest road, beside the roar of the descending streams, and now this battered exposure on another open shore, another bay, the unfortunately named Spit Bay, she's come to feel the wind's every shift, as if the weather itself is part of her. She's overwhelmed—bursting!—with this new comprehension. She *has* to share. The priest has fallen back and claimed Caroline's attention. Warren and the Scouts are well out of range, and Landon has stopped entirely, trying to light a cigarette, head bowed, hands cupped, one failed attempt after another.

Only Jaspar Goode is available, right beside her and visible once more in the open air. Unlike the rest of them, he looks comfortable, even aiming his face into the wind. His cheeks may be reddened and chapped, and his khaki camouflage might be soaked through, but he radiates calmness. Since Helen Hubka left, he's become chattier, relating fishing stories, telling tales on members of the considerable Goode family. His tone is different from that of the priest, who often confounds, but is equally singular, as if he's emerged from another time. Avis likes Jaspar. Avis trusts him. She finds herself babbling out her theory of the wind and is immediately flustered by the expression on his face. It's as if he's come awake to her. He pauses, gives her a long look.

"It's true," he says, finally. "People carry the weather inside them. I'm not sure which way the influence lies, if emotions cause the weather or weather reflects the emotions, but there's a real connection, you're right."

How thrilling to be taken seriously. Avis is so overcome she misses a bit of what the fisherman says next.

". . . in a book once," she finally hears, "up north on the boat."

He's still talking, his speech a kind of poetry, but the fanciful words are clearer and more astonishing to Avis than any she's heard in an English class (or science or religion class, either, for that matter). Jaspar Goode tells her how anger can thunder through a body, depression fogs the heart's true desires, and weeping cleanses the landscape of the soul. There's no barrier, his book said, between the physical world outside the body and the emotional world within.

"They kind of work together," Jaspar Goode says, "affecting each other in turn."

Wind, especially, the book explained, is the breath of the gods, and when it blows across the earth, it's like a deep sigh released, taking with it all the pent-up anxieties of beings much larger than mere humans. That same wind that tunnels through the landscape, scouring corners with ravaging precision, also swirls through mortal bodies, emerging as their own simple sighs, the tiny chugs of in-and-out, the hiccups of existence. *Doubt the wind within you?* the book asked. *Examine the pads of your fingers and toes and dispute, if you can,* the book had said, *the whorling, incomprehensible lines that are the marks of the exiting wind.*

"Go ahead," Jaspar Goode says, "check your fingertips."

Of course, Avis does. Of course, she can see the faint spiraling. Good Catholic girl that she's hoped to be, of course, she thinks *stigmata*. Signs of God.

Or gods.

"So, the wind is like breath?" she asks.

The fisherman grins. It's the first time Avis has seen him smile, and he is transformed from a handsome, often sullen man into a glorious boy. Not a pretty boy like Teddy. The fisherman hasn't an ounce of that terrifying charm that can switch without warning from seduction to scorn. Nor is the fisherman's boy like the Scouts, boys already wearing the faces they'll carry into middle age. No, this surprising man-boy is delighted, a curious child enraptured and elevated by a mysterious world.

"Yes, like breath," he says. "Exactly."

Miracles, she is thinking. Briefly, she wonders if she should consult the priest again, but a glance at that ridiculous pack bobbing along the trail ahead dispels that notion.

STATE PARK

MILE 31

It's nearly three when the walkers reach the state park, a patchwork grid of gravel pullouts and moss-slickened picnic tables. All the narrow lanes of the park are strewn with fallen branches. Not enough to obstruct the passage of a vehicle, but enough to signify the park's emptiness. The walkers note only a single trailer camper, a white metal box with turquoise stripes along the side, its roof furred with green mold. The camper sits in an unnumbered view spot well behind a wooden sign:

CAMPGROUND HOSTS

RITA AND DALE SELZNICK

No one seems to be around. As the walkers straggle into the campground, red-faced from the latest hill, they file toward the restroom pit toilets at varying speeds, each emerging with visible relief. Avis jots the time in her notebook. No one is claiming a second or third or fifth wind this time. Even the Scouts look exhausted.

They are all hungry again. They hand around whatever they have. Wearily, the boys pull out the pie and cookies their sister wrapped. Caroline attempts to empty her pockets of apples, but somehow produces one for every walker who asks and still, when her hand goes back into her pocket, feels yet another apple's reassuring curve. (*The loaves and fishes of the Kennedy Walk*, she wants to joke . . . to Jay and Jay alone.)

After marking their time log, Avis can't find her Life Savers, but—another surprise—her squashed peanut butter sandwiches are now at the top of her bookbag instead of in the inside pocket. Even her bookbag is being reconfigured by the walk, a worrisome thought. Her hand slips to the inner corner just long enough to feel again the round shape tucked within her sock. A relief and a worry all at once. More than half the day is gone, and her task remains undone.

No one's talking much. Jaspar Goode offers a flask to Landon, who refuses, and to the priest, who accepts, earning an amused half-smile from the fisherman. Cigarettes are lit and greedily inhaled. The priest unlaces his shoes and sprawls over a picnic table, his enormous pack leaning within arm's reach. As soon as the Scouts finish eating, they discreetly pick up cigarette butts and spent matches and deposit them in the ashes beneath a barbecue grate. They are still hungry, but prepared to endure.

Although Avis was relieved early on to move farther and farther away from the eyes of town and has become more at ease with forest and trail, the vacant park unnerves her. It's another clear sign that she's left a recognizable life. As she sits with these strangers in an empty campsite, she finds herself wishing desperately for her grandmother to drive up, the way she sometimes did when Teddy kept Avis from catching the bus, leaving her to wait alone on the deserted steps of St. James's, hoping the wrong car wouldn't spot her and slow. Teddy considered this a good game. He would somehow finagle his own ride or wave down the bus a block from school, and fate would take over for Avis. How did her grandmother know those days to take that particular route home from the grocery or the beauty parlor, to glance at the empty school, those stone steps, see Avis's red-plaid bookbag and pull over? It must have seemed as if Avis darted out of nowhere, her knee socks drooping, her skirt askew, yet her grandmother always leaned over before the girl reached the car to push open the passenger door, envelop her in the comforting scent of Cashmere Bouquet. Sometimes, Avis even made it home before Teddy, clambering out of the car and running to the back door and up to her room, into the closet, before he had a chance to punish her. Occasionally, her grandmother took her along on her errand, pretending they were shopping together as usual. She'd leave Avis with her own grocery bag containing a few tins of soup or a sack of bakery rolls, as well as a private treat. *Don't tell the boy*, she'd tell Avis. *Stick it in your bookbag*. But Avis would always pay for the special treatment, even when her grandmother dropped her off on the next block. Teddy would slam her on the side of the porch, root through her bookbag, scattering homework assignments, until he found her grandmother's gifts: candy dots on paper strips or Tootsie Rolls or even a pretty flower pin, so easy to snap into pieces.

If her grandmother drove up now, her big black boat of a Buick swaying from side to side, would she take Avis back to her parents and Teddy, or like the man at the café who'd been saddled with Helen Hubka and Denis, peel out onto the highway, heading straight for the law? She can't help imagining crawling into that wide backseat, her face pressed into the wool car blanket, a three-legged stuffed rabbit tucked under her chin. Her bookbag strap is broken again. The Scouts assess the situation, offer potential fixes. If only we had . . . Karl begins, annoyed at the lapse in his preparations. Before he can end his lament, Jaspar Goode is crouching beside them, a thin piece of rope in his hands, and he is repairing the strap using a kind of knot that transfixes the Scouts.

"Would you show us that one?" Oren asks, gesturing toward the knotted rope.

And soon Jaspar Goode has rope in both boys' hands and is illustrating a thrilling series of loops and turns.

"*You* probably know all these," Jaspar Goode says to Caroline when he notices her watching.

His grin, rare and swift, enlivens his broad face, undoing all the hard planes so that he is a recognizable Goode, cheerfully capable. But she's puzzled. Why would she know even one of the knots he's demonstrating for the Scouts?

"No, the most intricate knot we do in kindergarten is this one." She holds out her hand for the rope, winds a loop, and demonstrates: "The rabbit comes out of the hole, goes 'round the tree, and back in the hole again."

Of course, the Scouts know how to tie a bowline. That and a slipknot were the first real ones they'd learned. The other knots, the ones Jaspar Goode has been showing them, are from another planet; nothing matches them in the Scouts' handbook, and they could spend a day mesmerized by his fingerwork, weeks listening to him describe all the circumstances in which each knot would shine. But he's still looking expectantly at the kindergarten teacher, Mrs. Weller, as if they both share a secret.

"Did you learn those in the army?" Caroline asks.

"Marines," he corrects. "And no." He pauses. "Jay Weller taught me every one," he says.

For the first time in ages, Caroline fully beams. Jay and his knots! The walls of his shed were practically draped in rope and line. Jay's version of bookshelves, those ropes—knowledge waiting on every shelf. Jay Weller studied and mastered every known knot and a few that were mere rumors, and he had more than a few stories to share as he fashioned and formed.

"Did he ever tell you about wind knots? The wizards?" Caroline asks, tickled when Jaspar Goode tilts his head and raises an eyebrow as if to say, *Go on.* Caroline is thrilled that she can remember precisely how Jay would tell the story. She can summon up his exact words.

"A fairy tale, maybe," she says, "but Jay swore he knew a fellow who . . . well, the story goes like this."

"Long ago, in some northern seaport, Norway or Lapland or maybe Finland," she begins in her warm, low voice, a voice that has eluded her for months, a voice that has soothed and enthralled a near generation of kindergartners. From the start, her words are an incantation, and her audience is rapt, Karl's mouth actually hanging open.

Yes, Caroline tells them, this happened long ago in Finland, in that slip of real time that seems to have eluded history books, when country wizards frequented the open markets. In their simple stalls, tucked in a byway of the bustling market, the wizards sold wishes and charms, and, importantly, *wind* wrapped up in bits of knotted cloth. A stilled sailor, pale from worry and sheltered air, his ship reeking of readiness and despair, might beeline through the market's gray winter, clatter straight to the wizards' stall, making his purchase without a moment's thought to bargaining. He wanted wind that much.

Back on board, he'd untie the first knot, his fingers stumbling with unwarranted impatience, for results took no time at all to appear. Just as he smoothed the corner of cloth, the wind would begin to nudge, and the ship would regain its cradlelike rock, the sails unfurling and flapping with pleasure.

For a brief time, the knots proved miraculously helpful, but wizards don't share magic that easily. Soon some began threading gales into their knots—or hurricanes. Even the most kindly, the ones who promised a trio of sweet, bouncing winds, knew that eventually a dilemma would arise. The poor sailors soon discovered that not even magic could protect them; they had to rely on their own always-fallible judgment. If his ship were becalmed, for instance, the sailor would have to decide when and if he should undo another knot. The wind might come of its own accord. Then again, it might not. So many places where a ship could be stranded, ghosting on an orphaned sea. Days, weeks. Could happen over and over again. Who could predict the wind's return?

"They didn't have meteorologists then," Oren explains to Karl, who knows that.

Of course he does.

Caroline continues: "Sailors hoarded the undoing of those knots, knowing that once they were unraveled and the cloth unbound, the wind might only stick around for a short time before they'd be becalmed once more. The hardest of choices, because no sailor could believe that the hardtack and salted beef, the tins of fish and jars of mead and water would last as long as they were needed if the wind abandoned them. No sailor—not even the most dull-witted or naïve—could discount a curse or profess no need for miracles."

While Caroline is talking, Jaspar Goode fiddles with a piece of rope, looping and twisting, dipping and tightening, undoing. Knots appearing, then vanishing beneath his clever hands.

"If I were a wizard," he asks, open rope dangling from his fingers, "what should I weave into my knots to make this walk a success?"

"Light," says Karl, who already fears the setting sun.

"Water," practical Oren says. His throat is always parched.

The languid voice of the priest floats over from the nearby picnic table. "Peace and love," he says, as a real cleric might, without a hint of irony.

Caroline is still thinking about wind, specifically a current that will lift her off a not-so-distant cliff.

Avis, examining her fingertips, is imagining a wild wind, too, but one that will claim her in a different way entirely, a surge of amplifying breath that will remake the weather within her so that she becomes unrecognizable, fierce.

"You can't, though. Can you?" Karl asks.

Oren all but cuffs his little brother on the side of the head.

"He's kidding," Oren says. "Aren't you?"

Jaspar Goode shrugs, admitting nothing, not even when a few moments later he hands each of the Scouts a little bit of rope with a single knot waiting to be unwound, a single wish granted.

"Hang on to it, kids," he says. "You never know."

"And me?" the priest says. "Got one for me?"

"A piece of work," Jaspar Goode says, as with even more labor, he finishes another knot and passes it to the priest. Though it's not clear to Caroline if he's referring to the knot or the priest, she does notice a twitch playing at the corner of Jaspar Goode's mouth that might be mistaken for amusement. Pleasing others suits him, she thinks.

Early on, Landon remarked that the longer the stop, the more difficult it would be to keep going, and Warren feels that truth in every fiber of his being. He has to resist pushing along the group, even as he too sinks onto a picnic bench, unties his boots, and takes a half sandwich from Avis, another apple from Mrs. Weller. Still, it doesn't take long before Warren feels compelled to take a kind of roll call. Landon had convinced him of the state park stop because of a promised telephone booth and backup from the campground hosts. The telephone is smashed, the receiver broken right out of the cradle, and the campground hosts are either absent or pretending to be. No help at all, it turns out, yet still Warren must ask. He climbs atop a picnic bench, and Landon gives one shrill whistle.

The Question: Anyone want to drop out? Anyone need to go home?

Boy, oh boy, is that a loaded question! If Warren only knew. Avis looks at the ground, Caroline off to the distance. Is the priest even awake? Oren reads out the miles they've covered. Thirty-one! No one should feel bad about leaving now. Thirty-one miles! What doesn't hurt? Yet not a one of them scrambles to stand or raises a weary hand, not even the priest, who, yes, is still sprawled over a mossy picnic table, catnapping. Warren is suddenly piercingly aware that if, say, that wisp of a girl does decide to drop out here, one of them will have to get her to safety. Is Avis his responsibility? What about the Scouts? Or even Mrs. Weller? He hopes not, but can't help hearing the President's words in his head, entreating him to bear the burdens of others, to make the weak secure, to be strong, to sacrifice.

Truthfully, Caroline is wrecked. Not one part of her is not in pain. She must look a fright, too, without the scarf, her hair frizzed and blown into her own knots. And yet, even as the physical part of Caroline flails, she feels no hesitation about continuing. A small, crucial part of her has arrived at the forefront—clear and patient and observant. As if to reinforce his third tenet, Jay liked to quote Shakespeare—"Nothing is either good or bad, but thinking makes it so"—and this attendant Caroline seems to have taken that as her own motto for this walk to the end of the world. Her good deed will lie in letting go, in one quiet leap into the sea. She tries to think of it as a homecoming. Why just recently, after the last America's Cup, the President himself made a speech almost declaring it so. Caroline should have cut his words out of the paper, popped them in her mouth, and fully ingested them. She wishes she had them with her, but really, does it matter? She memorized them, half thinking she'd share them later.

Listen, Jay, she would have said, rattling the paper with the President's speech:

"All of us have in our veins the exact same percentage of salt in our blood that exists in the ocean and, therefore, we have salt in our blood, in our sweat, in our tears. We are tied to the ocean. And when we go back to the sea whether it is to sail or to watch it—we are going back from whence we came."

Jay might have snorted, but she thinks it more likely that he would've had a theory of his own that would lead to the same conclusion. Of course, the sea was home to him. Of course, he'd gone home. I may be going crazy, Caroline thinks. Why does it matter that the President agrees?

"Okay, then," Warren says to the group.

Caroline can see the boy is relieved beyond measure that no one has raised a hand, an emotion that's quickly wiped out when the trailer door slaps open and a wizened man carrying a trembling shotgun emerges and right behind him, a big gray-haired woman in a man's plaid jacket, a large cast iron pan raised above her head, her lips twisted together as if holding back a scream.

"Yeesus," Landon mutters, jumping to his feet with shocking nimbleness.

Caroline grabs Avis by the shoulders and pulls her back. The priest, reclining easily a moment before, rolls and tumbles to crouch behind the picnic table next to his pack.

"Whoa now," Jaspar Goode says, advancing toward the couple, his hands out in front as if confronting an angry animal. Within seconds, the Scouts and Warren are beside him. The sight of the towheaded Scouts interrupts whatever attack the old couple intended.

"Lord, Dale," the woman breathes, "they're children."

"Where's your truck?" the fellow demands.

"We don't have a truck. We're walking," Warren begins, ready to offer his spiel.

"Walking?" the woman interrupts. "Out here? All of youse?" She lowers her frying pan.

"That lady?" She points to Caroline. "That girl?"

"Walking where?" the man asks, squinting as if he can discern their route if he looks hard enough.

The woman isn't finished. She spots Landon. "That old fellow?" she says.

The priest has rearranged himself while under the picnic table and returned to the fold. His jaunty cap has vanished, and his dog collar is now on full display as he too approaches the couple.

"Dale," the woman says, "they've got a priest with them."

"You're a church group?" she asks.

Dale and Rita Selznick, the campground hosts, are well into their seventies, older than Landon even, but fierce as all get-out—and also obviously shaken. Confusion fights with fear and wins. The shotgun—no, a boy's air rifle—is lowered, the frying pan placed on the trailer steps.

Ten minutes later, it's clear that what was meant to be a quick pit stop has turned into something else entirely. Rita Selznick has brought out a plate of warm gingerbread, her freckled hands ever trembling, and Caroline sits with an arm around the woman's shoulders. Dale has led the men to the ravaged pay phone beside the pit toilets. But it's the collateral damage on the madrone tree beside the pay phone that incenses the old man even more. *Arbutus*, Dale calls the tree, using the Canadian word, the Scouts notice. They've all passed that tree. Most of them have been facing it for almost a quarter of an hour, but not one of them has spotted what Dale saw almost the instant he left the trailer: pieces of the broken pay phone must have hit the tree trunk hard. It looks as if it's been attacked, hammered and sheared, the ground around it littered with shredded red bark. Over an hour ago, Dale is telling them. A truck rumbled into the campground, drove the loop once, then again, then one more time. Rita was baking, Dale tying flies—both only gradually coming awake to the oddness of that rhythm, an idling engine, the rumbling truck passing, then looping again. Over and over. Must have cruised through six or seven times.

"Rough engine, dirty carburetor, I thought," Dale says. "Maybe someone having engine trouble. Not many campers this time of year," he goes on, "but it happens, so I thought I'd best check, see if he needed help, was about to open the door when we heard a banging, like someone beating his fist against a metal wall, then breaking glass. A drunkard? A lunatic? Delinquents from the boys' camp over the other side of Spit Town? Maybe someone trying to scare us. But why? Why drive in and destroy the only pay phone for miles?"

Why, indeed. A wire of unease courses through the walkers, each remembering Helen Huhka's freak accident, her seeping, bandaged temple and blood-soaked trousers, her astonishing silence. Mishaps on such a long walk were bound to occur, but violence? In another group, a group with fainter hearts, a kind of reckoning might take place at this point, and perhaps only a few walkers would continue. But although startled, a few of the remaining walkers are not surprised that more danger may be circling. When they think about it—privately, of course—it's a wonder to each of them that it's taken so long, that they've been complacent, that they almost believed the real trial would lie in the physical act of moving, when in truth, the push forward is the simplest challenge they mean to face.

High clouds are galloping by overhead, the eastern sky pitch-gray behind them, while farther off, a watery blue lines the horizon and weak gold light bounces off the snowy peaks of the Olympics.

"Well, look there." Landon points, and they turn to see the longest rainbow Avis has ever beheld. The priest, stirred, begins to sing,

Somewhere over the rainbow, way up high
There's a land that I heard of once in a lullaby

Rita Selznick joins in with her sweet, warbling soprano.

Somewhere over the rainbow, skies are blue
And the dreams that you dare to dream really do come true

"Do you know what Miss Hubka told me?" Avis blurts out. "She swore the President calls Judy Garland nearly once a month and asks her to sing that song for him over the phone."

"Really?" Rita Selznick says. "Can that be true?"

"For a fact, Miss Hubka said. They're exceptionally good friends, she said. The President and Dorothy, that is."

Even Warren privately thinks that alliance makes sense.

Avis tells them how Helen Hubka had also added that Judy Garland never hesitates. The moment she recognizes the President's voice on the phone, she begins to croon, no matter who she's with, no matter where. *Day or night*, Helen Hubka had said, adding, mysteriously, *and I should know.* As if Helen Hubka herself is always tuned into the President's line, waiting for something to happen.

"I love that movie," Rita Selznick says with a sigh. She's gone all dreamy-eyed.

"The President was a Boy Scout, you know," Oren is saying, offering up what is to him the crucial personal presidential detail.

"And a sailor," Caroline adds with a smile.

"Not just a sailor. A naval officer," Dale Selznick says, entering the competition.

"A naval officer who swam miles in the open sea with an injured man on his damaged back after his PT boat was destroyed," Jaspar Goode says.

Almost as soon as the words are out of his mouth, he offers Caroline a puzzling look of apology. But she and the rest of the group are mesmerized by the image of a skinny Jack Kennedy, their hero President, browned and shirtless, bobbing amidst the wreckage of his ship as he shifted a near lifeless sailor onto his back and began to swim.

"Miles?" Karl marvels. "How?"

"Determination, I guess," Warren says. "He did what he had to do."

"You know that desk of his, in the White House, that *Resolute*—that's made of wood from a shipwreck, too," Dale Selznick says.

They all pause again, considering this confluence of the President, their hero, and the shipwreck he lives with.

"His back must not have been that bad," Oren finally says, his voice thick with hesitation.

But Avis remembers something else, another bit of Kennedy lore her father shared with Teddy when he'd had his appendix removed and had to stay in bed for a blessed week.

"It *was* really bad," Avis says. "When he finally left the navy, the president was taken straight to the hospital and had to stay there in bed for months and months, from May until December. He almost died."

"That poor man!" Rita says.

"In bed? For months?" Warren is incredulous.

"Oh, it's true," the priest agrees. "He was given the Last Rites, in fact. But, of course, he's a survivor, isn't he? He'd had the Rites before, too, as a child. Came back from the dead twice."

Back from the dead. With that last remark, at least a few of the walkers remember their own private resolutions. The Selznicks are settling in for company. Rita puts on a percolator in the trailer, while Dale produces a tin of a cellophane-wrapped, red-and-white-striped peppermints and hands them out like Halloween sweets to each walker. Yet almost as if on cue, the walkers get to their feet and ready themselves once more.

"Wait a sec," Rita says. She holds up their departure one more time to clamber back into the trailer and bring out what looks at first to be a transparent folded fan.

"Take this, hon," she says, handing it to Caroline, "for your hairdo."

Caroline's hair is a lost cause, and the plastic rain bonnet Rita's given her will only preserve the mess. Both women know that, but Caroline is almost brought to tears by the kindness and surprises herself by planting a thank-you kiss on the old woman's cheek.

"It won't be warm, but should keep the rain off," Rita says.

Avis can't help looking up at the sky, pure and clear for the last hour.

"Oh, it will rain, sweetie," Rita says. "No doubt of that. You'll have some kind of little storm before the night is through."

Caroline can't take her eyes off Rita and Dale, this elderly couple now absentmindedly holding hands. She thinks of how she and Jay leaned into one another as they watched Ginny walk toward her plane and Africa. For once, a sweet memory isn't tarnished with grief or longing or even envy, but instead washes over her, gratitude to have had that luxury.

"Will you two be okay?" she asks, knowing they won't, that their time together, too, will be limited.

"Sure, sure. Now that Dale has the gun out and the pellets in his pocket, he'll be on guard the rest of the day. Also, our boy Randall stops in every night on his way home from work. Every day but Sunday. We may go sleep up at his house tonight, I think," she adds, a tiny trembling beginning anew.

Landon and Warren are having another confab with the map, this one with old Dale chiming in. The Scouts are called back, pencils produced, alterations made. The rest of the route was supposed to be a straight shot on the Old Highway to Spit Town and beyond, only the last leg on the road to the viewpoint. With that unnerving truck in mind, Dale offers another idea.

"Take out your compasses, boys," Landon tells the Scouts. Pencils and maps.

Only Avis, scribbling stop-and-go times in her own little notebook, lifts her head to see the priest drawing constellation pictures with his foot again, this time not far from the phone box and the strange red-barked tree.

Arbutus, Avis repeats to herself. *Madrone.*

Damage, she thinks. Ruin.

Why would anyone need a drawing for what was so clearly evident?

SURRENDER, AVIS

In the movie Rita Selznick loves so much, everyone abandons the aptly named Dorothy Gale as a terrible storm, a twister, descends. Down into the cellar go the three farmhands and Dorothy's uncle, pulling along her worried aunt, still hollering into the heaving wind for Dorothy, while a little farther afield, the kindly shyster, Professor Marvel, battens down the hatches of his traveling wagon.

"Poor kid," he says to no one. "I hope she gets home all right."

But she doesn't. Dorothy rescues her little dog Toto too late to gain admittance to the storm cellar and so hurries into the farmhouse, a frail refuge, it seems, because a moment later, the house shakes, Dorothy is knocked to the ground, and the twister carries the farmhouse away.

The first time Avis watched *The Wizard of Oz*, she'd been certain Dorothy died in those first minutes. As the farmhouse swirled away from Kansas, images from Dorothy's life flashed before her, just as Avis had heard would happen. When nasty Almira Gulch was revealed as the even more terrifying Wicked Witch, Avis knew she must pay close attention. And when the farmhouse crash-landed, and Dorothy opened the door to Oz, Avis was riveted by the vision of an afterlife not in heaven, not in hell, but in a place decidedly more interesting, a place where Dorothy didn't need to be saintly or evil but maybe something in between. In one swift stroke, she became a refugee, a hero, a thief, a murderer—everything, everyone, all at once. Oz made good sense to Avis—the mixture of gaiety and terror and personal dreams suffused with the imposter's constant fear of being thought to be something you were not. She watched raptly, never flinching, even as the winged monkeys appeared, even as the Wicked Witch filled the sky of the Emerald City with the dire command: *Surrender, Dorothy*. Of course,

Dorothy didn't surrender. Dorothy triumphed. Such a blow then when, at the movie's end, Dorothy wakes in that stark Kansas bedroom, back in her dim world, a child once more. Avis had never been so disappointed. Ruby slippers be damned. Avis would never have clicked her heels together, not even once.

"I want to go home," one of the girls in Teddy's found bomb shelter had cried.

"Why?" Teddy asked. In lantern light, the only light, the one he kept beside him, Teddy pointed out the shelves of supplies, mostly Spam, saltines, and peanut butter, the board games, the bucket toilet in a corner.

"We have everything we need," he said.

The other girls began to cry, too.

Teddy had been more than annoyed. He'd done so much work. He had found the empty bomb shelter in an empty wooded lot on the far side of the ballfield, an abandoned place in early winter, and stocked the shelves himself, readied for his game. *A good one*, he'd promised Avis. He had waited for the girls as they left the school together with Avis and walked with them, convincing them block by block to come see what he'd found, even as he pretended to shoo Avis away. He had led them into the shelter and put up with their flirting and their chatter and, too soon, their tears. Avis was late. Not long after the door closed behind them, Avis should have lit the cherry bombs and M-80s he had carefully set up around the bomb shelter. The girls would think the attack they'd feared for months hadn't been forestalled at all. This time, he wanted to be in the shelter with them to see the panic he could engender. Avis wasn't afraid of fireworks or matches, but he'd shortened the fuses a little to give her a little scare as well. A fabulous plan, but Avis, who had one job to do, was late, and the girls were getting tiresome.

No one would be hurt, Teddy had said. Just a good game. If she didn't do it, she'd pay again and again and again. Still, she hesitated, until finally she took out the box of matches Teddy had pushed at her. *Begin at the edges*, he'd told her, *and light the ones beside the door last.* He wanted to watch the terror build. But after Avis lit the first one and it went off too loudly and too quickly, nearly singeing her hand, she ran and struck a match on the one closest to the door. Once, twice, three times. She couldn't get the match to light. And just as she finally had, just as she'd managed to keep the flame long enough to light the two M-80s Teddy had left against the shelter, just as Avis herself began to run away, the shelter door swung open, and the terrified girls emerged, running right into the explosion.

In some ways, Teddy could not have engineered a more satisfying outcome.

"Avis!" he'd shouted into the mayhem of shrieks and screams. "What have you done?"

She could have run then. She could have been the one to go for help, to tell the truth. Instead, she'd submitted, following Teddy's every instruction, waiting with the bleeding, hysterical girls while Teddy sauntered to the nearest house.

"There's been an accident," he said, and he'd meant it, she knew.

Dorothy's ruby slippers remind Avis of her own burden, another en chanted object, if Helen Hubka is to be believed. The golden bauble hidden in her bookbag can't take her home to a placid Kansas bedroom surrounded by love, but one thing is for sure, at least for a little while, the stolen treasure Avis carries oh so lightly now, the treasure that pushed her on this walk, can keep her, too, from surrendering.

CARRYING ON

Must be Jaspar Goode who's placed the image in Caroline's head, she thinks, as the walkers begin again in a line that continually unfurls and turns and tightens. The walk now carries the illusion of honest work in that twining, and she can almost imagine Jay observing from a great distance as the walkers break off into their own threads. Even more fancifully, she imagines the twists and turns of the walkers are due to Jay practicing from afar the skill at which he excelled. Knotting, unknotting, pulling tightly, releasing. Pairing and separating, pairing again. (Alchemy. Physics. Is one more mystical than another?) In the distance, the Scouts pivot to allow Warren to take the lead, then file up so that Warren is between them. Jaspar Goode and Avis pull well ahead of Caroline, even as the priest, who's been keeping company near Avis, falls back and takes up with Landon for several miles. Theirs seems the oddest of pairings: the priest, chatty and discursive; the old typesetter, laconic to the point of rudeness. At some point, that duo breaks and the priest sidles up beside Caroline. Inexplicably, he's peeling a hard-boiled egg, which of course he offers to her.

"Share with me?" he asks.

She can't help smiling. How do you share a single boiled egg? One bite at a time, it turns out. Companionably. The egg smells faintly of stale beer and cigarettes, but it's oddly satisfying.

A few moments later, the egg finished between them, the priest cheerily lopes forward again, his now-familiar silhouette somehow vaulting this line of walkers and reappearing in the distance, not far behind Warren and the Scouts. Avis tramps along behind Jaspar Goode, mimicking his wide stride as best she can, as though trying to place her own shoes in his footsteps. The two of them seem to fade in and out, as if they've found a way to walk behind the dimming light, so that each time Caroline looks up, she has to struggle to discern Jaspar Goode's camouflage, his little Avis shadow. Caroline soon finds herself ambling along in Landon's company. Landon is the constant, she thinks. While the others shift company and positions, he holds the back of the line, his gait always steady, a brown cigarette (lit or not) always in hand. He waves one in her direction.

"Welcome to the caboose," he mutters.

"You don't mind the company?"

"Company? What company is that?" he says, a tiny smirk on him.

Landon, Caroline knows, is one of the Old Boys of town, the kind whose idea of a good joke is to notice a bygone high school acquaintance, now a proper housewife, practicing decorum in the busy line at the market, and call out to her. *Shirl! Good to see you in daylight again. Your old man out of jail yet?* What delight the Old Boy would derive from the stunned recoil of the crowd around the housewife, whose embarrassed laugh—*Oh, you!*—never came quickly enough to offset the shocked inhale, the exchanged glances, the furrowed brows that would follow the blushing woman right out of the store.

Caroline's too quick for him.

"Only the wisest, I hope," she counters, "for my sake. What is it the Bible says: *He that walketh with wise men shall be wise: but a companion of fools shall be destroyed?*"

"Good luck to you then, Missus," Landon says, but Caroline can tell by the deepened twist of his mouth he's amused.

She's "known" Landon for years, but doesn't know him at all. Her late mother-in-law used to blush whenever the Wills brothers' names were mentioned: Landon and Pete. But Caroline couldn't even manage to keep them in focus. Two gray-whiskered fellows, onetime randy bachelors. *So crazy good-looking*, Jay's mother would whisper, red-faced, as if releasing a confidence. Pete was pretty much a recluse now, a near rumor, who, according to Jay, sometimes appeared at the VFW, barely managing to finish a beer before he pushed off again. Landon wasn't much better socially, although he was a downtown fixture, showing up to typeset the weekly paper and set up the long newsprint rolls with pasted text. Caroline had taken her kindergarteners to the newspaper office on a field trip the year Warren was in her class, leaving with the end rolls of newsprint that served painting projects half the year. Landon had been there, of course, a bulwark between the roving line of children and his precious linotype machine.

"Watch out for the monster in the corner," Warren's father jokingly cautioned the kindergartners, and Caroline wasn't sure whether he meant the massive linotype machine with its grinding moving parts, those enticing metal letters, or the typesetter himself. When Warren's father suggested Landon might demonstrate to the children how to lay a line of type, Landon pretended deafness and went off to smoke in the breakroom, clearly irritated at the invasion and utterly immune to the charms of fifteen hopping, giggling, itchy-fingered five-year-olds.

For years, Caroline has found herself apologizing for that single field trip every time she and Landon cross paths, and she might again. She can feel the words coming when they pass by a tiny settlement of houses, six or seven bungalows, and a woman taking down laundry from a line pauses to gawk at them and wave. Caroline has been alone for so many weeks that this long day with company has skewed her perceptions. It's only as she waves back that she realizes how few other people the walkers have come across over the hours. True, they've kept to isolated byways and winter-silenced trails, but Caroline now finds it curious that they've been able to walk for so many hours without encountering more than a handful of souls. The hobo, of course. The café. Rita and Dale. Since they emerged from the woods, their route has steadfastly skirted nearly every sign of civilization. From time to time, figures appear beside them on narrower, adjacent trails— relations, no doubt, of those Forgotten Bay hobos. A head might jerk up at their approach, registering the murmur of the walkers' conversation, the red flash of a Boy Scout kerchief, before the figures swiftly ease farther into the shadows. Once, as their group waited to cross a narrow country road, a station wagon rolled by and an entire family cheered (or jeered at) them, the family's faces all but smashed against the car windows. Mostly, though, the walkers have moved through the day, across miles and miles, unnoticed and undisturbed by human interaction. If she had known it was possible to walk across the peninsula without acknowledging others, Caroline would have embarked upon this journey months ago. Other than the difficulty on Quarry Road and, of course, that unsettling encounter between Helen Hubka and wayward rocks, and yes, the ruckus at the state park, the terrain has been pleasant, the turns intuitive, curving away from any potential difficulties before they appear. While the Boy Scouts and Warren almost always stay at the front, often well out of sight, they are the best of guides, following Landon's revised map religiously and even notching trees to guarantee the way will be clear to those who follow. No need. If, say, the priest begins to wander toward one of those shadowy trails or Avis, deep in thought, misses a turn, Landon, at the far back of the line, seems to feel the mistake in the soles of his own worn brown boots. More than once, he's shouldered past to set a wayward walker straight. It's like a dance, this walk, and Landon is expert in all the steps.

"How do you know this route so well?" she asks him.

Of course, he doesn't answer straightaway. Caroline knows to wait. They walk in silence for whole minutes before Landon says, "Been walking out to the West End for years. Tried every which way until we found the ones we liked best."

"You and Pete?"

"Oh, sure, sometimes Pete, too. All of us. Me and Pete and Jenny."

"Jenny? A girlfriend?" Caroline teases, remembering her mother-in-law's stories.

"My wife," Landon says.

"You're married?" Caroline can't keep the astonishment out of her voice. "How did I not know that?"

Landon shakes his head and takes a long drag of his cigarette before exhaling slowly.

"She passed," he says. "Long while ago now."

"I'm so sorry," Caroline says, using those inadequate words. But she is sorry for him, truly aggrieved—and stunned. Landon, shrouded in his own smoke, has suddenly become more visible to her. Another man hidden inside a familiar façade.

"You know, I gotta confess I'm no big fan of Jack Kennedy," he says, "but he and I actually have something in common. D'you know he and his missus had a little girl before the one with your name? The first one didn't make it. Stillborn, just the same. Funny thing is, they gave that one the same name Jenny picked out for our girl. *Arabella*. Not a common name, I'd say."

"I'm so, so sorry," Caroline says again.

Then the old fellow does the most astonishing thing: He pats her arm, gives her hand a little squeeze. "Yup, I know you are, hon," he says.

In his surprisingly gentle voice, Caroline hears the town's knowingness and wonders if her plans have been sussed out, if Landon's been sent along on the walk for the sole purpose of bringing her back alive. With a pang, too, she remembers those little dresses of Ginny's riding along in the blood-spattered train case. Not for the first time on this walk, she wonders if she's being handed clues. C'mon, Jay, she thinks, help me out here. Tell me, tell me, why?

"It's the way of the world," Landon continues after a long beat of silence. "The folks gone, even Jenny's. Me and Pete are sitting in the front row now." He waves his brown cigarette around as if showing her the sights. "Might as well get a good view, eh?" he says. "As we carry on."

Carry on? Not Caroline. Is she a coward, she wonders? Or just wiser than this old man who's spent a good chunk of his life hurting and missing, hiding his terrible grief. What if she did carry on? What if she managed to embrace a life like Landon's, singed with bitterness, and head back to the classroom without the capacity for joy? Without a single real answer? Briefly, she imagines her kindergartners with Landon as their teacher. She winces at the image. No, she's not fit for living any longer. There is no cure for her kind of brokenness.

A trilling sound reaches Carolyn and Landon as if a real nature show's about to commence, but it's only the mind-reading priest whistling his way into song. The tune gradually becomes clearer as the whistle winds down and the priest's clear sweet voice warbles the words to an Irving Berlin song Jay used to sing (oh so badly) to Caroline.

What'll I do
when you
are far away
and I'm so blue?
What'll I do?

She slows, wipes her eyes, a new wave of exhaustion arriving.

What'll I do
with just
a photograph
to tell my troubles to?
When I'm alone
with only dreams of you
that won't come true
what'll I do?

Caroline feigns an urgent need to take a swig of water from Jay's canteen, and she and Landon end up pausing long enough to put distance between them and the priest's high, pretty song-ending whistling. Landon lights another brown cigarette. Together, they let the new silence gather until Caroline says, "He's not a real priest, is he?"

Landon shakes his head, spools out a thin stream of smoke.

"Course he ain't," he says as the smoke clears.

HIDDEN TALENTS

The blued hour of dusk, light seeping away, and the walk has become a trudge along what feels like an endless rutted driveway, dipping and rising between a mossy, swampy stand of trees. Firs, Avis guesses, using her new knowledge. Black firs and the thin white trunks of . . . alders—yes, she decides, alders—faintly glowing. But no God's rays in there, she notes as she tries to peer between the trees, no brilliant beams caressing fern beds. Night has already arrived in those woods. A putrid scent, not cow manure but something close. Rot. These woods are the stuff of fairy tales, dense and twisted and, aside from the alder trunks, nearly lightless. Nearly. There must be light, because shadows slink. More than one. Avis tries to quell her worries. No one else seems to notice. Far ahead, the Scouts and Warren are less than shadows themselves. They will all have to meet in Spit Town, if only for a brief check-in, so that Landon can make sure they remain on the right route. Mileage will be noted once again, as well as time. It goes unsaid that the usual offer will be presented, and although Avis can't imagine any-one yet accepting, she can see that Caroline's head is down, she's watching her every step, her gaze holding tightly to the sight of the so-called priest's worn black brogues or the kerchief tied to the end of his pack like a flag. They are all busy, navigating each root and rise.

Yet Avis wants to close her eyes. She wants to listen closely. She wants the two child Scouts to loop back and walk beside her, explaining away the shushing and crackles she hears in the adjacent underbrush. She wants to listen to them confidently chattering, telling her again about tiny harmless burrowing creatures or masterful impersonators or clever tricksters. Instead she hears—she is sure of this—a gutteral rumbling.

Never run, the Scouts had told her. *You'll become prey if you do.* Advice she should have been given at birth, she thinks.

The narrow lane pinches, widens again, and for a few minutes they are walking through what appears to be the remnants of an abandoned town. Not a real town, the boys would tell Avis, a *once-upon-a-time-town, an abandoned place.* The Peninsula is thick with such ruins, relics of a hopeful time when most commerce was dependent upon the great ships that traveled up and down the coast and through these waters. It seemed inevitable that towns would spring up—until the arrival of trains and the combustion engine, that was. End times for many burgeoning settlements. They sloughed into mere outposts for loggers or wayfarers, while the rest of civilization went to farm in Spit Town or work in the mills or travel south to the big city. Through the day, the walkers have passed the crumbled remnants of single cabins, some not much bigger than an outhouse, some with only a single wall remaining. Once, a plank door standing all alone in a blackberry thicket.

This is different.

Avis thinks the single block of buildings looks like a toy town or a dreamscape, fabricated out of jumbled images from all the television she's watched or the library books she's gulped down. Westerns mixed with fairy tales and historical biographies. *That* would be a post office; *that* a general store. *That* skinny tower? Would *that* be the school? Would there even be a school? A part of her wants to linger behind and try every door, roam from room to room. Teddy would hate this place. He'd take one look at it and know it would hold nothing for him. A light in an upper window catches Avis's eye and startles her, but it is quickly extinguished, even as she realizes it must only be the last shards of late-afternoon sunshine darting against the old, wavy glass. Even after they leave the buildings behind, they are still, it seems, in the almost-town. An abandoned lane runs parallel to the track they follow, reminding Avis of the ghost trails the hobos traveled along earlier in the day. Here the trees are more familiar to Avis, deciduous ones like at home, though these too are a tattered bunch. Funny that she doesn't know *their* names, even though she recognizes the broad canopies, the high crevices, the black limbs snaking toward and crossing one another. When the skulking shadows return this time, she recognizes them, too, even before a low growling, one that cannot be ignored or misunderstood, commences.

The sore muscle in Caroline's neck has announced itself again, pulsing painfully straight up the back of her head. She tilts her head from side to side in an effort to break its hold on her. Even her coat feels heavy on her shoulders, though she carries little in her pockets save those multiplying tiny apples. Ahead, the priest maintains his enviably light step. He munches from little packets of oyster crackers he must have picked up at the café and jauntily tosses around the bit of rope Jaspar Goode handed him back at the campground. Jaspar's gift knot to the priest is a pretty one, much smaller but akin to one Jay used to tie around the end of an oar. Jay called his fist of a knot a Poor Man's Turban, and as Jaspar Goode's simpler version sways with the priest's play, Caroline sees a polished oar ready to push off into rough waters. Perhaps because she knows the knot is meant to be stationary, to hold even another rope steady, the priest's constant swinging makes her uneasy, as if the knot itself might break loose and shoot through the air. She is about to call out to him with a warning when several things happen at once. Jaspar Goode appears beside Caroline, Avis, and the priest, pushing Caroline forward on the lane.

"Keep moving," Jaspar Goode whispers at them. But the priest takes one look over his shoulder and stops short, shrugging his pack to the ground. For a moment, it seems he might begin swinging his rope wildly, his own deep rumbling commencing.

"Oh, hell," says Landon. "Here we go."

Instead of springing into action, the priest appears to be praying, his head lowered as he turns to approach the trouble that's found them.

Before long, three dogs separate the priest from the others. Only three. None of them particularly big, but the noise, the noise. Deep growls escalating into snapping and snarling. Caroline feels them rumbling under her feet, sparking through her body. Every pain has vanished, replaced by a paralyzing fear.

"Keep moving," Jaspar Goode says again, close to her ear. "Slowly. *Don't* run. Don't look back."

With that nudge, Caroline puts one foot in front of the other, one hand reaching back as if to grasp Avis. But Avis doesn't take her hand, and as soon as she is out of sight of the dogs, as soon as the growls that burrow into the ground and throttle the air begin to fade, the fear that stiffened her legs turns electric, and against all instruction, Caroline is running. It won't take long, she thinks. Either the dogs will break free or attack and, packlike, run her down, or she and Avis will reach the others and, together, they'll form their own pack. Somewhere, not that far ahead, Warren and the Scouts are chugging along, oblivious to the danger. They hardly turn when Caroline, finally rushes up behind them, limping, her hair awry, and she can barely gasp out the story. Warren's ready to race back, but it's the young Scouts who stop him.

"Wait," they say to themselves as much as to Warren. "We should wait here."

The light continues to sheave away. In the silence, they imagine they hear snarling and yelps, the deep-throated commands of men. Yet for far too long, they hear nothing save the low wind. Where is Avis? Caroline is about to call out when the priest appears—with the dogs. She takes in a sharp breath. Her arm shoots out as if to protect the boys. But the priest seems unconcerned. The dogs circle and huddle around him, but their menacing aspect has seeped away. They are just dogs now, greedily milling about, waiting for the priest to throw them another scrap of whatever he seems to hold in one hand. The long rope dangles from his other hand, but Jaspar Goode's complicated knot has vanished. The priest winks at them as he passes, a newly ordained pied piper, and without another word, the Scouts and Warren follow, Warren shaking his head at what he presumes was Caroline's unwarranted hysteria.

Caroline lingers. Where *is* Avis?

Avis is in the trees.

More precisely, she is *standing* on a broad limb of one of the lost town's sycamores, high enough off that ground that the sound of her voice calling out to Jaspar Goode and Landon confounds the men until they tip their heads back and squint upward. The lowest branches are well above their own heads, and Avis, it seems, is even higher. It's as if the girl has flown there.

"Well, hell," Landon grunts. "How're we gonna get that one down?"

Jaspar Goode is already rummaging through his diminished rope supply when Caroline rejoins them. She, too, has to arch her neck and peer through the gloom to see Avis. The contours of Avis, that is, because the girl herself is barely visible.

"Hang on, Avis," Caroline calls out. She is well-practiced in calming anxious children.

But Avis doesn't hear her. Above the girl, crows are going wild, not complaining—more like congratulating. Bits of tree bark and lacy pale-green lichen rain down upon Avis like confetti. They, at least, know that the girl doesn't need rescuing.

"Whoa!" Landon says.

Caroline, too, cries out, startling Jaspar Goode. The three of them are riveted as they watch Avis seemingly stride through midair, across that broad sycamore right into another, landing lightly on a lower, narrower branch. From there, she twirls into a red leaf maple, and with another horrifying (thrilling) acrobatic feat, *onto* a slim alder, twining its trunk until she is back on earth, tramping through the undergrowth to join them again on the trail. With one last astonishing gesture, she tosses a handful of rocks she's been clutching over her shoulder, back into the brush.

Avis's long hair is full of twigs and leaves, one cheek is scratched, and her knuckles are reddened, but the slouch in her shoulders has vanished, and she is beaming, those uncanny blue eyes brightened, her face—her being—somehow *intensified*. The three adults can't stop staring at her, reconsidering, as she kicks mud from the spongy undergrowth off her once-pristine school shoes. For clearly, Avis is not the girl they thought she might be—a city child, cowed by nature, beset by shyness. Her bookbag, Caroline notices, is tucked within her buttoned-up coat. She's done this before, Caroline thinks.

"Glad to get you back on solid ground," Jaspar Goode finally says. "You'd make a good rigger, that's for sure."

A slight smile plays around the corners of his mouth, and even though Landon hasn't stopped shaking his head, he too can't seem to take his eyes off the girl until she herself breaks the spell.

"Look!" this newly assertive Avis commands, pointing ahead.

Perhaps it's because they are walking westward, but no one can remember the sunrise. Daylight crept over them in early morning, the black sky only grudgingly giving way to heavy gray clouds, that constant misting they've already consigned to a distant past. But the sunset, *this* sunset, cannot be denied. Before them, the retreating blue sky is streaked with pinks and magenta and a swirling, swelling orange, watery yellow light breaking free so that even now, in the gloaming, one final brilliance streams before them, paving the lane ahead with a pure, unwavering gold.

FIRST DATE

After she drops off her hitchhiker at the far edge of Spit Town—*Let him walk,* Remy would have ordered. *What are you? A goddamn chauffeur?*—Karin Johansson circles back to meet Remy, her heart thudding when she spots his old truck idling in wait. (*For her!*) In tandem, they rattle up the potholed road to the Spit Town dump, Remy plowing right into the chain that blocks the entrance. Who will notice a few more scratches and dents on that old farm truck? Shame about losing the Plymouth, Karin thinks. Not her style, but better than the truck, for sure. Of course, her conniving cousin had taken the best. But what does Karin care now? She has her sweet blue Chevy, waxed and polished and perfumed, not one hint of the Plymouth's stink. She even picked up a cute hitchhiker. That boy sure appreciated Karin's getup. She waits to see if Remy will be equally impressed, though it's already too dark for the full effect, she guesses, even though she's managed to flick on the dome light. He says nothing as he shoves a case of beer into the backseat and tosses a flask on the dash. He is, she notices, still wearing a workshirt stained with sheep grease and covered in what might be wood shavings. But Karin doesn't complain. Karin doesn't cower. That was her cousin's role. If anything, she grows steelier. She won't needle either. She'll give him room to vault whatever grudge he's stewing over.

"Your right headlight is out," he says as he rummages through her glove box for the flashlight he put in there the last time. His first words to her tonight.

His second: "Those the only shoes you got? You can't help me in those."

Karin glances down to where his flashlight illuminates her pretty heels. She raises an eyebrow, says nothing. No way she'd change out of these shoes, even if she had a pair of barn boots right beside her.

"Well, stay here, then," he barks.

Another woman might take offense, but Karin only hears affection. He's taking care of her, leaving her out of this last cleanup task. She sips from the flask as he empties the bed of the truck, hurling at least one crib into the abyss. She sips some more while he opens her car's trunk and unloads even more of their crap. She keeps her headlights on, a risk, but the narrow lane of light allows her to observe his tightly muscled figure as he hoists and pitches bundles into the great pit. Afterward, she watches too as he strips in the chill evening to change his shirt, and the smell of him, sour and earthy, carries the horse barn and their wild assignations into her car. Her man.

Remy gets a whiff of something entirely different.

"What's that stink?" he says. "You wearing aftershave now?"

Karin laughs, but he grabs her hand and leans in, sniffing.

"Not me," she says. "I picked up a hitchhiker."

"You picked up a fellow?"

He squeezes her hand so tightly that Karin feels her bones shift as if breaking and reconfiguring in the mold of his. A test, maybe. Or a gift, she thinks. She smiles at him under the car's dome light.

"Just a stupid high school kid," Karin says. "Chasing a girl in Spit Town."

His grip loosens. "A girl?"

"His sister, he said. A runaway," Karin elaborates. "Got the feeling he wants to teach her a lesson."

She's ready to explain, mock the boy for Remy, but he's lost interest. He's dropped her hand and is giving her instructions. He'll drop the truck off behind the Esso station in Spit Town, he's telling her. They can cruise around in her car. Or maybe they *should* take the truck. With that headlight going out on her car and all. It finally dawns on Karin that he's forgotten their date or wants it to take place in the car—with a half-empty flask and a case of beer. This, finally, is too much for Karin. She's waited months for this night.

"Nah-uh," she says, shaking her head. She shrugs off her beaded wrap so that he can see at least a glimmer of her tight blue sheath. *Goddamn*, she wants to shout, *Look at me!* But, as ever, she waits.

Her patience pays off. She can feel his mood loosening as he takes her in.

"What? Here?" His voice rumbles in a way she well recognizes.

Despite the welcome heat coming off him—for her!—Karin draws her line. He must get the full effect of her finery, unmussed. She wants to see him get riled up on her behalf, too, as heads turn in the cocktail lounge, and other men see what she can be.

"The Lounge. I'll meet you at the Lounge."

"Please yourself," he grunts, backing off her. (Yes, her cousin near-ruined him.) But he gets into his truck and follows her back down into Spit Town, even waits in the back of the bowling alley parking lot while she reapplies her lipstick in her rearview mirror and smooths out her skirt.

"Now that's a woman." He wolf-whistles once he sees her under the street-lights. Finally, he runs his eyes up and down, taking her all in—the dress, the makeup, those high, high heels—and Karin feels the tight casing of her being, the narrow-faced girl slapped over by desolation and rejection, fully crack open, and this marvelous creature, the true version of Karin, emerge, a little bent-shouldered at first, a little rickety on her heels perhaps. But no, it doesn't take long before she can tip her pointed chin up again. She has won. She kisses him, lets him rub her hand down the front of him.

"Good bitch," he murmurs into her hair as he maneuvers through the cars, past the bowling alley entrance, and into the brassy light of the Lanes Lounge, Spit Town's finest.

SPIT TOWN

MILE 39

The proper name is Spetletown, an aberration itself. Early German settlers apparently misheard or purposely translated the Indian word for the Olympic Mountains, *S'ngazanelf*, as "spet shelf," immediately assuming the word referred, not to the mountains behind them, but to the shape of the land, a flat stretch, long and slender, that jutted out into yet another bay; a spet, a spit. Hence *Spetletown*, sometimes called Spetleton, commonly known as Spit Town. The settlement sits smack in the rainshadow, so is seldom subject to the winter rain deluges that affect Warren's town. A sunny oasis in a gloomy land, the flat fields of Spit Town are also remarkably fertile, and the stench of cow dung, piercingly present in the new dark, announces the community well before the walkers reach the edge of the town's borders.

Warren supposes this is the second wind his track coach has rhapsodized over. A half hour before, they all were dragging, stumbling in the quickened night. The hot spot that developed on Warren's right heel was aflame, and he slowed to accommodate the pain, which mercifully vanished with a twist and repositioning of his sock. Mrs. Weller must have hit a similar snag; she was as close to tears as she could be. Avis and the Scouts might have been sleepwalking, dragging step by step, Avis no longer jumping at every sharp note, every scuttle in the brush beside them. Even in shadows, Warren could see the hitch in Landon's gait, the flinch he concealed by stopping to relight one of his thin cigars. Jaspar Goode showed what might be his fatigue by pausing and stretching. Only the priest seemed strangely unaffected, as if he undertook this walk every day of his life. The dogs he'd charmed had left one by one without consequence or goodbyes, as if remembering tasks or a waiting supper or responding to a far-off whistle. The priest hardly seemed to notice.

Warren is the first to use his flashlight again. As the beam arises behind them, the Scouts come awake, and soon their own flashlights are in hand. Too, as they crest the trail and begin the descent into Spit Town, a ripple runs through the winter-scrub grasses around them, as if they have been joined by shadowy runners, urging them on. Slowly, the energy of the walk is reclaimed. The wind tastes of that cow dung, but also wood smoke, and the combination conjures comfort. It's well past twilight now, yet hours before any moonrise. They've managed to regroup, and in a single line they tightwalk the narrowing trail, picking along as carefully as they did much earlier in the (same!) day when mud and puddles and massive tree roots littered the way forward. At the very point where the trail ends— a graveled edge of road—the beams from their encircling flashlights refract back and momentarily blind them. It takes more than a few minutes and a slowed group advance before they understand they've encountered a hill of broken glass, the far edge of the vast Spit Town dump, and skirt around it, half on tiptoe, leaping from one clear spot to another, until finally they reach the long, rutted track that is the dump road. A real road. Another two miles and they land, with deep relief, on a narrow, paved one that signals the next long leg before they enter Spit Town.

It's almost nine o'clock when the first of them file into the town proper and slump in front of the gas station Warren designated at their Spit Town meeting spot. The walkers are traveling as a group again when Warren announces the time, and young Oren the more important number. Thirty-nine miles. An admirable figure. Anyone might quit now and feel triumphant, but none of them seems inclined, though it's clear that it's nearing bedtime for the Scouts—and likely Caroline and Landon, too, and the priest has gone back to humming, a habit, Warren realizes, that is relegated to populated areas. As Avis fiddles with the phone booth's door, Warren pulls out a red coin purse, still heavy with nickels and dimes, before he sees the notebook and pencil emerging from her pocket and realizes she's only using the phone booth's light to record the time.

In Spit Town, nearly every business is shut up tight, including the gas station. The only ones open sit side by side: a cocktail lounge and the eight-lane bowling alley, both of which must also be near to closing. The priest finds a hose and faucet behind the gas station, and canteens are filled. Should they stop? Get more food? If only, Warren thinks again, Humtown had rallied behind them as other towns had their walkers, then they would have been met at critical junctures with fruit juice and sandwiches, big wide backseats in which to momentarily stretch and rest. Dry socks. Quarter-hour breaks, half hour at the most. No need for recalibrations, decisions. Instead, the walkers are on their own, and nearly every one of them is thinking it's damn cold and, look, lights are still on in the bowling alley.

"No more than fifteen minutes," Warren warns.

"Wait," Caroline says.

All of them appear unkempt, but under the weak glow from the phone booth, a still-glittering Avis looks downright feral. Landon offers up a clean cotton hanky, which Caroline soaks with water from Oren's canteen. She gently scrubs Avis's face clean and brushes off her jacket. She combs twigs and leaves from the girl's wild hair, smoothing and plaiting until a new Avis is revealed, taller somehow and more polished, with one long, silky braid held tightly by a rubber band the priest just happened to be wearing on his wrist.

"Okay, at least one of us is presentable," Caroline says, as she steps back.

An understatement, to be sure.

ON THE TOWN

Remy downs Rainiers and whiskey shots, one after the other, as if cauterizing the last of his open wounds. Cocktails are new to Karin, but she has contorted her initial grimace into a smirk, her approximation of sophisticated appreciation, and is steadily working through martinis. One, two—she is determined to order at least one more before the Lounge closes when she spots a fellow all dressed in black blatantly eyeballing her from the end of the bar. He's slipped off the varsity jacket, she notices, but it's there beside him for anyone to see. Who let the kid in here? And how long has he been there spying on her with Remy?

Do not, she orders him silently, *Do Not Come Over Here*.

But as one couple leaves, then another, Teddy shifts over a few stools, then a few more, until he's sitting mere feet away from Remy and Karin, who now can't escape hearing his conversation. They are among the last patrons, and though the kitchen has closed and the waitresses seem about ready to call it a night, the boy—that *Teddy*—is now charming the smitten barmaid with his tale of woe, the runaway sister, as if they have all night.

"I hate to admit it, but she's a thief, too," he's saying. "She may have gone off on this adventure to swipe a few things. She's stolen before."

"Like what?" the barmaid breathes.

"Oh, you name it. Jewelry, stamps, fancy gloves, rare coins. Even silly things like children's toys. She has a little blue suitcase at home, and I'm always finding treasures in there."

If Remy were sober, he might have put the pieces together right quick. As it is, the words initially drift over him without making purchase, an increasingly annoying blather that soon has him scowling at the pretty boy who's keeping the barmaid from delivering their final round.

When he barks at the girl, pointing to the drinks waiting at the pickup station, Teddy slowly turns to meet his eye, and Karin isn't alone in feeling a sickening spark hit the air. The barmaid hurries as she places their drinks down, spilling more than a little of Karin's third martini.

"I'm not paying for that," Remy snaps.

"Oh, let me," Teddy tells the barmaid, his eyes on Karin.

"Like hell you will."

Karin can feel Remy about to explode when another disturbance overtakes whatever might have happened between her man and the kid. Waitresses are rushing to the office. The counter girl from the bowling alley. All improbably gleeful as they barge through the lounge and toward the back office and storerooms, only to return with the fat boss who eyed up Karin but good earlier, all bounding past their table, the boss waving a Polaroid camera. Only moments later, it seems, the music in the lounge switches off midsong, and a man's excited voice booms over the loudspeaker: "C'mon, c'mon, everybody. We've got our own Kennedy walkers in the house!"

Inside the bowling alley, the bald fluorescence and overwhelming aroma of popcorn disorient the walkers as they enter. The Scouts land heavily on the leatherette bench curved around an empty alley. Jaspar Goode and Warren lope off to explain their group to the grumpy gray-haired cashier who had been all set to tell them the time for renting shoes has passed, the grill is cold, and the fountain already wiped down . . . all set to chase them back into the night. Instead, she calls over the wide-eyed fountain server already prepping her mop bucket. With a word from the cashier, the girl disappears into the adjacent cocktail lounge, returning with a trio of waitresses.

"Tony's got a camera. He's in the lounge office," one of the waitresses says. "Get Tony."

Only two groups of bowlers remain at this hour—one expert and serious, one considerably less so—bowling in adjacent alleys on the far side as if alternating expertise: *spare, return, gutter, return, strike, return, gutter, return, split, return.* The crack of balls landing and spinning on hardwood, the clatter of pins, and the shaking metallic clang of the new automatic reset mesmerizes the weary walkers. A few bowlers glance at the group, but only one, a big fellow in a dark blue shirt (like a uniform, Avis thinks) outright stares. In fact, Avis notices that he seems to be scrutinizing each walker, lingering on the priest and his pack. Then, as if in greeting, he raises an eyebrow at the sight of Jaspar Goode, but it's Landon who waves and offers a typical tease.

"Who let you out of uniform?" he calls to the fellow. "Get a night off for good behavior, did you?"

The fellow cocks his head. "Who says I'm not at work? Somebody's got to keep an eye on you, old man."

He winks, but once again glances toward the priest, then at Jaspar Goode, who responds with an almost imperceptible shake of his head. Avis catches it, though, and so does the priest, who jumps a little, knocking against Avis just as Tony, the boss, arrives.

A big man jiggling with enthusiasm, smelling heavily of cologne, Tony slows to shake hands reverently. He exclaims at the sight of Oren and Karl—*Swensons! Spit Town boys!*—and shouts out to the gray-haired cashier to *find these boys some fries and Coca-Cola!* He makes an announcement into the microphone as if proclaiming to a crowd. Most of the remaining bowlers pause their games to offer thin applause, startling Warren, who can't stop grinning. Tony brandishes his camera, and soon the walkers are scrunching together as best they can, like their own set of bowling pins, the Scouts happily in front. Avis ducks behind Warren. The priest sneezes at the last minute so that only his shoulder will be visible in whatever photograph results. Jaspar Goode's attention is diverted by something on his shoe. Tony offers to take another shot; he has one flashbulb left.

"You, kiddo." He motions toward the door. "Don't you want to get into the picture, too?"

They all turn, and Avis collapses into Caroline. Jaspar Goode catches them both, missing the moment a black-haired boy, wearing a Humtown High varsity jacket, saunters toward them.

Avis is fracturing. In the bright light of the bowling, she's splitting into pieces. When a hand pinches the sleeve of her rain jacket and pulls her away, she's shocked to see it's the priest propelling her away from the group, down the corridor toward the restrooms.

"The men's room," he's saying, "is far too narrow."

Avis is not exactly sure what he is telling her or how, seconds later, she ends up alone in the ladies' room—a cavernous pink palace of a lavatory with a separate mirrored makeup room—the priest's ridiculous pack slumped beside her. No windows here, no back door, and she's left her bookbag behind her on the bench, not expecting to be more than a few feet away while the photograph was taken. Now it's sitting there in full view. He will recognize it at once.

The priest needed to shave, he said. He'd pulled out a battered leather dopp kit and what might have been a towel, leaving the open pack undone as he hoisted it through the swinging door of the ladies' room. "Won't be but a few minutes." He winked.

But why not leave this enormous pack out in the bowling alley? Why leave it with her? Avis closes her eyes. Teddy's triumphed again—of course, he has—and she will pay dearly once her bookbag is undone, her treachery confirmed. Almost without thinking, she rolls up her sleeves and begins to rummage in the priest's pack, looking for something, anything, she might use to save herself. Something sharp. Something heavy. A slingshot slips into her coat pocket. But she'll need more than that. It doesn't take long before her fingers close around a familiar roundness, that odd ridge. For a moment, she is stunned, then scattershot questions hammer at her. How long has he had it? Since he first took her bookbag, tucking it in with his own belongings? Why? And why leave the pack open now, where she can easily find and take back the treasure? Is he testing her? Avis has little time to parse the so-called priest's meaning. She only knows that she can't keep the stolen treasure, not with Teddy here, and for some reason, the priest can't either. When the door opens again a few seconds later. Avis visibly jumps, and the hand clutching the gold egg flies into her pocket.

"You okay?" Caroline asks. She's hugging her own coat, and her face is pale.

Avis stammers out an excuse about looking after the priest's pack. But, wait, that's the truth, isn't it?

"Would you hold this, too?" Caroline asks, handing her the coat before rushing into a stall.

Of course Avis will. Caroline's coat has such deep pockets.

"Whew," Caroline says when she returns. "I didn't realize how desperate I was."

Avis is still as can be, cradling the coat as if she's been tasked with guarding a true treasure. Caroline washes her hands, avoiding the mirrors. Instead, her eyes flick to the side, to Avis's exposed forearms, the girl's sleeves rucked up by her tight grip on the coat.

"You didn't get those today," she says after a long minute, nodding toward the bruises and the constellation of little scars.

"No," Avis says.

"Your parents . . ." Caroline tries as she dries her hands. She thinks that one of those marks, a vivid red circle, can only come from a cigarette burn. She's seen those before, unfortunately.

"No, not my parents. My brother . . . we . . . I . . . had . . . an accident," Avis says, falling back into the worst of her habits. "My fault."

If they were in her classroom, Caroline would have bent down to look Avis in the eye, to catch her and hold her long enough to let all the usual excuses lose substance. She might have stroked the girl's hair. She certainly would have said, as she does now, "No, honey. Not your fault."

In the silence that follows, Caroline feels the weight of what Avis cannot say or cannot say right. The words might finally emerge, and they won't be lies, but they can't be all true either. Too much, she thinks. We all have too much inside, too many private lands that few others have visited, and the task of explaining, of making visible, is too great. Caroline understands the silence, knows, too, the need for it to be broken. They have miles yet to walk, she tells herself. She won't upset the girl here, but neither will she let it, or her, go.

"Oh, boy," she says as she retrieves her coat and tugs it over her shoulders, sagging a little with the weight. "What was I thinking, filling my pockets with apples? They get heavier with every mile. Honestly, I can't believe any are left, but they must be, because . . ."

A "shave-and-a-haircut" knock on the door jolts Avis again. With Caroline's help, she drags the pack to the door, and the priest hauls it out easily. He's a new man. He's shaved, slicked down his hair, and changed into a clean black shirt that makes his collar looks fresh. He even smells a little like incense. *Welcome back, Father Dan.*

Avis hurries to push down her sleeves, but the movement does the opposite of what she intends and draws the priest's attention, too, his eyes lingering on the marks on her skin. He says nothing, but as he and Caroline and Avis return to the group, the priest puts one hand on Avis's shoulder as if blessing or claiming or . . . absolving her.

Yes, Caroline thinks. Priest or not, the man misses very little.

Back in the bowling alley, the mood has changed. Most of the bowlers have left or are in the process of hurriedly putting on their own shoes, well away from the far corner where the walkers have clustered and where voices are raising. The big man in the uniform shirt hesitates at the door, a bowling bag in each hand. Again, his eyes linger on the priest before his attention is diverted by a couple who have arrived in the bowling alley from the adjacent cocktail lounge, the fellow already shouting as he comes into view. Is a fight about to start? The big man's companion pulls him away. *None of our business. One night off; that's all I've asked.*

Warren is surprised to see Karin Johansson, all dolled up with a cocktail in hand, hanging back by the rental counter. Scrawny, red-haired—she was graduating as Warren was entering high school. She works as a filing clerk at the courthouse now in the same office as Denis's mother and has a reputation for making even the simplest transaction difficult. He doesn't think he knows the man, much older, a hard wire, but Landon and Jaspar Goode—even Caroline—clearly recognize him. That fellow's wound tight as a tick, hands curled into fists at his side. He's barely among them before he's leaning into Landon as if he thinks he's Lyndon Johnson embarking on a nose-to-nose bullying session.

"A girl stole it!" the man is yelling, jabbing a finger in the group's general direction.

Beneath the priest's hand, Avis is shaking.

"Stole what?" Caroline frowns.

"Stole it right out of my house! I put that yellow handle on myself."

"You." He turns on Caroline. "You're just like your old man, creeping around my place. Mind your own damn business. No wonder he got himself killed."

"And you," he yells at Jaspar Goode. "Don't think I haven't seen your truck rumbling down my driveway middle of the afternoon. Bunch of god-damn thieves. What else did you spirit away?"

"Don't be an ass, Gussie," Landon says, not yielding an inch. "No one's stolen anything."

Caroline glances at Jaspar Goode. Of course, Jay never ventured onto the Gussie farm, but the man's attack unnerves her. Unlikely, too, Jaspar Goode had visited the place, but why does he too suddenly look so pained? Still, all the walkers remember Avis emerging from the woods with the yellow-handled blue train case. They know exactly what is missing and where it might be, but not one of them is inclined to tell Remy Gussie.

"Denis's jacket," Oren blurts out. "He's wearing Denis's jacket."

While Gussie has commanded everyone else's attention, the Scouts have been keeping an eye on the interloper, the black-haired boy.

Oren points to the name on the back of the varsity jacket.

"Clayborn," Oren reads. "Isn't that Denis?"

"Sure is," Warren says.

Clayborn. Like the sheriff? Karin Johannsson, sipping on her martini by the counter, sputters as if amused. Of course, the kid's a fake, a thief himself. The black-haired boy slips off the jacket and dangles it from one finger to read the name himself.

"Found it on the ground by the highway café," he says. "Didn't want to see it ruined."

Sure. He must have, and yet why do his words feel like a lie? He hands the jacket to Warren, who hasn't even realized he's had his hand out.

"Glad to help," the boy says.

Without Denis's jacket, the newcomer might be a beatnik, all dressed in black from head to toe, that pretty hair a touch too long, and Caroline realizes where she's seen him before.

"He's the paperboy, isn't he?" she whispers to Landon, who looks at her as if she's suddenly become dumb as a rock.

"My brother Pete delivers the paper," he growls. "From his truck. Been doing that for almost twenty years, girl. You know that. Sometimes Cullie Goode helps out."

"But I've seen him," Caroline insists. "I know I have."

"Could have, I guess," Landon says. "He's Avis's brother."

And he's not done.

"Is this what you're looking for?" Teddy says to Gussie, holding up Avis's bookbag.

Put that down, Caroline wants to snap, the way she might at a particularly bothersome kindergartner who'd once again snatched away a classmate's favorite crayon.

"It's not a goddamn pocketbook," Gussie says, sending a scorching glance the boy's way.

"Bookbag," Teddy corrects. "And maybe what you're looking for is inside." He undoes the buckles, rummages around until his hand emerges with an overlarge balled pair of gray socks.

"What's in here, I wonder?" he says. "Doesn't feel like . . ."

With a flourish, he unrolls the socks to extract a worn, dirty-white leather baseball.

"That's not yours," Karl pipes up.

"No, it definitely is not," the priest says, pivoting to scoot Avis behind him before he snags the ball from the boy's hand. "I had that signed at Wrigley Field, myself."

The expression on the boy's face is disturbed but not, it would seem, by the question of ownership.

"There must be . . ." he says, beginning to search again.

"Enough, goddammit!" Gussie explodes.

But now it's Landon leaning in closely. Landon pressing near Gussie to mutter: "What's it been—only a few months—and you're dating? Shouldn't you be out looking for your family instead of swilling lady drinks in Spit Town with little Karin Johansson?"

The insult hits its mark more than the insinuation, and Gussie's rushing forward when the sound of breaking glass stops nearly everyone.

"Oopsy," Karin says, while Gussie takes the opportunity to plow his fist toward a distracted Landon.

He might have done serious damage, but Jaspar Goode is right there, spinning a now-flailing Gussie around into his own sights. With his wide shoulders and tattooed forearms, his camouflage and wind-burnt face, the look of Jaspar Goode alone should have stopped Gussie cold. But Gussie's clearly plastered. His hands are scrabbling along the damp floor amid the broken glass, but before he can gain purchase on a shard, he's stopped again. This time it's the manager, Tony, who seems more than experienced in expelling rabble-rousers. He all but lifts Gussie over his shoulder, ass in the air, and carries him straight out the door into the pit of the parking lot. Jaspar Goode follows. He waves a wincing Landon back, but not before sending one significant glance in the direction of the black-haired boy, as if he might like to grab him as well.

"Well, this is a night all right," the gray-haired cashier says in the direction of the girl in the cocktail dress.

The corner of Landon's jaw stings, but he wants to have a word with that girl, too.

"Your poor aunt and uncle know you're out here with that creep?" he says over his shoulder, in the direction of the gaudy, smirking fool, wobbling on her high heels.

But Karin Johansson is already gone. While the others are consumed by the spectacle, she's pushed away from the counter piled with battered pairs of sweat-soaked bowling shoes, wound a chiffon scarf around her spray-stiffened hair, and slipped back down the hallway to the cocktail lounge. She'll make her way to her Chevy in the far side of the parking lot, where she'll run the heater, listen to the radio, smoke one Salem after another, and wait. Perhaps he will come find her; perhaps not. Their first official date, and she could drive straight home now, if she chose. But she'll wait a little longer. If nothing else, Karin is expert at waiting, at never saying a sideways word, at knowing all the proper times a woman should disappear—if she wants to go on her own terms.

LAST BUS TO HUMTOWN

Teddy's found nothing, and without proof, he can't punish her for something she hasn't done, can he? Since the café when the priest returned her bookbag, wonderfully lightened, Avis must have known. Known the priest had relieved her of an enduring burden. Startled at first, she's come to think of his act not as theft but as a kindness. How could she not? Even now, as the priest catches her eye and smiles, Avis, who knows the true, twisting smile of the wicked, sees only gentleness and mirth and, too, something she has never seen before—recognition. He had to hand it back, but that didn't mean he was hanging her out to dry. He'd given her the ladies' room, a chance of her own to divest and be free. Only a short time before, her world had seemed to end, and it would have, too, if not for the priest, for Caroline. Standing between them, her shoulders straightened, her chin tilted up, suffused with a calm she does not recognize, Avis waits for Teddy to claim her.

Tony, the manager, returns, a little out of breath.

"All good?" Landon asks him.

"Sure thing," Tony says. "Your boy's just having a final word."

The fountain server, who quickly swept up the remnants of Karin's martini glass, now hovers at the group's edge with bucket and mop out. She shoots the gray-haired cashier a questioning glance. Should she mop around them? Wait? The cashier tips her chin. Get on with it. Haven't they had enough excitement? And look at the time.

"Seven minutes!" the cashier calls out into the near-empty alleys. "Last bus to Humtown in seven minutes!"

Astonishingly, although he still holds her bookbag, Teddy hasn't seen Avis. His eyes lap the group again and again with no sign of recognition.

He even wanders around the counter, raising the ire of the cashier, who's counting cash and shoos him away.

If he doesn't spot her, he'll have to run for the bus. Teddy won't risk being stranded in Spit Town. *Seven minutes* and Avis will be safe, and yet she does not crouch. She does not hide. If anything, she stands taller. She waits.

Has she finally succeeded? Is she truly invisible in full sight?

In front of her, Oren fiddles inside his knapsack, hoping for an overlooked oatmeal cookie. Instead, his hand emerges with his own bit of gifted rope from Jaspar Goode. He's utterly forgotten his wish, that charm, and undoes the fancy knot to gain a clean strand of rope. You never know when it might come in useful, he thinks.

"We should go," Warren says.

Hats are retrieved; coats buttoned; packs adjusted. Caroline pulls out the plastic rain bonnet Rita Selznick offered and ties it on as if for protection against a storm that may be coming. Avis's hat is tucked in her bookbag, which dangles still from Teddy's hand, his proof she must be here. The priest, that mind-reader, hands her the blue watch cap he wore all morning. She tugs it on and is almost to the door when Karl calls out.

"Avis, the time!"

With that, Teddy is onto her, elbowing past Warren and the Scouts.

"C'mon, Sis," he commands. "Time to go."

"Avis can't leave," Karl says, horrified.

"Of course not," Caroline says.

"Avis is with us," the priest says, coming up between sister and brother. His hand migrates to Avis's shoulder again.

Caroline arrives on her other side, sliding an arm around the girl's waist.

Another time, Avis would not have dared even glance at Teddy, certain she'd wither under his demands. But Avis is no longer alone. Avis is no longer afraid.

"Bus!" The cashier calls out, more than a warning in her voice.

No one moves.

"Go home, Teddy," Avis says, straightening her back.

"Has she told you what she did?" Teddy says. "Has she told you about the girls she maimed. Girls in the hospital, all those burns and broken bones. Has she told you about her friend who nearly lost an eye. Accidents, she calls them. How many of you will get hurt today? And how close will you be to my sister when you do? Poor accident-prone Avis. She's a thief, too, isn't she? How did that baseball get in her bookbag, anyhow? And whose little toy is this?" He holds up the bunny Avis rescued all those miles back, wagging it before the Scouts, who are deeply offended by the suggestion that the stuffed animal might be theirs. No one moves. Caroline's arm remains around Avis. Landon, still smarting from Gussie's rogue punch, begins to mutter. Even Warren finds himself moving in, closing a circle. Other girls might be hurt or go missing or be swept away by strange boys, but not their Avis.

For once, she does not flinch when Teddy surveys her with a smile meant to distract, the smile he deploys as he readies his strike, that simple push that will put her within reach of the tight, twisting grasp he's perfected. She doesn't even seem to mind that he's swinging her open bookbag, nor that when he tosses it behind him, it upsets the fountain server's bucket, splashing water over the floor behind Teddy and soaking her bookbag. Instead, a wire of electricity zings between the siblings. Avis is more than visible now. Teddy might be looking at a kind of mirror, one that reconfigures his image, weakening it, so that he appears smaller and far more superficial. His sister's singular stare, shockingly identical to his own unsettling turquoise gaze and absent that familiar gratifying fear he inspires, confuses Teddy enough that he hesitates and misses the moment Landon takes hold. Of course, Teddy pulls back his clever catlike move. But one shoe lands in water, and the boy slides against the fountain server's bucket, saved from a real fall by the priest's surprisingly muscled arm.

"Let's go, son," Landon says, ignoring every flailing effort Teddy makes to shrug him off. The other walkers follow, Avis in their midst, as the priest and Landon propel Teddy into the brisk night air, through the parking lot, to a near-empty bus, which idles brightly on the curb, Jaspar Goode on the bottom step.

"Well, here's your last passenger, Bertie," the fisherman says to the driver as he pulls back to allow Landon to deposit Teddy inside. "Right on time."

Landon gives a final push and barely frees himself before the doors suck shut. (Embarrassingly, Teddy tries to bite the old man as he releases his grip.) The bus pulls away swiftly, as the walkers bunch together on the sidewalk to chronicle the passage of retreating red taillights, block by block by block, until they wink out of sight. If Teddy is protesting, no one can tell.

He'll get off, Avis thinks with surprising calm. He'll demand. He'll sabotage. He'll certainly come after her again.

Okay, then, she thinks, feeling the others press closer to her. Let him try.

"You all right?" Jaspar Goode asks Landon.

"You bet," the old fellow says. "Kid's got worse aim than one of those snappy pocketbook dogs."

"You?" he asks Jaspar Goode.

"Oh, yeah," he says.

Caroline waits until the men shift off the curb and she can touch Landon's sleeve. Her voice is low, but Avis overhears bits of her questions.

"Will he get away with it?" Caroline is asking.

Of course he will, Avis thinks. Teddy always does.

". . . those poor girls, all three of them," Caroline says, and Avis is astonished. She wants to cry out, *How do you know?* And she might have, too, if not for Landon's reply.

"Men like Gussie never really escape," he says. "Even when they think they do."

"Karin Johansson. Does she know what she's getting herself into?"

"Hate to say it, but she might be every bit as bad as he is. Did you see how she looked at him? She's proud of the bastard."

"You can't think she's involved in that business."

"May not be what you think it is," Landon says. "He's mean to the bone, but he just ain't that smart."

"Um . . . Avis," Karl's whisper wakes her. He doesn't need to continue.

As Avis completes her duty (notebook, pen, and watch), the bowling alley's neon sign is extinguished behind them, and Oren sighs loudly. Avis realizes that in all the fuss the Scouts didn't get to eat the fries and cokes the manager planned to send over for them. She's about to apologize when Karl pipes up again.

"Thanks, Avis," he says.

Oren surprises her, too.

"We're glad you stayed," he says, holding up the dripping bookbag he'd rescued after the bowling alley scuffle.

"Hey, Oren," Avis says, after she resettles the damp bookbag on her shoulder. "You've got something there." She points to the side of the boy's head, and before he can react, she reaches out, her hand brushing his tousled white hair to pluck a coin from behind his left ear.

"Here you go," she says, placing the Indian Head nickel in his hand. "For your collection."

HER REWARD

He never could stand a witness. You'd be better off running blindfolded into the dark. If Remy saw her skulking about, witnessing his humiliation, he'd be even more steamed at her. Karin knew enough to keep away from the parking lot and whatever send-off Jaspar Goode and the Lounge boss were giving her man right before his truck tore away. Is their date over? Because of . . . what? That Teddy's invisible runaway sister? Nah, Remy might have hightailed it toward Humtown, imagining that she's scurrying right behind him, and once he sobers up a little, he'll hoot at the clever way she stepped up when he was so badly outnumbered. Karin, his tough girl with her low-cut dress, her heels, her red mouth. Yeah, he'll be back for her, pissed in every possible definition of the word, but he'll see this night out. Karin's head swims as she totters to her car. But, boyo, isn't she proud of herself?

In the shelter of her Chevy she lights another cigarette. She'll wait.

A bus pulls up. The bowling alley empties out. All those patriotic fools stomping back into the night. *Thieves!* Remy had hollered. Well, they certainly stole this night from her, the bastards.

The light of the red neon bowling pin is extinguished, and first the waitresses emerge from the cocktail lounge's back door, then the bartender, then big Tony with a bottle under each arm and a ring of keys swinging from one hand. Soon Karin is alone in the back of the parking lot, her radio playing softly, a few cigarettes left, her plaid car blanket wrapped over her beaded sweater and that tight blue satin sheath. She waits and waits, an interminable time, a full hour, maybe more. What is the point of driving back to Humtown, to her parents' bungalow, tiptoeing down the hallway to her childhood bedroom, the one—goddammit—she's certainly quit? She's about to stretch out on the Chevy's big bench seat when she hears footsteps on gravel, her passenger door opens, and the shock of the dome light half blinds her.

"I knew you'd wait for me," he says as he climbs in beside her.

His hair is disheveled, one hand is cut, his clothes are strangely wet. He is, she realizes, actually shivering in his thin black shirt. She hands over her car blanket, hardly registering he's had his hand out.

"Whew," he says, snagging a beer bottle from the case behind her seat. "Opener?"

"Glove box," she says before she can stop herself.

Before she knows it, he's swigging Remy's beer and squinting at a scrap of paper in his hand, some kind of map.

The goddamn nerve. This is her reward for waiting? Still, once Teddy's claimed a place in her car, what can Karin do but finally drive away?

"No, that way," he says, pointing into the night, as if she doesn't know exactly where he wants to go.

NIGHT MAPS

Paper maps are no good in the dark. The night's sightlines must be drawn, not by a pencil or a finger moving across a printed grid, but by suggestion. A speckled reality of edges and shapes.

Glancing light on a puddle. A stick rolling underfoot. The come-hither wave of a high cedar frond or the gleam of wire fencing like a knit-edge on their world.

On a clear night, of course, the map must move skyward. Find Polaris. Cassiopeia. Perseus. The heavenly compass shall lead you. But on a night like this one, soaked in pitch, with dense clouds refusing to yield more than a wedge of star-blistered sky or a glimpse of a waxing moon, the only map—god help you—must lie within.

"Ready?" Warren calls out, but for the first time that long day, his voice is unsteady. Who will lead the walk now? Not him. Fatigue has crept into Warren, stiffening even his young limbs. The encounter with Avis's brother—a stranger in Denis's jacket—unnerved him so much so that he'll walk three more miles before he realizes that he's left that precious item on a bowling alley bench. Then it will seem as if he's the one who left Denis behind, and he'll be consumed by renewed feelings of doubt. What if neither of them completes the walk? If his father arrives at the End of the World parking lot to greet a handful of adult strangers and three little kids? The Scouts, those ever-eager adventurers, hang back as well. This is their town. They know its spidering network of narrow, humpback roads, its unmarked shortcuts, ancient orchards, and tidy farms. They know where beaver ponds hide and what field migrating geese blanket yearly without fail. They know the locations of silos and barns and the 4-H sheds and half-a-dozen relics of abandoned buildings. Their sister has shown them where a field of blue flax appears every June and where, reliably, you can pick early wild blackberries in abundance. They know all this, but they are children, who up until now have been forbidden to roam in the night, so are blind to this dark place, this foreign town they know so well. Too, the lure of their own home, their own warm beds, waiting not far off seems to drag on them. As the line shuffles and reshuffles, in unspoken agreement, the boys step back and cede to Avis, lighting her path from behind with their flashlights.

In the end, of course, it's Landon who must take the lead. The old man has already proclaimed this last leg to be the most straightforward of all: six straight miles on the main road, the last four on the paved lane that winds to their final landmark. The new Avis, that ever-surprising creature, falls in line right beside him. To begin again, they amble up the main drag of Spit Town, which has quieted considerably during their stop in the bowling alley. The cruisers are gone, and the few others still on the road—the lovers, drunkards, and troublemakers—seem to be pursuing their own agendas, almost all heading out of town back to the lowland farms or up into the hills. One old car rattles up from behind, its muffler belching, its wavering headlights arching over them. As it draws alongside, a window is unrolled, a garbled shout expelled. More shouts might have followed, but the two whitehaired Boy Scouts turn as one to stare into the car as it slows, spooking those mischief-makers. Two children on the roadside in the middle of the night?—that will give them nightmares, Caroline thinks with more pleasure than she'd like to admit. She too likely startled them: a lady tramping up the highway, wearing a plastic rain bonnet without a raindrop in sight. Moments later, a newer model sedan, sleek as an otter, glides past, purring as if to erase the scare. In the first hour after Spit Town, only a few more cars pass. The walkers tense as headlights appear, relax as they vanish, and as the road breaks free of Spit Town's environs and hushes altogether, the walkers could be forgiven for feeling they were trudging outside the world, outside time, held within the cindered air. Yet no one hesitates. No one even stumbles. From afar, one might confuse this state with a magical somnambulance, consciousness all but retreating, leaving only a modicum of awareness in charge so that bodies move, entranced and directed by rhythm alone. For a good mile or two, they travel in near silence, steady footfalls on the graveled road edge, the muddied gullies, the occasional soft gift of tarmac. Anyone might have harbored the fleeting thought that this, the final leg of the Big Walk, would be suffused with a singular peace. In truth, almost all the walkers are walleyed, whipped, dimmed with a fatigue so deep each step feels miraculous, all their blind attention riveted on the slim tunnels of light carved from pale flashlight beams. Far off the road, a raven cronks relentlessly as if traveling through the landscape with them. Or perhaps the sound belongs to not one raven but a string of them, uncharacteristically trying to be helpful.

Wake up! they warn. *Wake up! Wake up!*

Fewer than five miles out of Spit Town, a vehicle with a broken headlight rolls past, winking at them and setting hearts to pattering. A few moments later, the odd half-light of the single beam grows in front of them, gaining uneasy speed until the car flings past. Again. And again. Three times the car laps them, until on the last approach, the driver slows, trolling mere feet from the walkers, allowing Jaspar Goode to hear the unmistakable sound of bottles clinking against one another.

"Look out!" he shouts. "Get off the road!"

His words barely register. Yet the obedient group leaps as one into brush, even as a bottle explodes in front of them, shattered glass raining inches from their faces as the car peals away.

"Everybody okay?"

"Turn off your flashlights!" Jaspar Goode orders.

"What good will that do?" Warren asks, even as he obeys. "If they come back, they'll see us standing here as soon as they drive by."

Landon stubs out his cigarette. "We can get off the road up ahead, I'm pretty sure," he says.

"Maybe they won't come back," Warren says.

"They will," the priest says. "They always do."

"How far?" Avis asks.

"I don't exactly know," Landon admits. "There's an old gate right about here, but it's been a while since I had to take that route."

"A wood gate?" Avis asks. "With a metal ring?"

"Jesus, girl, don't tell me you can see in the dark as well as fly?"

"It's just there, I think," she says, pointing into the abyss. "Only a little behind us. I noticed it when we passed. We have to get through those bushes, though."

"Go on, then," Landon says. He hands her a clean white hanky. "Take this and wave it when you've got the gate open and are on the other side."

Avis plunges forward, and it's as if the earth has swallowed her up.

"Avis," Caroline calls out.

"There's a ditch," the girl's breathless voice rings back from somewhere below. "I'm okay."

Only a few moments later, squinting, Landon spots the white flutter he needs to usher Caroline and the Scouts forward into what seems impenetrable brush.

"Watch the drop," he warns.

As Warren ducks forward, Landon says, "Get 'em all to hold tight to the middle of the track if you can. I think there's a hell of a ravine down there if you miss your step."

The priest is next. He is as surprisingly surefooted as Avis, but his backpack gets stuck halfway through the bushes so that Landon and Jaspar Goode both have to wrestle with it until the priest and his pack are free and he too can disappear into the dark.

"Go on," Jaspar Goode urges Landon, spotting a pinprick of light growing in the distance, but Landon waits for him, and only once Jaspar Goode is through the thicket does Landon leave the road behind. Avis flaps the white hanky over and over until, stumbling downhill over roots and ground vines and rocks, all arrive on the other side of the gate. Seconds remain to close the metal ring and huddle deeper into the woods, where they are subsumed by a darkness so dense no one dares move, not even as they hear the car's slowing approach. The driver has misjudged their position. From the woods, the walkers hear the vehicle pass and can see the brake lights go on well down the road. Tires rumble.

"They're pulling over," Warren says.

The walkers breathe as one. Landon's voice scratches the dark again.

"Huddle close," he says. "Avis, get that hanky deep in your pocket."

"You boys," he adds, "keep your heads down in the middle here. Caroline, take that darn plastic bonnet off."

A horn blasts with what can only be sinister intention. No one jumps, but more than a few hearts thump uncontrollably. Momentarily, the engine cuts out and all lights vanish, but if a car door cracks open, they can't hear it.

"Hold tight," Jaspar Goode whispers.

Finally, a headlight springs on, and the car creeps off, creeps and creeps, the red taillights slowly bleeding away, until with a screech, the monster speeds back onto the road.

"Is that Gussie, do you think?" Warren's voice is strained.

"Seems too patient," Landon says. "And that ain't his truck, is it? Sounds like a Chevy."

"He'd be shooting, too," he adds, "just for the sport."

"Thanks for that, Landon," Caroline says.

"Karin Johansson has a Chevy," Warren can't help but say. He's seen it up at the courthouse, parked beside Denis's mother's car.

That foolish girl, Caroline thinks. That horrible, foolish girl.

"Whoever that is seems to have marked us for a challenge," Jaspar Goode says. "We need to move on."

"How?" Caroline says. "Where?"

"We'll go slow," Landon says. "Our eyes will adjust, I'd bet."

"Won't take much longer," he says. But he, too, is squinting, and when the huddle they've made breaks and he presses forward, he knocks Karl over.

"Hold on," Jaspar Goode says. "Landon, where does this track go anyway?"

"Nowhere," the old man says disconcertingly. "Big old field some fellow wanted to develop. But other side of that is . . ."

". . . the cliff path," Oren's voice arrives from beside Caroline. "We hiked it with our troop."

"Oh, *that* field." A faint sound suggests Karl is nodding.

"It'll get us where we want to go," Landon says. "Maybe even a little faster. Least it might in daytime."

"I don't know," Warren says. "How can we walk miles when we can't see? Maybe we should just take a break here and wait a few minutes."

"And what? Get back on the road with our flashlights and hope they've tired of us?" Landon says. "Or let them track us through the woods, following our lights? No, we walk in the dark, a mile, no more."

"It'll work," Avis says, remembering her invisibility lessons. "Cover one eye."

"Girl . . ." Landon growls.

"Listen to her," comes the priest's voice, strangely commanding.

"Cover one eye," Avis instructs again. "Just for a minute."

"We don't have a . . ." Landon begins.

But they are an obedient lot. Even Jaspar Goode's right palm rises.

"Hold on, hold on," Avis says. "Don't move. Now . . . take your hand away quickly and look toward my voice, but not directly at me. Look to the side, kind of next to my feet."

"Well, what do you know," Caroline says. "I see you. Sort of."

"Me, too," says Oren.

"It's a pretty narrow path, isn't it?" Warren says.

"But you can see it, right?" Avis whispers.

"I can," he marvels. "Kind of. Enough."

"You better go in front, Avis," Jaspar Goode says. "Can you do that?"

He's asking her to lead, but more than that, Avis realizes he's asking her to take up his own role. He's recognized her as a fellow rescuer.

Tentative at first, the line is soon in sync. In the deep quiet, the walkers sink back into woods, night folding around them. Their footfalls land more gently, the tunneled forest path somehow entering their hearts so that the separation is less distinct. Soon, they can hardly imagine a need for more light. The forest does not stir or tremble as they pass through. It is, and always has been, fully awake, a state Avis suddenly longs to claim.

So, it's true, she thinks. I'm alive.

ANOTHER KNOT,
ANOTHER RESCUE

MILE 45

How can you tell the truth about a story that happens almost completely in the dark? What do you have but glimpses and snatches of sound and the memory of that crackling sensation that tells you someone is close, too close, or the eerie shuffling, so subtle that later you won't understand how you even registered it, that informs you the companion you'd counted on, the one you swore was right behind you, has vanished?

Caroline can't help thinking about Gussie's ranting. Jay at his farmhouse? Jaspar Goode's truck ripping up the gravel in his driveway? The little blue train case with the yellow handle. Ginny's clothes inside. The path they traverse is riddled with roots and requires constant attention. Yet Caroline feels a part of her disengage as she tries to unravel this latest Jay mystery. Despite the narrowness of the trail, she presses to one side to let the others go by until she can stop Jaspar Goode with what she recognizes now as his own familiar gesture, one hand pushing through the empty air.

"*Did he?*" she asks. "Did Jay borrow your truck before the storm?"

For once, Jaspar Goode doesn't pause or hedge.

"He did."

"Why? Do you think . . ." she almost can't say it.

"I don't know," Jaspar Goode says, "but I've been . . . I haven't . . . I don't . . . but . . ."

"Tell me." She all but begs. "*Tell me.*"

He doesn't know, he really doesn't, he insists, but he can't stop thinking about Jay and that boat.

That boat?

After Halde Bens's visit, he tells her, Jay had indeed gone to talk with Mick Craven. He'd figured out what Craven had been up to and wanted to make some kind of deal with him. Money might have changed hands. Or an old favor may have been called in. The result seemed to be that only certain information would go to the Feds, who Jay assured Craven were close to knowing everything. In exchange, Jay arranged to have Jaspar Goode deliver the much-disputed boat to its new owner in Seattle.

"I thought Jay was squaring the debt," Jaspar says, "maybe for the Shuffler."

The fisherman had planned to do it right away, the very day the storm hit. But he'd been stuck. He'd had . . . an . . . an appointment that Friday he couldn't miss. *Saturday*, he promised Jay, and though Jay wasn't entirely happy about the delay, that became the plan.

"But your truck?"

Earlier that week, Jaspar Goode had bought a truck from a fellow in Spit Town. It had come with a good tow hitch. Jay needed, he said, to help a friend tow his car to a garage that afternoon. Jay had been gone only an hour or so, and Jaspar Goode hadn't thought about that since.

But how had Jay picked up the train case? Caroline wondered. When had he brought it home and filled it with Ginny's baby clothes? And why? *Aileen Gussie?* It suddenly made sense. Of course. Jay was trying to help that poor woman.

What was his plan? The train case—was it to put Remy Gussie off the scent? Aileen's mother would know for sure something was off the minute she saw those baby clothes. Nothing like the ones she made for her grandbabies. Fancier, like those old Mrs. Weller, Caroline's mother-in-law, used to sew. Lord knows, Aileen's mother wouldn't say a word about that to Gussie, who wouldn't know the difference in any case, who wouldn't wonder as she would, a ridiculous hope rising. Borrowing the fisherman's truck . . . well, Jay wouldn't have wanted Gussie to spy a vehicle by his house and recognize it as Jay's, set a trail for him to follow. Caroline shares her speculations with Jaspar Goode.

"But I guess Gussie saw Jay up there, anyways," he says with a nod. "In my truck."

"No, not then," Caroline says. She remembers a late September morning when Jay woke from his familiar nightmare.

"They're just babies," he'd told Caroline, who had thought he'd been rehashing his dream. She could see now, with a burnt clarity, that he'd been talking about Aileen Johansson and her little ones. She must have finally come to him in the boatyard, that brave girl, and Jay had tried to talk to Gussie, to sort him out—a fruitless endeavor. Only once he realized how much danger the girl was in had he started devising her escape. The boat and whatever mess the Cravens were involved in must have seemed providential.

Jay, the Rescuer. What a plan that would be, to spirit the battered wife and her children onto the sailboat, sail them away in the dead of night. What a perfect, beautiful plan. Until the storm.

Oh, god, she could scream, but she's too deeply exhausted. Beside her, she feels a trembling and realizes that Jaspar Goode, the big fisherman, is crying.

"I'm so sorry." He weeps as she tightens her arms around him. "I'm so, so sorry."

They might have stood there, unmoving in their shared anguish, if not for a light patterning the trees onto the path before them. Landon, returning with his own flashlight, wondering if they are all right.

"This isn't the time to split up," he tells them. "We've got to keep together, keep moving. It's easy to get lost out here."

Prophetic words. A mile or more into the woods, Karl hears a whoosh, like a fish plunging into deeper water. A second later, behind him, the priest trips over a root. A stumble more than a fall, but the enormous pack continues its forward movement even as the priest begins to right himself. Karl sees the outline of the priest's figure falling and hears the *oomph* of the man's breath and the clatter of God knows what banging around or spilling out of the enormous pack. Karl can't make out his brother, and his first thought is that the priest has fallen on top of Oren. He does what he can to pull the priest upright, yanking on that slippery black coat. Not a difficult task. The fellow seems more surprised than hurt, and Jaspar Goode and Warren are soon at each side, easing the priest fully to his feet and recalibrating the enormous pack so that steadiness prevails.

"How do you carry that thing?" Warren asks. "Doesn't your back hurt?"

"It does now, son," the priest says.

"Where's my brother?" Karl says.

"He must be up ahead."

"No, he didn't pass me. I'd know."

"Oren!" Karl calls.

Avis lets out her piercing two-fingered whistle, and Karl, remembering his own store of essentials, is about to find his own whistle, when a weak echo, a faint cry, responds. Avis whistles again, and the priest joins in with a more melodic version. The stillness is broken by footfalls—the others returning, answering the whistle themselves.

"Oren?" Karl calls out again. "Orie?"

Three-quarters of an hour since they broke from the highway. Karl doesn't care if it's safe or not to turn on his flashlight now, if they make all the noise in the world. With Jaspar Goode and Landon, he flails the woods with light, skirting along the trail edges to look for a break, a flattened edge.

When the priest whistles again, they pause and wait. Whistle, pause, wait.

Oren's voice is faint, but Karl finally hears him.

"Where are you?" Karl calls.

"He's over there, I think," Avis says, pointing off to the side. Their flashlights, surprisingly, aren't all that useful. The light skitters over unfathomable shapes, blotting out all but the briefly illuminated—is that a leaf? a branch? a possum?—so that context is extinguished as well. What they can make out is how narrow the path they've been traversing is, the sharp drop-off to one side into brush, into a slight gulley or a deep ravine.

"I think we'll see better without those lights on," Landon says. "Maybe he can get his own flashlight out, direct us."

"Turn your flashlight on, Orie," Karl shouts.

"Can't," comes the weak reply.

"I'll climb down," Karl says.

"No way," Landon says. "We'll have two of you stuck down there."

"Not if I go by rope," Karl says. Already, he's pulled out his gift from Jaspar Goode.

"With that scrap?" Landon says.

"We can tie it together with your pieces," Karl says to Jaspar Goode. The kid is working hard to undo Jaspar Goode's fantastic knot, an artifact he'd hoped to treasure and study. He has to work it around with his teeth, biting and loosening until the knot lies limp and he can unravel the last of it with one quick twist. Meanwhile, Jaspar Goode himself is performing the opposite, blindly weaving and knotting. It's not long before he holds a long length of rope in his hand.

"That should work," Jaspar Goode says.

"You think?" Landon says. "We don't even know how far below he is."

"Excuse me," the priest says. "You can get Karl down to his brother with the rope, but how will we get Oren back up here if he's hurt?"

"Hey, look." Avis's voice rings through the dark.

"Don't tell me you can see down there, girlie," Landon says, turning his head in her direction, fully shocked to see her, almost clear as day.

"Well, anyone can," Avis says.

"My god," Caroline breathes, "the moon."

Of course, the moon has been there all along, but while rope has been unknotted and retied, while whistles have been blown and answered, the night clouds above have dispersed, allowing what certainly must be a full moon or damn near it to take center stage on the night sky.

"It's like someone flicked on a lamp," Warren says.

Otherworldly, Caroline thinks. And then corrects herself, because this black-and-white world feels far more real than any others she might imagine. Otherworldly, she decides, only means not *your* world. Not the world you've known. In the daylight of Humtown or Spit Town, a boy who'd slipped into a ravine would not appear as Oren now clearly does, ten feet below them, engulfed by salal as if by roiling waves, his white-blond head bobbing. And Jaspar Goode's slide to rescue would certainly have looked less like a plunge into wild unknowable waters. But here, now, everyone holds their breath as if they too are descending when Jaspar Goode swings off the path and slides down the hillside, when he lifts Oren up as easily as if he were a kitten, and Warren and Landon bend and scramble to grab him, Jaspar Goode pushing from behind, before making his own way back to them.

No, not otherwordly. Of *this* world.

Oren's right foot is hurt. "It's not broken," he tells everyone. He can wiggle his toes. Yet when Jaspar Goode places him upright on the path, the boy crumbles.

"Right," Jaspar Goode says.

He relieves Oren of his rucksack and tries to pass it to Landon.

"Can you . . . ?"

"I'll carry it!" Karl all but yelps.

In seconds, he has his brother's rucksack, identical to his own, strapped to the front of him, Jaspar Goode hoists Oren onto his back, and without another word, the walkers are off again, entering yet one more version of this reclaimed night.

MULTITUDES

A netherworld glanced with moonshadows and the shushing echoes of nightwork. All the walkers move in sync, their footfalls seemingly gentler. Every step feels surer, the air, clearer. Their own deeply wearied bodies ease. The blind treachery of night is gone, replaced by a black-and-white moon-drenched world. They *trust*—in this gift of moonlight, in the frazzled gorgeous undefinable space around and within them. No one's talking now. Not even when they reach the big field, where swales of new grasses, etched bright, sway around them, and old tractor ruts, corrugated heaves of half-frozen mud, sparkle with bits of mica. Not even when they pass through what must be a full colony of tender rabbits grazing obliviously in clear view do the walkers remark upon the wild dream this night has become.

When did the walk cease being a race, a human feat of endurance, an ordinary, if lengthy, journey? When did they truly begin to travel effortlessly through space and time? Because, of course, they are.

Karl and Warren daydream. Karl of thick meat stews and buttered biscuits, of his 4-H rabbits waiting for his care, of the way he'll shyly present the number on his pedometer when he reaches his sister's car. Warren is visiting Monday at school, how no one will know, and he and Denis will say nothing, but then the President himself will telephone and the principal will put him through to the classroom intercom and head after head will turn in wonder.

Avis rocks within an open boat deep in the night. It rocks and rocks as if held within a wild cradle. Icy waves splash over, taking her breath away with each surge. Her little leather shoes are soaked through; she can no longer feel her feet. But she is not alone in the boat. She is bundled within a heavy wool blanket and an arm holds her close and safe. No, she is not alone.

Farther and farther behind them is wreckage. A flare of fire, a floating copse of blackened wood. And, somewhere, not far off, a foghorn is calling and the faintest of lights is signaling land.

Oren, his right cheek resting on Jaspar Goode's shoulder, fights sleep by imagining it's he who's walking at Jaspar Goode's height—he who is a full-grown man, tromping through a foreign jungle. He falls into the jangle of Jaspar Goode's own cavernous memories, riven with blasts and flashes of light, a bobbing boat on a turquoise sea, a landscape of impenetrable islands.

Landon has dropped like a stone into an endless pool of recollection. Somewhere in there is a day of fishing, and he is hip-deep in a fast-moving, green-gold river, rod in hand, sun flashing, the two dearest people in his life mere feet away.

Caroline leans beside Jay on the back-porch steps, deep summer, early evening, cold bottles of beer beside them. The lush garden's been watered, and a fine mist lingers. Supper is waiting, but their heads tip together so that, for a while at least, for an eon perhaps, they are breathing as one.

"You idiot," she murmurs to him. "You glorious idiot."

The priest, perhaps astonishingly, is having another heart-to-heart with his God.

What a marvelous world one enters when walls fall between *here* and *there*, *then* and *now*, *if* and *why not*. When borders vanish. Who in their right mind would ever want to go back?

SUNDAY

March 17, 1963

THE END OF THE WORLD, 12:30 A.M.

MILE 50

The parking lot at the End of the World is all lit up. At least a dozen cars with headlights on, a radio playing Ricky Nelson. Someone has set up a long table with a camp stove. The edges of an oilcloth flap in a constant wind, and the smell of coffee simultaneously singes and comforts.

How long have they been waiting? For the first time in hours, Warren flicks on his flashlight, causing a loud cheer to erupt in response, and when Warren and Karl, then Jaspar Goode with Oren on his back ramble into view, they are rushed. Hair is tousled, hands are shaken. The boys' Scoutmaster is there. So is Tony, the bowling alley manager. Despite his injury, Oren can't stop grinning. Karl desperately needs to pee. He throws his pack and Oren's into the open trunk of his sister's car and dashes toward the blackest edge of the parking lot. Even his sister knows not to stop him. Jaspar Goode gently unloads Oren onto the car's backseat and stretches deeply.

"Twisted his ankle," he tells the sister. "*He* thinks he'll be fine."

The sister can't help but laugh.

"How long did you have to carry him?" she asks Jaspar Goode.

"Hours," a returning Karl answers for him.

Oren slowly scrambles out of the car, hops to stand beside Karl. He can't miss this final moment. Their triumph. Without their rucksacks, he and Oren are two grinning little boys, glinting in their deepest fatigue.

"What time is it?" Oren asks his sister, and when she answers, he looks to Karl, who will hold those numbers tightly until Avis and her notebook arrive.

Warren's father, suddenly proud, slaps the boy's shoulder, a gesture that Warren feels as a ringing sound, a cheering peal. His father has a camera in hand, flashbulbs ready, and with the illumination of headlights, just might get a photo for the front of the paper. Denis appears, ragged and worn after his own long day. He's shivering inside a borrowed Spetle County Sheriff's Department windbreaker. Warren feels a stab, remembering the forgotten jacket. No sign of Avis's brother or that raving Remy Gussie, but a Spetle County Sheriff's car is parked at the entrance to the lot.

"My ride," Denis says, following Warren's gaze. "Lots to tell."

A young deputy eases by, landing a playful punch on Denis's arm.

"Some friend you got here," he tells Warren, nodding at Denis. "Boss wants to hire him."

Before Warren can ask any one of the questions swirling between them, his own father is back by his side.

"You did it!" his father is crowing. "How was it?"

He's waiting. He's listening. A real question: his father's highest form of praise.

Warren feels his back straighten with the recognition, but he can't yet answer, because, of course, the walk isn't over.

"We have to wait for everyone," he says.

Landon's brother leans against his truck, smoking the same slender, odorous cigars with which Landon peppered his walk. Pete Wills raises two fingers in greeting when he spots Jaspar Goode. Shakes his head.

"You know, Bobby may have, but JFK hasn't done this walk himself. He gathered a few of his fancier friends, including that Prince Radziwill, got 'em all together down in Palm Beach, then set *them* off on the fifty miles. Our Hero followed for a few miles, sitting in the back of a white Lincoln convertible, waving little American flags and sipping on a daquiri. His health, apparently, wouldn't allow him to participate. No lie."

"Which part?"

"Some of it. All of it."

"Well, at least that's better than nothing," Jaspar Goode says.

"I did notice you're alone," Pete says. "Get your man?"

Jaspar Goode shrugs, joins Pete on his tailgate.

"Doubt it," he says. "Got someone else in my sights."

"Hellava way to make a living," Pete says. "But here's a bit of good news," he goes on. "The sheriff arrested the Shuffler today. Got a tip from an unnamed federal officer, apparently, about a shed up by the mill. Turns out, the Shuffler has a story to tell about that sailboat and Mick Craven, thank you very much."

"That's something, too, I guess."

"And Mrs. Jay?" Pete Wills asks, squinting into the dark.

Caroline spots the parking lot hoopla below as they near the forked end of the cliff path. Civilization to one side, the roaring Strait to the other. She can't help but notice how the swaying trees behind them—how far away the forest seems!—mimic the swelling waves ahead. She feigns a need to address a flapping, muddied shoelace one last time, waits until Landon, the priest, and Avis pass, and steps off the trail.

Will they say she slipped? Will they say *She must have thought, yes, I've come this far, I should see the cliff. Silly woman.* Caroline thinks she is prepared for joy, but when she sees the vastness, when she hears the high roar of the sea below, she feels undone by . . . not doubt, not sorrow, exactly, but a throbbing resignation.

Yes, she fell, they'll decide, and not one of them will be wrong.

What sixth sense makes Landon turn back? Or is it the priest, hesitating at the sight of their illuminated welcoming committee, who first begins to retrace his steps? Or maybe Avis, alert to Caroline's absence and keenly aware of her own unsatisfied task? Or, perhaps, all three. They've been listening, haven't they, this bunch, listening to one another's unspoken dreams and terrors hour upon hour, following thoughts like footfalls that can barely be separated from their own. *Here I go,* one thinks, and the remaining walkers can't help but hear her murmur, *Come get me.* They turn together, a thin moonlight tunneling the cliff path, all but propelling them to the cliff edge where Caroline—weary, fragile Caroline—rocks unsteadily.

It's a moment that will be with all of them for the rest of their lives, there at the End of the World. Far below, waves batter the haystack rocks, enormous swells that leap and stretch onto the graveled shore.

Shipwrecked, Caroline thinks. I've been shipwrecked just like you, Jay, and all I want to do is fall back into the sea with you. She is dizzy with longing, one foot sliding forward, when a small cold hand slips into hers.

It's a sensation she recognizes. Muscle memory. She can't help squeezing back, and as she does, she finds herself pulled gently onto solid ground.

"We're almost there," Avis says. She has to half shout to be heard. "We did it."

A quaver in the girl's voice wakes Caroline to another concern and sets her to wavering as she feels a little ridge on the girl's hand. Avis with her bruises and scars. Avis, levitating in the trees. Avis, claiming her place among them as the bus winks away down deserted Spit Town streets. Avis, going home. Not alone. She can't go alone.

No, no, no! *Not fair!* Caroline thinks.

And, too, what about poor Jaspar Goode? How will he feel if he fails at this crucial moment?

No justice, a familiar voice seems to whisper in her ear.

Ah, c'mon, Jay, Caroline protests. *Really?*

The absurdity of having come so far only to trudge back into life. Caroline hears Jay's voice teasing her with his fifth tenet, and she has to smile, too, even as Avis's hold on her takes her back one step and then another until they're standing beside the priest and old Landon.

"That a girl," Landon says.

Lights are still blazing below when they regain the trail, and Avis's hand remains curled within Caroline's.

"Boy, look at all the cars," Avis says, stopping short on the rise of this last hill.

"A full congregation," the priest agrees.

"For *us*," Avis marvels. She pats the pocket where her notebook waits with its record of their time and the Scouts' good deeds and not a scrap of information about her own journey, her great relief.

"The President would be proud, I guess," Landon says, jarring the others a little. They've all but forgotten *him*. "Warren's probably gonna pine for a Kennedy *parade* when we get back."

"God forbid," Caroline says.

"Indeed," the priest says faintly. "Blessed are the meek."

Avis turns to grin at him. It's the most reverent sentiment she's heard from him all day, and one aimed right at her, it seems, but the priest and his enormous backpack are no longer beside them. She doesn't have to point. Caroline and Landon, too, can make out the shadowy outline of a figure striding back toward the field and the woods, having satisfied whatever mission he's been on.

"Not a priest," Avis says, looking after him.

"Nope," Landon says.

"Well," Caroline says. "He is something, that's for sure."

"Shall we make wishes," the priest had suggested in those last moments near the cliff's edge. He'd kicked up a black rock, white-striped and glistening with moonlight, and hurled it over the cliff, his lips moving wordlessly with a prayer, a wish. Even burdened by that ridiculous pack, he demonstrated the ease of a seasoned ballplayer with a high arc of a throw, graceful and strong. To everyone's surprise, Landon followed suit.

"Why the hell not?" he said, flinging his own found rock off the cliff. "I get a wish or two of my own, don't I?"

Avis cast about. She couldn't make out any rocks. Not even a stick of wood.

Caroline, ever the kindergarten teacher, came to the rescue. "Here," she said, reaching into her pocket for one last apple. She could feel two left, and for once was not surprised at all. She handed one to Avis and grasped the last one, misshapen and heavy, in her own hand.

"Ready," she said as the girl watched her intently.

Off their wishes flew, and it may have been the weight of her own thwarted desire or a trick of that miraculous moonlight, but as Caroline's apple rose and tumbled into the night, she could have sworn it glowed like real gold and never fell at all but traveled on and on into the far reaches of that long, peculiar night.

ACKNOWLEDGMENTS

I couldn't have conjured companions more charming and stalwart for my own journey with this book, and I thank them all: the endlessly giving and indefatigable Gail Hochman; the brilliant Nicola Mason and everyone at Acre Books; my longtime neighbor and friend Arletta Gould, who chatted with me endlessly about everything from the telephone operators of her youth to the never-told details about a long-ago (unpunished) triple murder in our small town; my good buddies Joan Jonland and Leslie Schwartz, who hold and share so many crucial memories with me and always, always make me laugh; JoAnn Alber, who lets me travel occasionally with her into the true world and, vitally, reminds me of why I might be here, and her partner, Dave Fraser, who was kind enough to relay the story of his own Kennedy Walk in 1963; Jess Walter, Debra Magpie Earling, and Rikki Ducornet, who so generously read and endorsed this novel (I am immensely grateful and owe them each a long night at the bar—oh, wait, that would be for me!); and Peter Scovil and Duncan Scovil (reader extraordinaire), my dearest companions on the sweetest and the hardest stretches of the road.